THE
PERFECT
DATE

BOOKS BY JULIA CROUCH

THE
PERFECT
DATE

JULIA CROUCH

bookouture

Published by Bookouture in 2023

An imprint of Storyfire Ltd.
Carmelite House
50 Victoria Embankment
London EC4Y 0DZ

www.bookouture.com

ISBN: 978-1-83790-678-9
ebook ISBN: 978-1-83790-676-5

To Uncle

ONE

Holding her breath, Caz hurries the dogs through the stinky underpass. She breaks out the other side onto the grassy brow of Racecourse Hill, and gulps in the fresh air.

She comes here every Thursday morning, and each time she reaches this spot she is taken by a sharp rush of possibility – the smells, the endless sky, the distant sea stretched out beneath it like a piece of silk. As ever, despite the horrifying Incident that forced her away from London and her teaching job, she is grateful that she is here, now, doing this.

She is finally moving towards a sort of peace.

Today, the onshore breeze carries the bright tang of salt with it and the four client dogs tug on their leads, keen to run free. She unclips Joe, her own mostly Border collie rescue mutt – whose training is impeccable – and he sets off, nose to ground.

The others look expectantly up at her, but she shakes her head. 'Not after the sheep, guys.'

Yesterday, Henna the red setter went after a ewe who had strayed through a gate left open by some careless idiot. Luckily the ewe, who had her lamb beside her, wasn't having any of it. She stamped her foot and charged, and it's unlikely that Henna will be going after any more sheep any time soon. But it did teach Caz that this particular spot isn't great for letting her client dogs off their leads at the moment. Not while the urban sheep are just the other side of a gate used day and night by urban humans.

Mungo the Dalmatian, who has been limping like a diva, lifts his paw for Caz to inspect. Somehow, even this early in the season, he has managed to get a grass seed embedded between his toes. It takes a while and involves her Leatherman tweezers, but only one treat, to get it out, because he is learning well.

He is learning well because, as an added extra to her dog-walking services, Caz turns pain-in-the-arse dogs into little treasures. Which is why, even after only three months in business, she's having to turn new clients away.

'Perhaps you could expand,' her mum, Ruth, said when Caz told her how it hurt her to say no to customers. 'Employ someone to help out.'

But Caz doesn't want that. The whole point of moving back to her childhood home after the Incident was to reduce stress, simplify life and get back in touch with a better side of nature. The very thought of having someone relying on her for their income raises her heart rate.

Putting the Leatherman back in her dog-walking bum bag, she straightens and gets ready to steer her pack over the hill and down into the community orchard, one of her favourite spots at this time of year with its free-for-all blossom.

But Joe has disappeared.

She whistles for him, the special high-pitched sing-song they have established as a non-negotiable demand for him to return.

No Joe.

'Joe!' she yells.

Again, the whistle.

He doesn't return.

He always returns, though.

Except that one time...

Rooted here, with four dogs on leads all jumping around like they know something is up, Caz's heart races, her breath comes short.

Time stops, the grassy hill tilts towards the sky, because that other time he didn't return was the start of the Incident, the moment that tore up her world.

Just as she is about to enter full-on panic-flashback mode, there he is, running towards her from where the Thursday-morning walk normally finishes. He has his ears back, his eyes wide, like he's got something urgent to tell her.

She reels herself in, becomes the boss again.

The others, sensing the release, start barking.

'Quiet!' she commands.

Apart from Joe, they obey.

'Sit!'

Apart from Joe, they sit.

'Jesus, Joey. Where the hell have you been?' And 'Quiet,' she says to him again, in take-no-prisoners mode.

But he keeps on, and the others take their cue and ramp it up once more.

A worm of dread stirs in her belly.

Don't be stupid, she tells it.

It's lovely up here. Stop expecting bad things.

The worm settles.

'Quiet!' she yells at the dogs.

She should be ignoring them: it's the only long-term way to stop dogs barking. But they've worked themselves up into such a lather, and she's beyond best practice.

Twenty minutes into the hour-long walk and they are still

here, just the other side of the underpass. She will not be giving tired-dog-value-for-money to the owners this morning.

Her phone buzzes in her bum bag. She pulls it out in a tangle of unrolled poo sacks. It's a message from Harry, a guy she met on the SeeMe dating app. She's been out with him twice so far but already feels he's pretty special, and she's looking forward to their date tonight at the Mesmerist for cocktails and hopefully then some.

She pauses before opening the message, already half convinced that this will be him cancelling, because why would such a hottie want to spend time with a scruff bag like her? Always, with dating, she tries to have no expectations whatsoever about anything – to do so only leads to disappointment. Since the Incident, however, this philosophy has become central to her world view. It's self-preservation.

She hands the still-agitating Joe a biscuit to buy herself a couple of seconds of screen time. It calms him for a bit, but of course then everyone wants one.

'Quiet!' she shouts again. Good job it's so early and there's no one around to hear the harshness in her voice. That would most certainly not be good for business.

She opens up the message.

You are very special.

He signs off with four kisses.
Is that a bit odd?
No. It's nice.
She allows herself a brief moment of hope that this could be *it*, that Harry could be the One who doesn't turn out to be a complete arsehole.
Unlike her dog, who is being exactly that right now.
'What *is* it, Joe?' She squints at her mutt.
Having got her attention, he turns and tears off.

Bollocks. She should have put his lead back on.

The other dogs strain to follow him.

'Joey, come!' she calls, but he has run back along the foot-path to where it forks and bends, where he sits like he's waiting for her to follow.

The worm stirs again.

Again she tells herself to get a grip.

Pulled by the others, who have caught Joe's mood like it's a virus, she catches up with him. But he's off again. He repeats this running-ahead-and-waiting move three more times, before heading off into the grass, nose down, tail up.

Then, sharp like an accusation, he stops sniffing and looks up at her.

She can smell it, too.

Fifty feet above her head, a skylark pipes. It thinks she is disturbing its nest.

As she steps towards Joe, she sees it: the hand first, curled like it should be holding something soft. But instead, the empty fingers are stained with old, black blood.

The belly worm writhes and flails, and prickles form on Caz's scalp.

This man's body is full of holes. There is a lot of blood.

Flies buzz.

But under that, there's this horrible stillness.

TWO

The dogs howl and pull at their leashes, trying to get at the remains.

She hasn't looked at the face yet.

Like that feeling you get standing on top of a cliff when you want to jump off, she has this sickening urge to bend towards him, to look, to touch.

Tasting acid, she fights it down.

Instead, she keeps him in her peripheral vision, buying time before she processes the whole of what she knows is in front of her. Frighteningly calm just for this moment, she ties the dogs to a fence post, well out of the way.

She knows dogs. Their howling and baying won't be stopped now.

Joe sits calmly, though. He has done his job, brought her here.

Good boy, Joe.

She returns to the body and, breath coming in short gasps, looks at the face, tries to put the items of it together. Those brown eyes staring emptiness up at her, those soft, full blue lips.

Her gasp appears like it's from someone else.

She doesn't want to believe it. Hands shaking, she pulls her mobile phone out again, fires up SeeMe, taps the profile picture of Harry, her date for tonight, so it fills the screen.

A nice face, brown eyes, soft cheeks, youngish-looking for thirty-five. Soft, full lips. Red.

Lips she kissed.

She holds her phone so she can see both the bloodied face in the grass in front of her and the face on the screen.

It is, then. This body lying in front of her.

Harry.

The man she was seeing, the man she had hopes for, has been killed.

Joe whines and licks Caz's face like he does in the mornings. She opens her eyes. She's lying in the long grass, nearly nose-to-nose with Harry. This should have been tonight, after the Mesmerist, his place or hers – although hers would have been unlikely, as she's sleeping in her single childhood bed at the moment.

Banishing this sick, redundant thought, she rolls over and jolts herself up onto her feet, waving her hands around her head, trying to wipe this all away.

She clips a lead on Joe and ties him up with the other dogs.

Then she leans away into the grass on the other side of the path and empties her guts: coffee, early-morning toast. An apple.

But didn't Harry message her just now?

She looks again at the message and her scrolling finger freezes.

You are very special.

Who wrote that?

She lets out the breath she has possibly been holding since before she passed out.

Stop it.

It was sent through the app. There must have been a delay. It happens. Since a recent upgrade, the app has developed more bugs than Joe brought with him from the streets of Romania.

Then she does what she needs to do and, shakily, calls the police.

The call handler tells her to stay where she is.

They arrive within ten minutes, along with an ambulance she didn't ask for, because really what's the point. The blue lights strobe the air above the road a couple of hundred metres away from where she crouches, her back to Harry's remains. Two police officers – an enormous man-mountain and a tiny bird-woman, who seen together in different circumstances would make her smile – appear on the other side of the race-course with two paramedics. They duck under the white fencing and hurry across the grass, which was newly mown for the race held here yesterday.

The tiny policewoman greets her and guides her gently away towards the dogs.

Glancing over her shoulder, Caz sees that even the para-medics look shaken at what they are dealing with. They stand well back and peer at Harry's remains. One looks at the burly policeman and shakes her head. The policeman nods, pulls out his handset and calls it in.

The dogs are going mad. To distract them, Caz reaches into her treats pouch and throws handfuls of liver drops onto the grass around them. Instantly they give their entire beings to snuffling and hunting.

She envies them their ability to so completely switch focus.

The policewoman – who has introduced herself as Lisa – leads her through a brief recap of how she discovered the body.

'Do you have any idea as to the identity of the deceased?' she asks, her notebook at the ready.

Caz shivers and looks at her. 'Why?'

'Just asking. Brighton isn't such a big place, and with you being out and about with your work, perhaps you might have seen him up here?'

'I didn't really look too closely,' Caz says. She has learned the hard way that telling the whole truth can get you into a lot of trouble, so she's not doing that again.

Lisa makes a face. 'Don't blame you.'

The dogs have started bickering over the remaining treats.

'Can I get this lot back to their owners?' Caz asks. 'And I've got to give my disabled mum her breakfast.' She winces as she says this, knowing how much Ruth would hate this description of her.

'Hold on a tick.' Pointedly not looking at the body in the grass, Lisa goes over to her colleague, who, now death is established, is hustling the paramedics away to clear the crime scene. They exchange a few words. In the distance, more sirens sound. Soon this once-peaceful spot will be fenced off, tented over and surrounded by press and gawkers.

Lisa returns to Caz. 'He says yeah, we'd best get the dogs away before they contaminate the scene even more.' She hands her a business card. 'This is me. I've got all your details, Ms Sessions, so give me a buzz once you're sorted with this lot and you can come down to the station and give us a full statement.'

'Call me Caz.'

'OK, Caz.' Lisa takes her by the hand, a gesture that feels oddly intimate in this crime scene. She fixes her with her kind blue eyes in a way that makes Caz feel dirty for lying about not knowing Harry. 'And I want you to know that this sort of thing – finding a dead body when you're out on a walk – is extremely rare.'

Caz nods blankly.

Lisa squeezes her hand. 'It won't happen again, I promise.'

She blinks. She can't look her in the eye any more.

It had better not happen again.

Because as well as not telling the police that she knew Harry, if the subject comes up – and why on earth would it? – Caz has decided to withhold another truth.

This is not the first time she and Joe have discovered a body.

She's keeping it to herself because the first time – the Incident – nearly ended everything for her.

That it has happened again – this new Incident – well, it has to be a horrible, horrible coincidence.

Doesn't it?

THREE

'Yum,' Ruth says as Caz places a mug of tea and a plate of scrambled egg on toast with mushrooms and tomatoes in front of her. 'You know you don't have to do this for me.'

'But I want to.'

Ruth nods at Caz's coffee, which is all she can face after her morning from hell. 'Aren't you having anything?'

Caz usually has a second breakfast after her early, energetic start to the day.

'I picked up a flapjack from Hilltop Cafe,' she lies.

'Are you sure you're OK? You look a bit peaky to me.'

'Gee, thanks. No, I'm fine.'

'Are you sure?'

'The dogs gave me the runaround this morning.'

'Was it you, Joe?' Ruth asks as she tucks into her breakfast. Joe is sitting at her feet, looking patiently up at her, hoping for at least a corner of toast.

'Course not.' Caz scratches him behind the ears. 'It was Henna again.'

'Darn that Henna—' Ruth stops speaking, fork halfway to her mouth, and catches her breath.

'You OK, Mum?'

Ruth screws up her face – as much as she can with the scar tissue – breathes in, then lets it go. 'Back's not so clever today.' Her Leeds origins show more strongly in her voice when her guard is down like this.

'Have you taken your painkillers?'

Using her good hand – the one with all four fingers – Ruth tips the usual five teaspoons of sugar into her mug and shakes her head. 'You know how they mess with my guts. I'll have a spliff in a bit, once my breakfast's gone down.'

Ruth bears her scarring and pain so bravely. She doesn't like talking about the accident, but over the years, Caz has established that the car she was travelling in with Caz's father, Dan, was sideswiped by a lorry on the road between Harrogate and Leeds, where they lived at the time. It rolled twice and ended up in flames in a ditch. The emergency services managed to drag Ruth out of the passenger seat before the fire claimed her completely, but Dan, who was driving, was not so lucky. He died at the scene.

Caz has always taken strength from her mother's forbearance, even in the shameful teenage years when she was embarrassed by strangers staring at Ruth's facial scarring, her scary-looking right hand, the way she walked.

What are Caz's current issues compared to what her mother went through – still goes through every day? Ruth has enough on her plate. Like she didn't need to know about the Incident when it happened, she doesn't need to be bothered with what happened today with poor Harry.

For a moment Caz wonders if she should join her mother in her morning smoke. But turning up at a police station stinking of cannabis is so not a good look. In any case, although she makes an exception for Ruth's medicinal use, she doesn't really approve of numbing yourself with drugs.

Out on the kitchen work surface, her phone vibrates. She

wants to ignore it in case it's another delayed message from Harry. But she can't stop herself.

'Just going for a pee,' she says as she gets up, grabs the phone and heads for the damp bathroom at the back of the tiny kitchen.

The WhatsApp isn't from Harry, thank God. It's from Marcy, owner of Bridget Jones, the Maltipoo Caz walks every weekday except Thursdays.

Her shoulders relax and drop. But not all the way, because Marcy is not just any old client. She was Caz's best friend from primary to secondary school and on into university.

Was.

They only reconnected after Caz returned to Brighton. It's complicated, and Caz hasn't the mental space to think about it right now, but she has to look at the message because it's probably work-related.

She settles on Ruth's closed toilet lid and taps the message open.

Cazzer, it starts. For nine years, no one called her that, and now Marcy is back in her life and here she is, Cazzer again. Like nothing ever happened.

Ha.

> *Gotta go up north cos mum had a fall & is in hospital. Any way u could look after Bridge for me? Back Wed if all OK. If u & Joe can move in & take care of the house & garden 2, that'd be gr8 & I'll put £2k in your bank now & leave cash 4 expenses.*

Caz's eyebrows disappear into her fringe.

Marcy's gorgeous house sits at the end of Woodbourne Close, a tree-lined cul-de-sac of detached homes up by Hove

Park. When Marcy reconnected with Caz, to make amends – or at least that was Caz's reading of her motive – she took a fistful of her business cards and spread the word round her neighbours; so the early-morning dogs all live in the close.

Marcy has a heated outdoor dog-friendly swimming pool, bifold doors that open onto the garden, and although Caz has never been upstairs, there must be at least five bedrooms.

She stands and looks at herself in the mirror. 'But do you really *deserve* that gorgeous house, Marcy?' she asks quietly, so Ruth can't hear. 'Cow-face Marcy,' she adds, tasting the words like salty popcorn in her mouth.

She leans on the basin, which is cluttered with Ruth's hippy home-made toiletries, and focuses on her own eyes.

'Shut up,' she tells herself. She has no space for that anger right now, even though she relied on it to keep her sense of self and pride going over the last nine years. 'Shut. Up.'

Instead, she tries to look at it objectively.

So far, it's been a day of extremes. First all the horror on the racecourse. And now here's Marcy offering her a chance to live not only rent-free, but handsomely paid, in massive luxury, right next door to her morning clients so she doesn't even have to schlep all the way across town for pickup.

If she believed life worked like that, this could be karmic pay-off.

She rereads the text, just to make sure she's got it right.

She could also have a proper snoop into Marcy's world, beyond her fake 'oh, life is always so peachy' social media accounts that Caz used to stalk before she came back to Brighton.

And given that she is currently living in her childhood bedroom in Ruth's tiny two-up two-down in the crowded hilly tangle of the Hanover district, it's a no-brainer.

Except...

Except Ruth needs her.

Her mum is sixty now, and the toll of the constant pain and the bouts of PTSD-fuelled depression is showing on her, slowing her down. Added to that, three months ago, the grab rail that helps her up the stone steps from the pavement to her front door broke away from the wall as she was using it. She fell backwards, cracked her head, broke her right wrist and worsened the already dire situation in her spine.

By a dark stroke of luck, this accident coincided with Caz's issues after the Incident, so, having been all but sacked from her teaching job in London, she didn't have to think twice about returning home to help her mother recover from the fall and to stand by her side as she faces an uncertain old age.

She even felt a perverse touch of gratitude to the Incident for making the decision so easy for her.

But she is not grateful today. Today she wishes she could wipe both old and new Incidents clean from her mind. Or, better still, turn back the clock so that they never, ever happened.

She can't, of course, but a week at Marcy's will give her time to process what's just happened without having to hide it from Ruth.

She flushes the unused toilet, runs the tap just long enough for Ruth to think she is washing her hands, and goes back to the knocked-through living/dining room to talk it over.

'I managed without you OK for the last ten years. I think I can do a week,' Ruth says when Caz tells her about Marcy's text, but not unkindly.

'Are you sure?' Caz says.

'Do I ever lie to you?' Ruth fixes her with that stare she has that contains everything mother: love, pride and a sharp, keep-it-real dash of challenge. 'Plus it's two whole grand in your pocket.'

Caz's phone buzzes. It's Marcy again.

Can u let me know asap, Cazzer? Stressed out my box here.

Caz glances at her mum, who still has that fierce look on her face.

'OK then,' she says. She summons a smile, then turns back to her phone.

I'd love to!

Marcy's reply is instant.

Cool! Gotta fly. Dad's got dementia & can't look after himself with Mum in hosp. U got a key, so let urself in & make urself @ home. Any Qs just get back!

And only then does Caz realise how weird it is going to be to stay in the house that by rights should be hers.

Her fingers tingle at the unjustness of it all.

She finishes the washing-up and goes to give Ruth her post-breakfast cuppa. She finds her sitting in one of the two old armchairs in the little lean-to conservatory, almost hidden among all her artworks and plants. She is resting her fingerless right hand on the smooth marble of the Mother sculpture she made back when she was pregnant with Caz, before the accident stole her ability to hold a hammer. Her other hand holds her morning spliff.

Even now, Caz's rattled heart is warmed by the sight of the little bag Ruth keeps her stash in. Caz made it for her when she was about six, embroidering a shaky butterfly on a scrap of hessian and sewing a twisted rope strap onto it. It has stood up amazingly well, given its more than daily use.

Joe, who is always drawn to Ruth, sleeps on her feet. Bright sunlight filters through the greasy glass roof and gilds the two of them so they look like modern-day saints.

Caz hates busting up all this serenity, but she has to go to the police station before picking up her lunchtime clients.

'Got a one-to-one with a nervy new dog,' she tells Ruth, crossing her fingers behind her back for the lie. 'You sure you're OK with Joe for an hour or so?'

'Course.' Ruth smiles up at her and exhales like a sleepy dragon. 'I'm going to miss him while you're gone.'

'We'll be back before you know it. And we'll drop by every day.'

'Honestly, Caroline,' Ruth says, rolling out the big gun of Caz's full name. 'I'm not an old woman.'

Nearly, though, Caz thinks. *And then what will we do?*

A brief picture hits her of the two of them, mother and daughter, both traumatised, sitting in these two battered chairs, smoking away their days.

It's almost seductive.

She blinks and shakes her head.

She can't let that happen.

Not to Ruth, not to herself.

FOUR

Harry is a murder inquiry, so the team in charge has changed. Instead of lovely PC Lisa, Caz's interviewer is DS Dave Collins, who couldn't look more like a slimy cop if he spent a week in a costume and make-up department. His suit hangs lank from his too-thin frame, his dyed-black hair slicks greasily back from his balding temples and there is something unappetisingly grey about his complexion.

His attitude feels a bit off, too. His bloodshot eyes hover around Caz's chest when he greets her. Weirdly, it doesn't feel pervy, though. It's more like he just can't be bothered to look up at her face.

Still, she'll only have to put up with him for an hour or so. After all, she's just the person who found the body, so she won't have anything to do with him after today.

This is what she tells herself.

Unlike last time, when she naïvely told the truth and then had far too much to do with the detective in charge.

That was back in London, though. Safely fifty miles away, another world. There are so many crimes, so many reports, so much underfunding both there and here. If she keeps a low profile, the Brighton police won't make a connection, will they.

Will they?

She turns it over and over in her mind.

No. Of course they won't.

He ushers her to a grim little interview room where another detective is waiting, her face inscrutable underneath a peroxide crew cut. Collins introduces her as Detective Sergeant West. She nods unsmilingly then returns her gaze to the laptop sitting in front of her.

'So, Miss Sessions,' Collins says, partly through his nose.

'Call me Caz.'

He doesn't skip a beat, just steams on through this formality of an interview. 'Tell us in your own words and your own time what happened this morning. You don't mind if we record you, do you?'

'Of course not.'

Caz tells them him about how Joe made the discovery, how she fainted, how she called the police.

'Do you know who it is yet?' she asks when she's finished.

DS West sighs and raises an eyebrow at Collins, and Caz's ears grow hot. Does she know she's bullshitting? Has she blown it? Shouldn't she just tell them the whole story here and now?

But that would make everything more complicated than she could bear. She's just got to get through this and then she's done. She can walk the dogs, go to Marcy's, have a bath then go to bed and shut down the day.

And that other day, eight months ago.

Collins closes his notebook and shakes his head. 'He had nothing on him. No phone, no ID, no cards, and he's not on any of our databases either. We're hoping someone will notice he hasn't turned up for work or come home.'

Caz breathes out, slowly and quietly.

'Your dog was great,' Collins says as he makes moves to

wrap up – switching off the tape recorder, picking up his note-book. 'Once attended a body washed up on the seafront where the dog who found it thought he'd discovered a lovely big snack. Had a proper tuck-in. Terrible mess.'

Caz winces. 'Joe's a good boy.'

'Almost like he's done it before,' Collins says, pocketing his pen and winking. Caz suddenly feels sick.

As she stands, the silent DS West looks at her with cold grey eyes.

'Nice to meet you.' Caz smiles at her.

'Likewise,' West says, not taking Caz's outstretched hand. Her voice is flat and clipped, and once again Caz gets the feeling she has been rumbled.

But Collins leads her to the exit. He shows her out of the interview room by holding the door open at the top and ushering her under his cheaply suited armpit.

She can smell his sweat.

Can they smell hers?

Back in her old childhood bedroom, Caz gathers her stuff for the stay at Marcy's. She is not a high-maintenance sort. Her packing involves the basics – soap, a toothbrush, her Nivea/Vaseline/sunblock skincare regime and some deodorant. She rarely uses a hairbrush, so leaves that behind. Her two suit-cases are full, however, of seven complete sets of leggings, vest, fleece, socks and underwear, and three lots of waterproofs. She doesn't want to wash everything every day, and has discovered to her own cost that picking up a client's squeaky-clean dog when you are plastered in mud doesn't inspire confidence. She has even installed a warm dog shower in the back of her van to give a quick hosing and towel-off to any mucky clients before returning them to their owners.

She also packs a couple of cheap fleece blankets to protect

Marcy's no doubt pristine furniture from Joe, who thinks he is the king of every sofa he encounters.

Finally, after her usual good-luck touch of the Spice Girls poster that has lived on her bedroom wall since she was six, she hauls the two big bags down the narrow stairs.

'Mind my paintwork with those suitcases,' Ruth says from the sofa.

It's a long-standing joke, because the stairway wall is as scuffed as Caz's dog-walking boots.

She says her goodbyes, promising to call in tomorrow, and with Joe at her side, climbs into the little electric van she leases for her business.

She feels strangely unanchored. She has hardly started to process the morning's events, and now she is moving from living among all that is familiar to the utter weirdness of staying in the home of her nemesis. She feels like she is in a bubble, separated from normal life and normal people.

As she switches on her van, the radio kicks in and it's Beyoncé singing about how her soul can't be broken. In an attempt to channel Queen B's fortitude, Caz sings loudly along as she heads off to pick up the lunchtime dogs. She's decided she's just going to take them to the puppy park.

No more walking in the wilds today.

No more tempting fate.

FIVE

The lunchtime dogs all returned to their homes, Caz turns into Marcy's driveway and parks up in front of the house. While Joe shifts excitedly on the passenger seat, she sits and takes a couple of deep breaths, tries to settle herself.

But still the sediment disturbed by what happened this morning whirls on. It's been a day and a half, and then some. If only it hadn't started like it had, and she could fully dive into the fantasy that this is her house and she's just coming home.

Yet every time she closes her eyes, she sees poor Harry, blood, mutilation...

She has learned to shut the less gory but equally shocking first incident from her mind. But already she can feel it seeping around the edges of this fresh vision, bleeding in.

She clambers out of the van, lets Joe out of the passenger side and, sorting through her big bunch of clients' keys for the one that will let her into Marcy's house, makes her way to the front door. Bridget Jones is barking excitedly on the other side – she knows the electric whistle of Caz's van. Knows it means FUN!

Before she puts the key in the lock, Caz pauses for a

moment, stands back and takes in the house. Unlike the others on the quiet, tree-lined close, which still look more or less the same as when they were built, Marcy's has been completely renovated, with sleek white render, grey steel windows and cedar cladding.

It's lovely. It looks like a house in LA.

Not that Caz has ever been to LA.

And with that thought, up flares the realisation she has suppressed since the first time she stood here after returning from London. If Marcy hadn't betrayed her, Caz would probably have visited LA several times. She would have been accustomed to first-class travel. She would have seen more of the world beyond sunny resorts in southern Europe.

She pulls a face. Oh, boo-hoo, Caz.

Unless she deals with them right away, these thoughts about how this house should have been hers are going to spoil her week here.

She shakes herself. It's totally irrational.

For one thing, as she has been trying to tell herself ever since she and Marcy reconnected, Mark was never Caz's property. If, as she had assumed ever since they started going out in sixth-form college, he had truly wanted to make a life with her, then Marcy wouldn't have been able to 'steal' him.

It was at the superhero party Marcy held to celebrate the end of their university finals – yes, she, Mark and Marcy had been such a close-knit group of friends that they all slipped off to Manchester University together.

Unhealthy. She knows that now.

She has quite often literally kicked herself that she went to the party as Robin to Mark's Batman. Every other woman – Marcy included, *of course* – took the opportunity to smoulder in male-fantasy Lycra.

It was a typical klutzy Caz mistake.

Was it any surprise that Batman left her and her green cape

and baggy flesh-coloured tights behind to sneak off with skin-tight Wonder Woman?

Bam! Holy Betrayal, Robin.

But of course, the affair between Marcy and Mark hadn't started at the party. Two weeks later – two weeks during which both her boyfriend and her best friend completely ghosted her – Marcy cornered Caz as she was moving out of the grim little flat she and Mark had shared.

'Why do you think I didn't flat-share with you two when we moved out of halls? We've been trying to stop it for over a year,' she told her. 'Neither of us wanted to hurt you.'

Caz put down the rucksack she was manhandling into the van she had hired for the move and slapped Marcy hard, somewhere between her sharp cheekbone and her lovely hazel eye. A slap she knew would result in a massive puffy shiner marring that gorgeous face.

It was not her proudest moment, but even now she thinks, *Really, Marcy? And that was supposed to make me feel better?*

Marcy had been her best friend for ever. They sat together all the way through school, until their different aptitudes – Marcy's for design and the visual, Caz's for numbers and facts – found them drawn down different streams. Marcy brought Caz out of the shell that widowed and traumatised Ruth had built up around her only child. Repeatedly she saved her when she was out of her depth – both metaphorically at parties and pubs and once, quite literally, when she dragged her drunk from a stormy sea. She was Caz's hero, her shield, her champion, and Caz had truly loved her more than she loved herself.

And then she – and Mark, too, although Caz has always partly excused him, because, well, men think with their dicks, don't they – did *that* to her.

The slap wasn't enough. With a fury so violent it shocked her, Caz wanted to kill them both. To smash their heads together until they cracked like runny eggs.

After she'd moved her things into a new shared house with three boring maths graduate girls, Caz took a detour while returning the van. She parked up outside Marcy's place – a typically cool warehouse conversion she had somehow bagged for virtually no rent – and waited until she and Mark came out. Despite the darkness and the rain, Marcy wore her big Jackie O shades over the results of Caz's blow. Mark had his arm around her like he was protecting her from wild tigers.

Because, in a way, he was.

Caz gripped the steering wheel. She was now over an hour late returning the van – a previously unthinkable transgression for good girl Cazzer. But she was broken, so former rules no longer applied.

The entwined M&M – as she had taken to thinking of them – walked a couple of hundred metres down the road. Caz turned the key and started the engine. She rolled slowly out of her parking place. Picking up speed, she roared up behind them.

Somewhere between the edge of the road and the kerb, an image of her mother flashed up in front of her, as vivid as a three-dimensional avatar. She was shaking her head.

Because of this, thankfully, Caz didn't turn the wheel. Didn't mow Mark and Marcy down. Didn't reverse over them again, and again, and again.

She did look into her rear-view mirror as she passed them, though. And behind her shades, Marcy clocked her and flinched. Despite everything, the best-friend telepathy was still hanging on in there. Marcy knew exactly what Caz had thought of doing.

So instead of slaughtering them both, she drove on, parked the van and steadied her shaking hands as she paid the late hire fee. She told the boring maths girls she wasn't staying. Instead she was going to return to Brighton to live with her mum and do teacher training. The more miles she could put between herself and M&M, the better.

Particularly for them.

To stop herself from going over and over this same old same old, she focuses on the stunning magnolia standing in front of Marcy's house, its glorious blossom like velvet candles. So beautiful. She will have the best of it this week, before the petals fall. She breathes in the scent of the Scots pine next to it.

A beautiful welcome.

It almost calms her.

It should have been hers.

But perhaps Mark making a fortune after they graduated was more down to Marcy being so dynamic than to his own business acumen. Unlike Caz, who is sometimes too laid-back for her own good, Marcy is a Type A, a person who makes things happen. As well as that fateful end-of-university celebration, she organised all their joint birthday parties when they were growing up. It was Marcy who, once they were old enough to go away on their own, suggested, selected and booked the holidays they went on. And then she argued with her parents and moved out when she was eighteen to pay her way through university by working in Topshop.

She must have softened over the years, though, to drop everything and go and help her mum and dad in their hour of need. But then Marcy would never turn down the opportunity to look like a hero, to don a little metaphorical Lycra.

Caz taps herself on the cheek, a tiny little slap, and tells herself to stop being such a bitch.

All's fair in love and war.

And anyway, rather satisfyingly, Mark and Marcy split up last year in a messy, money-wrangling divorce, the details of which Marcy splurged all over her Insta.

While she was watching all this from the anonymity of a fake account, Caz sometimes got to thinking what a waste of a marriage it had been. If Marcy hadn't stolen him, her daydream went, Mark would have had a happy lifelong partnership with her.

Then, in her more cruelly masochistic moments, she stands her image of herself up against the gorgeous reality of Marcy.

If anything, it is surprising that Mark held out that long.

Stop it, stop it, stop it.

The dead body from today flashes across her vision again.

Poor Harry.

No more dreams for him. No more regrets.

If nothing else, he has put all this in perspective.

SIX

The reeded glass front door isn't double-locked like it usually is. Marcy must have left in a real hurry. Caz lets herself in. It's perfectly normal to her now to do this, but when she first started dog-walking, she was amazed at the trust her clients put in her – not only handing their dogs over to her, but also the keys to their homes.

For reassurance, she has a criminal record check certificate, but so far not one of her clients has asked to see it. To repay this trust, she never takes the piss. She abides by all the requests they make for their dogs – don't let this one off the lead, don't feed treats to that one. She even gives Henna the filtered water his owner supplies, even though he drinks heartily from every single puddle.

Above all, she never ventures any further inside her clients' houses than necessary. So even though she's a nosy sort of person, she only knows their hallways, utility rooms and kitchens, and has no idea what most of the living areas and any of the upstairs rooms are like.

She bends to greet Marcy's dog, who is beside herself at this unexpected visit. 'No walk right now, sorry, Bridge,' she says, ruffling the creamy fluff behind the little dog's ears.

Now that she's inside, Caz is itching to have a good old rummage.

Marcy's cool warehouse flat used to be as messy as you'd expect from an art student. Her look was also what might be called eclectic. But over the years she has honed her style, and when they reconnected, Caz was surprised by her new, sophisticated take on arty as a look. Pink tips on her afro, sure, but *expensive* pink tips.

The dropping-off glimpses Caz has had of this place show that Marcy now keeps her living space equally well groomed. Compared to the dark, cluttered corridor greeting visitors to Ruth's house, this entrance hall is gleaming clean and clear.

This hall that could have been hers...

'Stop it,' she says, and the two dogs look up at her, wondering what they've done wrong.

She straightens up, takes her dog-walking headband off and runs her fingers through her knotty hair. She has to be a better person about this. It was a long time ago, water under the bridge.

All that.

It takes her a second to register that the burglar alarm, for which she has the code, is not beeping. Also, it reeks so strongly of cinnamon and orange in here that it's making her eyes water. Joe, whose nose is twitching, instantly finds the source of the smell. The diffuser that normally sits on the console table under the mirror has fallen onto the floor and spilled its oily contents on the expensive tiles.

'You been jumping up, Bridge?' she asks the little Maltipoo. The table has two drawers, which contain her treats and walk gear, so it's highly possible.

Mindful that the scented oil could ruin the flooring, Caz takes a photo to show that it was like that when she got here.

Just in case – the worst part of her whispers – this is some sort of trap set by Marcy.

Telling herself off again, she hurries through to the kitchen to get some paper towels to clear up.

She knows the kitchen, because she comes in here to put out Bridget's water and food bowls when they get back after Marcy has left for work. Usually it's pristine, with wiped-down counters and absolutely nothing left out. But today it looks like Marcy really did have to leave in a hurry, because her bowl and mug are still on the breakfast counter, and she's even left half her muesli and blueberries.

Of course it would be blueberries.

They're probably organic, too.

From bloody Waitrose.

Caz wipes up the oil spill in the hallway, then puts leads on Bridge and Joe to take them round the block, just in case the excitement of her unexpected arrival has stirred up the goods. But then she remembers she is not at Ruth's place, where there is only a small courtyard out back and she has to take Joe to the grassy patch at the end of the street. No, Marcy has a vast, dog-proof back garden. So instead she lets the guys out of the bifold doors in the living room while she sets off, envy tucked firmly away, to explore her home for the week.

Six doors lead off the galleried landing at the top of the staircase. Working left to right, Caz finds four guest rooms that wouldn't look out of place in a five-star hotel. Despite the en suites for each of those rooms, the fifth door opens onto a lovely additional limestone-lined bathroom. The final one reveals what an estate agent would call the master suite, presumably where Marcy sleeps.

Where Marcy used to sleep with Mark.

And here are more surprises. The bed has not been made, a damp towel lies discarded on the sheets, and a nightdress and what look like yesterday's clothes – a white blouse, one of the designer business suits Marcy wears when she's queening it at the upscale menswear boutique she owns, and black underwear far lacier than Caz would ever dream of buying for herself – are strewn across the floor.

When Caz lifts the towel, there is blood on the bedsheet, which, given the horrors of the morning, pricks her nerves. But when she takes the towel to hang it in the en suite, she sees the open box of tampons on the top of the bidet, puts two and two together and tells herself to calm down.

Engaging her empathy so hard it almost hurts, Caz acknowledges that poor Marcy must have been really distracted to have gone away and left her bedroom like this. It also poses something of a dilemma. Her first impulse is to tidy up and wash the bed linen, but would that be seen as meddling, or worse, snooping?

'No, it's just kindness,' she says as she steps forward to strip the bed. And anyway, there was no indication from Marcy as to which room she should take, so it stands to reason that she would have looked behind all the upstairs doors. She'll just quietly clean up and then stay in the largest of the spare rooms.

With the linen bundled in her arms, she pauses to look out of Marcy's bedroom window, which has a view over the sweeping back garden – well-kept lawn, pool, garden studio, fashionable horizontal cedar fencing and grand mature trees. Again, a far cry from Ruth's little courtyard with her pots of baby tomato plants, leggy old geraniums and algae infestation. Caz has plans to spruce it up a bit now spring is here. Perhaps she can find a cheap way of putting up fencing like that...

And then she notices the dogs. Joe is at the end of the garden, standing guard by a massive old apple tree in full blossom, barking at Bridget, who seems to want to get past him.

'Joey!' she calls out as she runs down the stairs, dumping the laundry in the utility room before tearing outside to stop her boy bullying poor little Bridget. But when she reaches them, she sees that he is actually stopping Bridget from running out of an open gate behind the apple tree. Caz pokes her head through the gateway. A twitten runs down the backs of the gardens of the neighbouring houses and out onto the adjoining road.

'Blimey. Good boy, Joe.' The little alleyway is full of weeds – nettles, mostly – trodden down by locals, who must use it as a short cut to the Tesco Metro at the garage on the corner.

She gives a treat to each dog and closes the gate, releasing the nib on the Yale so that it's locked from the outside. Marcy must have left it open, which again surprises Caz.

For a second, she feels sorry for her. How much energy must all the straightening of her naturally messy approach to life take? Perhaps one day, after this house-sitting gig, Caz could teach her to relax and chill out a bit more, accept that she doesn't have to be perfect.

Perhaps one day they can erase all that bad air between them.

She is just wondering if this is actually what she really wants when, from the other side of the slatted fence, a woman screams.

A full-throated, high-pitched, mortal-danger scream. Completely out of nowhere.

Once again, Caz's overworked adrenaline jolts around her bones and she sees blood on grass, and Harry's empty eyes, and hands closing around a neck...

She lurches, the dogs start barking.

SEVEN

'Hello?' Caz calls, trying to peer through the slats between her and whatever is going on next door. 'Are you OK?'

'Marcy? Is that you?' The voice on the other side bursts out in a high, panicked, breathless register.

'No, but are you OK?' Caz asks again.

'I can't...' The woman breathes in and regroups. 'He just jumped straight out at me.'

Caz can barely believe this. Not after everything that has already happened today. 'Who?'

'They hide in the earth and you're just clearing a few weeds and *boof*! Right in your face.'

'What?'

'Bloody frogs.'

'Jesus Christ,' Caz says, partly out of relief, partly out of annoyance.

There's a beat of a pause from the other side of the hedge, then a mascaraed eye appears in the gap in the slats. 'I suppose Marcy's not there, then?'

'No.'

'Never is, is she? If you see her, can you tell her I really need
to talk to her about her extension plans.'

'She's away at the moment. I'm her... friend.' It still feels
odd to say it. 'House-sitting.'

'Do you know anything about her extension?'

'No, I—'

'Tell you what, meet you out the front and I'll give you the
plans she sent me, with my list of objections. You could hand
them over to her when she gets back.'

Caz shrugs and heads for the gate to the front garden.

Seems Marcy has a knack for putting people's backs up.

'...but perhaps *you* can make her see sense.' Marcy's neighbour
has laid a set of architect's drawings out on the bonnet of Caz's
van. 'Just look at this.'

'It is big,' Caz says, trying to sound as uncommitted as
possible.

With a firmness bordering on madness, the woman has
scrawled BLOCKS MY LIGHT!!! Several times on the plans,
accompanied by arrows pointing to an outline of her own
extension.

'You can just let her know when you see her that I'm
putting in my objections and I'll fight it to the death if necessary. Hey.' She smiles at Caz as if, despite having stood in
Marcy's drive for the past ten minutes bashing the set of drawings and ranting at her, she is seeing her for the first time.
'You're that dog girl everyone raves about.'

'That's me,' Caz says. 'Dog girl.'

'You certainly look the part!'

Caz smiles. She doesn't know how to take that.

The neighbour certainly looks *her* part, which Caz has
already nailed as entitled middle-aged Karen having a moan
about the ambitions of the young woman next door. She is

dressed like a well-heeled crafts teacher – everything she's wearing is probably organic and hand-made, and her hair is long and thickly plaited down her back. Her feet are clad in a Birkenstock/Hunter welly crossover; her voice is equally well heeled.

She extends a gardener's hand. 'Colette Stevens. I emailed you about Roget, but you said he was too big for the group walk.'

'Ah, the Pyrenean mountain dog! Yes, sorry, my van's too—'

'And you're madam's old school friend, yes?'

Caz nods, wondering how much else Marcy has let on about their relationship. Not the betrayal part, she bets.

Colette moves a little closer and leans in as if they are sharing a secret. 'How long is she away for?'

'A week.'

She snorts as if that's an outrage.

'Her mum's had a fall, and her dad has Alzheimer's, so she's got to go and sort things out for them,' Caz says, some old best-friend muscle jumping to Marcy's defence.

'Well, at least we'll have a break from the parties.'

'Perhaps I'll have parties.'

Colette laughs as if the very idea is absurd. 'Since Mark left, it's been all noise. I mean, what's the point of having a sound-proofed house if you leave the doors open all hours while you're entertaining? Constant shrieking in the pool, too. And now she's had that DJ studio installed in the garden. Again, expensively soundproofed, but she leaves the bloody doors open while she's spinning her discs or whatever it is she does. Horrible music.'

Caz blinks. She doesn't have Marcy down as a DJing sort, but there are loads of young women doing it on Instagram, so it's possible.

'Tell you what,' Colette says. 'I'm having a little dinner party tomorrow night to introduce my new fella to the neighbours – he's just moved in.' She gives a conspiratorial shiver of pleasure. 'It'll just be the immediate houses around us. You have to come.'

'I'm only here for a week. I don't think—'

'I won't take no for an answer. Now, what's it like inside?'

'Eh?'

'Her house,' Colette says, nodding at Marcy's front door.

'It's nice.' Caz isn't going to let this woman go poking around Marcy's stuff. That's *her* prerogative.

'She's very stylish, isn't she? Likes the nice things. Pity she and that husband split up. Though I could see it coming. All that dashing around. Nice shop she's got, though. I bought Jon a smashing shirt there the other day. Cost a fortune, mind, but then quality's what you pay for, isn't it?'

Caz smiles, not quite knowing what to say. She's strictly a Sports Direct person these days.

'Eight tomorrow night, yes?' Colette lifts the plans from Caz's van bonnet, rolls them up and hands them over. 'See you've gone electric. Is it any good? I'm thinking of getting one.'

'It's great,' Caz says. 'Do you know if there are any street chargers near here?'

'Madam's got one in her garage,' Colette says. 'For her snazzy Mini. I'll show you. Got the bipper?'

'This?' Caz fishes Marcy's house keys out of her pocket. There's an electric button device attached to the fob.

'That's the one.' Colette grabs the keys and points the thing at the garage door, which opens slowly like a well-oiled metal jaw.

Marcy's little silver Mini is sitting there.

'That's odd,' Caz says. 'I just kind of assumed she would be driving up north.'

'She doesn't strike one as the kind of girl who would take a train,' Colette says.

'She's definitely not the kind of girl who would take a train.'

'Perhaps she flew.'

. . .

Later, Caz lies in the sunken tub in Marcy's en suite bathroom, soaking in Marcy's expensive bubbles, lit by three of Marcy's costly scented candles. She has managed to get her own Relaxing Music for Dogs playlist up on the waterproof bathroom Bose system, and the soothing tones wash over her.

She has half decided to replenish the bathing luxuries she plans on using while she's here, but the thought still lingers annoyingly that they are, by rights, hers. That Marcy stole them.

So she probably won't.

Her muscles begin to let go of the day. She has walked her evening clients hard, eaten as much of a Deliveroo burger with fries as she could stomach, and her body is ready for rest. Yet, despite all this, when she closes her eyes she sees Harry. She tries to shake him out of her head, but then, moving from the edges of her vision towards the centre, there it is, the image she has so far successfully kept at bay.

Ash's face.

The face of the dead man Joe found eight months ago, out on their regular early walk on the canal towpath near where they lived in London.

The face that was so distorted it was barely recognisable.

Except that she recognised him.

She splashes the bathwater to try to push the thoughts out of her mind, but it doesn't work.

She recognised him because she had dated him.

Like she dated Harry.

Since this morning, she has held this knowledge away from her like a fragile glass ball, like something that might shatter and pierce her skin and make her bleed if she grasps it too tightly.

She and Ash became lovers more quickly than usual for her, and she allowed herself to hold a small piece of hope for a future with him. One night, in a crowded bar in central London, she even told him about what happened with Marcy and Mark, the Batman and Robin story, and how she was estranged from them both. It's not a story she shares with everyone, and his reaction to the betrayal was gratifyingly horrified.

So it hurt doubly when, thanks to an anonymous note, she discovered that he was also a rat. She never found out who was behind the note, but she suspected it was the mother of his three children, who was still very much married to him.

And like that time with Marcy, her rage flared. She sent messages to him containing unfortunate threats, which, when she discovered his body and told the police the entire truth, made her the number one suspect.

She was arrested and kept in a cell overnight for questioning. Those messages were used as evidence against her, the threats about strangling him read out to her in interviews.

'And then you "find" the poor man, strangled in a park,' DS Chowdhary said, leaning across the table, her beautiful eyes full of question and accusation. 'Quite a coincidence, eh, Caroline?'

But then, when the initial autopsy report came in, it turned out that when Ash was killed, Caz had been present all day at a searingly dull in-service training course.

The police finally let her go, with no apology whatsoever.

It was the head at the school where she worked who confirmed her alibi. When she got home, he called her and told her that until the case was resolved, she should not come in to work. In a release of the anger built up over her time in custody, she told him he could stuff his bloody job. The last thing she wanted was to face a classroom full of students or a staffroom full of whispering colleagues. He agreed so readily it felt like a sacking. She suspected he didn't want to deal with a potential scandal rippling through an already challenged school.

Then Ruth had her fall and Caz knew she had to make a

new start. So she moved back home and tried to leave everything behind in the past.

And now this has happened, and it has pulled it all back out of the box she thought she had packed securely away.

'They're linked,' she says to the bathroom tiles. 'They have to be.'

'No,' she replies for the tiles. 'They were murdered in completely different ways. Ash was strangled, Harry was stabbed.'

'Shut up,' she says.

'So of course they're not connected. Not the same modus operandi. That's what they say connects killings on the telly.'

Talking to the tiles. She's losing it.

She swishes the bathwater around her belly, tries to pull herself together.

And now there's the weirdness of all this, all Marcy's stuff, the scent of Mark not yet fully gone from the place. And the encounter with Colette, and the invite to dinner tomorrow.

She'd rather find another dead body than go to that.

'Actually no, scrub that,' she mutters.

Today has been too, too much.

But sometimes life is like that. You just bimble along and nothing happens, then everything lands on you all at once.

She slides down under the water. 'It never rains, but it pours,' she says, bubbling the words up to the surface. 'You wait hours for a bus, then five turn up at once.'

It's a thing. If not, why are there so many clichés about it?

Her scalp crawling like she's got head lice, she surfaces and, drying her hands on a flannel, grabs her phone. What she needs to do is delete that app. SeeMe. Seamy, more like. Whoever named it should have read it out loud. She's sure there's no link, but as far as she knows, it's the only common denominator between Ash and Harry.

Apart from herself. And yes, she knows how it would look if slimy DS Collins got hold of that information.

There's a lot of stuff in the press about police forces not talking to one another, not joining up the dots, not bringing criminals to justice.

She hopes that's going to work in her favour. In any case, there's no way she's putting herself through what happened to her in London again. She'll never forget the shame of being arrested and carted off in a police car. Nor the terror when the nightmarish possibility struck her that she – a total innocent – might be charged with murder. And all that horror heaped on top of the trauma she was already going through after finding an actual murder victim, the first dead body she had ever seen.

Even so, despite the urge to instantly wipe the SeeMe app entirely from her life, before she deletes it, she screenshots Harry's profile and all their communication and files it on her Dropbox next to where she put Ash's stuff.

Just in case this isn't the end of it.

Just in case she needs all the help she can get.

EIGHT

The most disturbing thing about the night's sleep Caz has after her horrific day is that it is so deep and thorough. Her Fitbit awards her an unprecedented score of ninety-two. Perhaps it was the comfort of being sandwiched under the duvet between two excessively needy dogs. Bridget, who is clearly usually shut in the utility room at night, couldn't believe her luck when Caz allowed her up into the bedroom. Even though Caz often has words with herself about anthropomorphising dogs, it felt too cruel to shut her out while Joe had full access.

She wakes, however, with a tightness behind her eyes and a headache that can only partly be explained by the stiff gin and tonic she poured herself from Marcy's well-stocked drinks cabinet after her bath.

The pain reassures her that she is human and feels and hurts like other people.

Leaving her van charging next to Marcy's Mini, she walks her earlies in Hove Park, just round the corner from the house. Compared to the Downs, this forty acres of urban greenery is tame, manicured and, even at this hour, buzzing with joggers and people walking their own dogs – what she likes to call the amateurs. But she's grateful for the company of strangers this morning, even though she's not really giving the dogs the runaround they deserve or need to wear them out.

Back at the house, she is just clearing up after her breakfast – a conscious re-creation of what Marcy had yesterday – when the doorbell chimes, making her jump and drop her bowl. She curses loudly as it cracks and splats leftover muesli, yoghurt and blueberries across the sparkled terrazzo kitchen floor.

Bridget and Joe, both on edge in their new domestic set-up, bark like there's a serial killer on the other side of the front door. Whoever it is, the shape they make behind the reeded glass is tall, wide and unmistakably male. In her annoyance at the breakage, Caz forgot to look at the doorbell camera screen on the kitchen worktop. She hesitates while the dogs snarl and snap, and wonders if she can just tiptoe back and take a look, or whether the caller has spotted her.

'It's just someone ringing the doorbell,' she mutters to herself. 'Get a bloody grip.'

But she feels oddly exposed in this large detached house, where, unlike back at her mum's place, the neighbours can't see all your comings and goings.

'Not *another* hound, Marce?' a male voice booms, and instantly Caz knows who it is and stands down her guard. 'Hold it back, please.'

'Bloody hell,' Caz says as she opens the door. 'You're such a wuss, Damian.'

'Caz?' Her tall, immaculately dressed caller blinks in surprise. 'Well, that's incongruous. Mind me trews!' he says to the dogs, who, having decided he is zero threat, are trying to get past her to jump up in greeting. 'New season Westwood, RIP,' he explains as he smooths his tartan trousers.

'Smarty pants.' Caz holds the dogs' collars while Damian breezes past her and through into the kitchen. He clearly knows his way around.

He puts his laptop bag down on the table and turns to look at her. 'What the hell are you doing here anyway, and where's Missy Marcy?'

'Don't I even get a hug?'

'Come here.' He opens his big leather-jacketed arms and folds her up in that way he has that, ever since she and Marcy first met him, has always made her feel so protected.

Damian, Marcy and Caz were the coolest kids in sixth-form college. Well, Damian and Marcy were. Caz has no idea why she was included in their gang, except perhaps for the fact that they all had absent fathers: Caz's died in the car crash, Marcy's was an emotionally withdrawn tyrant, and Damian's was a mystery, someone his mother refused to talk about. When the big falling-out over Mark happened, unlike all their other mutual friends, who naturally sided with Caz, Damian trod the line between her and Marcy with such skill that he managed to keep both as close friends and confidantes.

Perhaps his historical dislike of Mark, which dated from their early schooldays, also helped. He felt both glad that Mark was out of Caz's life and sorry for Marcy because she had somehow been duped into loving him.

True, in recent years he has seen more of Marcy, because he now manages her shop. It's ideal for Damian, who says he's like a stick of rock with *Brighton* and *fashion* written right down through his centre. However, despite relying on Marcy for his livelihood – and he *loves* his job – he has always said, 'If it comes to it, I'm Team Caz, babe.'

Indeed, it was with glee that he came to her with the news of Marcy and Mark's split. She didn't burst his bubble by telling him she already knew. Shame means she'll take her secret social media snooping to the grave.

This was shortly after she found Ash's body. Damian is her only friend who knows about that, and she told him that if she hadn't been in such a state, she would have thrown a party to celebrate.

He releases her from the hug and steps away. 'Proper bezzies with Marcy again now, aren't we?' he says. 'She got you moved in?'

'Nah. I'm working for her, too, like you.' Caz explains about the house-sitting.

'But me and her are supposed to do breakfast here today to talk through stock for next season.'

'I think it was all a bit of a rush,' Caz says. Once more she finds herself defending Marcy.

'She's normally so on things like that, though,' Damian says. 'She'd twist my balls off if I didn't turn up for a meeting without letting her know.'

Caz explains about the breakfast things, the state of the bedroom. 'She must be proper worried, Dame. None of that sounds like her.'

He shakes his head, then claps his hands. 'Well then. Aren't you going to get me some coffee, now you're Marcy's bitch? And we can have these.' He opens his bag and pulls out a box of macarons from the expensive patisserie up by the station.

'Yes, boss.' Caz salutes and heads for the espresso machine.

Damian bends to make a fuss of the dogs. He presents as brittle, but he's all heart, really. He briefly watches her struggle with Marcy's ridiculously complicated coffee machine, then, without any fuss, steps in and takes over.

It's a bright, sunny morning, so they take their coffee and macarons to the sunloungers by the pool. As they cross the patio, Damian holds his phone to his ear, trying to call Marcy to rearrange the meeting.

'No reply,' he says. 'Again, that's one hundred and fifty per cent out of character.'

'She's probably at the hospital with her mum, or looking after her dad or something,' Caz says. 'Leave a voicemail.'

'She said she'd fire me if I ever did that,' Damian says.

'So strict.'

'And she was only half joking.'

Caz smiles. 'Cow.'

'Anyway, what is this sudden devotion to the parents? I thought they'd emigrated.'

'Me too,' Caz says. 'Perhaps they came back. Brexit or something. What happened to your hair, Dame?'

He strokes his bare scalp. 'Shaved the last bits off. Bum fluff, really.'

'Goes nicely with the beard.'

'Almost bear.' Damian smiles and bites a chunk out of his macaron.

The pool steams in the still, chill morning air.

'Is that right?' Caz asks as they stretch out on the slatted loungers. 'It's always heated?'

'It's for Bridget, really. And Marcy can afford it.' Damian throws a ball into the water for Joe and Bridget, who launch themselves in after it. 'Who would've thought it, her inviting you of all people to come and stay in her house. Bet you've had a good nose around.'

'Haven't actually.' Caz holds her hand up in a Scout salute. 'I'm a good girl.'

'You didn't go round the place touching all the lovely things and singing "It should have been me" in your best Yvonne Fair?'

'Eh?'

He calls up the song on his phone and plays it to her.

'Turn it down,' she says, as the chorus winds up, and the singer's anger explodes all over the lyrics. 'Colette,' she mouths, pointing over the hedge.

'Ah. We don't want to upset Crappy Colette, do we?'

Caz sighs. The song has brought the high she got from

seeing Damian crashing down. 'It *should* have been me, you know,' she says.

'Still, Caz? You are so much better off without him.'

They watch the dogs, who are now paddling towards the steps to get out of the pool.

Caz flexes her fingers. She doesn't want to talk about it, but she can tell Damian does. To be fair, it comes from a kind place.

'And look,' he goes on, 'Marcy didn't get him either. Well, she got his Mr Smart-Arse High-Tech Start-Up money, but she didn't get to keep his soul. You're well off out.'

'A good man is hard to find.'

'Ooh. Another song!' Damian picks up his phone and starts scrolling though Spotify.

'Stop it, please,' Caz says. 'I've got to go to dinner at Colette's tonight. The last thing I need to be doing is putting her back up.'

'You've got right in there, haven't you? She's not been quite so welcoming to Marcy.'

'I think Marcy annoys her no end,' Caz says.

'Poor Marcy.'

'Seriously?'

'She's very alone, Caz.'

'That bed she's made for herself.'

'But look at the way she reached out to you when you came back home.'

'Huh.'

When Caz returned to live in Brighton, she got a card from the now-wealthy divorcee Marcy: *Dear, dear Caz, I hear you're back in town. Can we meet? I don't want to put you under any pressure, so please let me know yes or no through Damian.*

So Caz went ahead and used Damian – who knew nothing of Marcy's overture – to arrange to meet her in Mrs Fitzherbert's, the city-centre pub where back in the day they used their fake IDs to buy cider.

She also chose it because it is named after Maria Fitzher-bert, the mistress of the dandy King George IV, who he married then violently disowned. This personal joke made her feel a tiny bit dirty, and she had to remind herself that having a little laugh on Marcy was nothing compared to what Marcy had done to *her*.

But Marcy – looking gorgeous in her designer gear and that pink-tipped afro – was oblivious to the slight. Her delight at Caz arranging to meet her was so beguiling that, after they had downed a second large glass each of Pinot Grigio, Caz decided to bury the hatchet, albeit with a tiny part of the handle still showing, just in case.

The dogs bound towards Damian, and Joe drops the ball at his feet while Bridget Jones shakes water all over him.

'Oh no. Your lovely trousers,' Caz says.

'Didn't really think that through, did I?' Damian says. 'I'll never get on with dogs.'

'They're better than people.' Caz picks up the ball and throws it over to the other side of the lawn. 'Present company excepted.'

'Have you had any more luck with that dating app?' Damian asks.

And here it comes again. Seeing Damian briefly swept the memory away. For a moment, Caz feels like filling her pockets with cobbles from Marcy's landscaping and jumping into the pool.

Instead, she takes the ball from Bridget and chucks it back into the water. Then she turns to Damian and tells him what happened yesterday morning. As she describes this discovery of the corpse of yet another man she had been dating, his eyes grow so round she's afraid they might pop out of his head.

'My God, Caz, that's awful. How are you?'

'I don't know.'

'I can't believe it,' he says.

'Me neither. It's like I attract horror. Like mine's the kiss of death.'

'Don't go there. Things don't work like that. It's just a horrible coincidence.'

'Just bad luck?'

'What else could it be? It's not like you've got any enemies or anything, have you? You're the nicest person I know.'

Caz pulls a face and wonders why this feels like an insult. 'Worse than bad luck for poor Harry, though.'

'Hold on. Harry?'

'Yes. So?'

'Do you have a photo of him?'

Caz goes to her Dropbox, finds Harry's profile picture and passes her phone over to Damian.

'Jesus,' he says, squinting at the screen. 'Oh no.'

'What?' Caz says. 'What is it, Dame?'

Frowning, he hands the phone back to her. 'He was one of Marcy's favourite customers – even though he only came in at sale time. So handsome. She was going to use him for an Insta shoot for the late-summer collection.'

'So you knew him, too?'

Damian nods. 'And him and Marcy. They were kind of close.'

'What?'

He shrugs. 'I don't know any details, so don't ask.'

'Fucking hell.'

'I can't believe it.'

'*You* can't believe it?'

'Look. Wait till Marcy gets back before you tell her, eh?'

Caz's cheeks burn. She has been flayed with this, sent to hell a second time. 'You mean protect poor little Marcy?'

Damian holds up his hands. 'Forget I said anything.'

'What about me, Damian?'

'I love you, Caz. You know that.' He looks at her, but she can't read his expression.

Is this right? Is this yet another coincidence? Caz is so confused; she can't quite unravel all the implications of it.

'Brighton's a small place,' she says, still so full of anger that it sounds like an accusation.

'It is.'

Joe bounds up again all wet and drops the ball in front of her. She throws it extra hard to expel some of the fury she's feeling towards Damian; fury even she knows is unfair.

He watches her, then moves to the side of his sunlounger to make a space for her.

'Come here,' he says.

She lies down next to him, and as he puts his big arms around her and holds her tight, she burrows her face into his chest.

'Jesus. Poor Harry,' Damian says. 'I can't believe it.'

'It's so horrible.'

'Look up,' he says. He's holding his phone above them, in selfie mode.

She sees herself, her hair nestled into his beard. Safe. Protected.

'We're alive, Caz,' he says. 'And we've got each other. We're the lucky ones.'

He taps his screen and captures the moment.

NINE

'Come on in, darling.' Colette greets Caz with a waft of amber perfume and wraps her in a hug that's all gauzy sleeves and clattering bangles. Behind her, a giant blonde dog waits in line for his greeting, as if he knows that Caz is all about the animals.

Caz hands Colette the bottle of nice red she has taken from the pretentious 'cellar' installation on Marcy's kitchen wall and obliges the dog with a ruffle behind his ears.

'You love that, Roget, don't you?' Colette says. 'Too bad Caz's van is too tiny for you, boy, isn't it?'

It's hardly surprising that she's being sensitive at the moment, but Caz can't help feeling a little bit under attack with this.

'Come on in, dear, and meet the others.'

Caz wants to take the bottle back from Colette, run to Marcy's, lock the door and spend the evening watching reruns of *Friends*. Instead, she lets Colette lead her through the hallway and into a living room overlooking the back garden. Although similar in size and built around the same time, this house couldn't be more different to Marcy's. Colette likes Persian rugs, Indian lampshades and walls covered in splashy abstract oil paintings. Jungles of plants sprout from every corner. The other four guests sit uneasily on a giant modular sofa that looks like a multicoloured series of slumped bags of concrete. One of them, a heavily made-up blonde woman in her sixties, is perched on the purple part of the sofa, coughing in a mildly alarming way.

Looking at the smartly clad neighbours brings on another urge to make a swift exit. Caz didn't pack for middle-class dinner parties and feels decidedly underdressed in her one pair of clean jeans and neatest T-shirt. She would have ransacked Marcy's walk-in wardrobe, but as she is two sizes bigger, it would have been a depressing exercise.

Colette claps her hands. 'Hey, everyone. Meet Caz, Marcy next door's house-sitter and dog-walker to everyone in the close but me.'

'Hey, dog-walker girl.' A tall, well-built man with the faded looks of a retired rock star approaches Caz and places a glass of champagne in her hand. Caz has a strange feeling that she has met him somewhere before. 'Jon Ashdown. Colette's bit of rough. Nice to meet you.' His tattoos, Mancunian accent and deep gravelly voice go some way to illustrating his point, although his super-whitened teeth and expensive-looking shirt redress the balance. Colette breezes across the room with a platter of some sort of brown dip and tortilla chips and scoops Caz away from him.

'That's not how it is at all,' she says, rolling her eyes and steering her over to the other guests. 'Jon and I are absolute soul-mates, and this party is to welcome him to our end of the close, along with Peter here, who is going to be next door indefinitely sorting out his late uncle's house.'

'Big job.' The man called Peter levers himself up from the too-low sofa and holds out his hand. 'Dear old Ezra was a bit of a hoarder.' He has a kind, handsome face. His firm chin, chiselled cheekbones and clear blue eyes make Caz think of a young

Peter O'Toole – a reference she can dig out of her brain thanks to Ruth's insistence on only watching pre-1970s movies. And he has interesting, pixie-like ears, which soften his good looks, make him appear vulnerable.

'My mum's a bit like that,' she says, in an attempt to make small talk.

'Well, if she's anything like Ezra, she must be an interesting woman,' Peter says.

'Although Ezra was a bit of a nutter,' the coughing woman says. 'No offence,' she adds, winking at Peter.

'None taken.' Peter smiles. 'He was what you'd call singular.' He has, Caz realises, a touch of Bristol in his voice, a West Country burr that she instantly warms to.

'He believed the end of the world was nigh and would tell you all about it if you lingered too long putting out the dustbins,' the man sitting next to the woman says through lips that look like they would be more at home on a fish. 'What they call a prepper, I believe.'

'And this is June and Clive, Marcy's neighbours on the other side,' Colette says, taking Caz's elbow and moving her towards the couple.

June coughs again. 'Sorry. I've tested negative. I won't shake your hand, though, just to be safe.'

Clive's hand feels hot and clammy when Caz takes it, and he holds her fingers just a second too long.

'Pleased to meet you, darling,' he says, those fish lips glistening.

Peter catches her eye as she pulls her hand away and they share a small conspiratorial wince.

'So this is the entire turning-circle end of the close,' Colette says. 'Except for Nicola, of course.'

'Nicola?'

'Doesn't ever go out,' she whispers, as if Nicola can hear her from her house, which must be at the far end, beyond June and Clive. 'Hasn't since 1982, they say.'

Caz feels ridiculously young in this crowd. Not the neighbours she would choose if she were Marcy.

'I'll be serving up in five minutes,' Jon says, and disappears into the kitchen.

'This is delicious,' Caz says as she bites into the slow-cooked pomegranate-jewelled lamb Jon has served up. The champagne and two glasses of wine have slightly softened the edge of her post-traumatic state.

'Never ever go out with anyone if they don't cook,' Colette says, beaming across the table at her boyfriend.

'I'll bear that in mind.'

'Although Jon has many other talents.' Colette throws another admiring look at him. He holds his finger to his lips.

'Do you have a boyfriend, Caz?' asks Clive, who is sitting opposite her. A pomegranate seed flies from his mouth and lands on the tablecloth between them like a tiny blood clot. Caz takes a deep breath and tells him no, she's single at the moment.

She might not have been had the night with Harry at the Mesmerist happened. She might even have been out with him tonight, too. Or they might have been staying in, enjoying Marcy's house, erasing the ghosts of Mark and Marcy from the master suite...

She eyes the lamb: dead flesh, wet with fat and red pomegranate juice. Perhaps, she thinks, Ruth has a point about being a vegetarian. She puts down her fork.

Peter, who is sitting to her right, leans in and asks her if she's OK.

She is not OK. She wants to stand up, turn round and run away, but instead she just paints on a bright smile and says that she's fine.

'What happened to your uncle?' she asks, to try to move her brain on.

'He just collapsed and died, poor old bloke. Heart. Three weeks ago,' he says. 'The police called – I'm the last of the line – and I shot down here.'

'How's Rupert?' Colette asks.

'Rupert?' Peter asks.

'His poodle.'

'Oh. Roop! I got him rehomed with a lovely lady a couple of streets away. Old friend of Ezra's who adores him. I'm just not a dog person.'

'Pity,' Colette says. 'I'd have had him.'

'Roget would have had him for breakfast!' Jon says.

'What's going to happen to his house, Peter?' June asks. 'Are you going to stay?'

Peter shrugs. 'Don't know yet. I'll certainly be here a while. There's a lot of work to sort out.'

'Work?' Caz says.

'He was a sculptor,' Peter says. 'There's a garden studio full of pieces, and two of the bedrooms are stacked floor to ceiling with stuff – maquettes, sketches, so on.'

'Should be worth a bloody fortune.' Jon places another two bottles of red wine on the table. 'Now he's a goner.'

'Jon!' Colette says.

Caz turns back to Peter, as Jon tops up her glass for the fourth or fifth time. 'Was he famous?'

'Not wildly, but he sold steadily, it seems. I've found the name of the gallerist who held his last show, so hopefully he'll come round and help me sort out what to do with it all. It'd be a pity to see it go to waste.'

'You're laughing, mate,' Jon says.

'I've seen some of it.' June wrinkles her nose. 'Not my cup of tea.'

'I just want to honour the old man's work.'

'My mum was a sculptor, too,' Caz says.

'There's a coincidence,' Peter says.

'Was?' Colette asks, looking at Caz as if she is seeing her in a new light.

'Oh, she's still very much here, but she was badly injured in a car accident and had to stop. When she was pregnant with me.'

'That's awful,' Colette says.

'It's OK. She's OK. She paints now.'

'Brought you up on her own, did she?' Jon asks.

Caz frowns, wondering how he has made this leap. 'Yes. My dad died in the accident.'

'My mum was on her own, too,' he says. 'Disabled as well. It's tough.'

Caz's scalp starts itching. Jon is making a lot of assumptions here. 'We got by. Get by. I've moved back in with her. While I get things going with the dog-walking.'

'That's what I like,' Jon says. 'A bit of get up and go. You and me, girl. We're cut from the same cloth.' He winks at her, and she realises he is quite drunk. Possibly has been since she walked in. 'Working class, single mums. I know how it is.'

Caz thinks about pointing out how wrong he is, that in fact she is solidly middle class, and while her mother is disabled, she's certainly not the feeble invalid Jon is no doubt picturing. But it would open her up to yet more questions, and she'd really rather just eat her food and get out of here.

Luckily Colette picks up the conversational gauntlet.

'Jon likes to point out how privileged I am.' She addresses the whole table with a smile crafted to be charming, but which is actually quite terrifying. Her voice slurs. She too appears to have overdone the wine.

'You don't have to work for a living like me and Caz here,' Jon says.

Colette laughs. 'I bloody work my arse off, Jon, and you know it.'

'I mean proper physical labour, love, not sitting at a computer playing with numbers.'

'Like you made your money from physical labour!' she says.

Caz can't work out if she's furious or playing with him.

'And what is it you do, Colette?' Peter asks, leaning forward to draw Colette's murderous gaze from her 'soulmate'.

'Futures,' Colette says, which Caz thinks has something to do with money. 'And I'm bloody good at it.'

'Guess you have to get up early with the dog-walking?' Jon tops up her glass yet again. 'I don't think I could do that.'

'I'm used to waking at the crack from when I was a teacher up in London,' Caz says.

Clive holds out his own glass for more wine. 'All that walking keeps you in nice shape, though.' He licks his lips.

'Excuse me?' Caz says.

Before she can stop herself, she imagines stabbing him in the eye with a fork.

Colette stands. 'Is everyone finished?'

The dessert, a white chocolate cheesecake, is as delicious as the main course.

'I had a spell working in a kitchen a few years back,' Jon says when Caz tells him how much she is enjoying the food. 'Pastry chef.'

'Which restaurant?' June asks. 'Clive and me, we eat out a lot.'

'Not round here,' Colette says, so quickly that it's clear she's trying to shut the subject down.

'Not round here,' Jon agrees, nodding like he's been slapped down. 'But I do love making a pud.'

'How long are you house-sitting for Marcy?' Peter asks Caz.

'Until Wednesday,' Caz says. 'She's up north looking after her parents.'

'Tell me about her.' Colette licks cheesecake from her spoon. 'What was she like at school?'

'Lovely girl,' Clive says as Caz opens her mouth to reply. 'Keeps herself to herself, though.'

'I'm glad that Mark's out of the picture,' June adds. 'His car was so noisy and so vulgar.'

'You know what they say about a man with a red Ferrari,' Clive says. 'Let it be known that I drive a beige Granada.' He and June laugh at this joke, which is delivered with not brilliant but clearly well-rehearsed timing.

'Mark left early every morning,' Colette explains to the rest of the table, 'and often didn't get back till late, and his car made an awful racket.' She turns to June. 'But now we've got Marcy's parties. Letting her hair down now she's single.'

'You went to school with Marcy?' Peter asks Caz.

'You from Brighton, too, then?' Clive says. 'Like me and June?'

'Have you met her?' Caz says to Peter.

'She was really kind when I moved in. Brought round a cake and said how much she admired Ezra's work, how she'd bought one of his pieces for her shop.'

'Oh, her shop!' June says. 'Daylight robbery. And the clothes – I certainly wouldn't buy that sort of thing for Clive.'

'That's one of her shirts,' Colette says, pointing at Jon.

'Oh,' June says. Caz swears her legs are literally back-pedalling under the table. 'Well, *that's* a lovely shirt.'

'Thanks.' Jon smirks and lifts a jug from the middle of the table. 'More cream, anyone?'

'She's hard-nosed, Marcy, but then you have to be to be a good businesswoman,' Colette says. 'She's going to need a ton or two more steel when I start fighting that bloody extension plan, though.'

'We were at school together from primary,' Caz tells Peter.

'It must be great to have such a close friend.'

There's something about this man. He seems so sensitive to her awkward position here that she has to stop herself from telling him about how actually not great it had been having Marcy as a friend.

Perhaps it's because he's the nearest to her in age. She's never been good at guessing how old people are, but he must be no more than forty-five. And his good looks are almost other-worldly. She has dated a couple of men in their forties before, but they turned out to be nightmares, like vampires sucking away at her youth. Peter feels different, though.

Despite that, she doesn't think there's a spark.

Perhaps he's gay.

Perhaps she should introduce him to Damian, who is endlessly looking for Mr Right.

Perhaps she should just forget entirely about dating and pairing up and all of that.

As Caz, a little drunk, trips her way down Colette's driveway and back up Marcy's, she is suddenly plunged into darkness. All the street lights go out, just like that. She gets her phone out: it is midnight. Some green energy-saving thing, no doubt. It doesn't happen down where Ruth lives, nearer the city centre, but up here in the 'burbs...

She's never liked the dark. A shiver runs up her spine and across the top of her head.

She switches on her phone torch and runs to the front door, glad of the sensor light that kicks in. Behind her, she can hear June and Clive making their way home, her coughing then laughing like a drain at something he murmurs to her.

She lets herself in and is greeted by two overenthusiastic dogs. But in the middle of his welcoming ritual, Joe drops the slipper he always brings and starts barking at the door she has just closed behind her.

'What is it?' She opens the door again. Joe gets down on his haunches and growls.

Something rustles down in the shrubs that shield Marcy's house from the road.

Caz's scalp prickles again.

'It's just a fox,' she says, but as Joe looks up at her, she knows he believes that as little as she does.

She bolts the door, sets the alarm and heads for the stairs. The dogs seem keen for her to go into the living room. Joe even bats her leg with his nose.

'No, guys. Six a.m. start. Bedtime.'

Reluctantly they follow her upstairs.

Just before she goes to sleep, she texts:

Hey Marcy. Just met the neighbours. Lolz! How's your mum?

There is no reply.

TEN

Her early Saturday session done, Caz lets Bridget and Joe back in through Marcy's front door. Once more, she took the local dogs to Hove Park, which, even at this hour, was busy with people setting up the weekly Park Run. She's not sure she'll ever be able to go out into the countryside again.

All she wants to do now is go to bed and nurse her hangover. Champagne then red wine is never a good plan, particularly in those quantities. She is still trying to piece together the events of the evening. There are a few black holes, but she remembers feeling uncomfortable with a couple of creepy men. As well as hung-over, she is exhausted. Despite the alcoholic anaesthesia, last night's dreams featured so many bloody collages of mutilated men that she kept on having to wake herself up.

But if she doesn't do her weekly admin now, it's going to be hanging over her for the rest of the weekend.

'Not that we've got any plans,' she says to the dogs. 'Apart from walking Spicer tomorrow and visiting Mum.' Damian will be busy at the shop, and all her other old friends have either moved on to more exciting lives or are cocooned with their children. Still, at least she's got Marcy's house to enjoy, even if she's rattling around in it.

She heads to the kitchen to make some desperately needed coffee, but again, like last night, Joe and Bridget want her to go into the living room.

'I'm not a sheep,' she says to Joe, who is pulling out all his genetic programming and herding her across the hallway. 'OK!' she says, holding up her hands. 'If it makes you happy.'

While Joe pushes the backs of her legs with his nose, Bridget runs through the door.

A curved metal arm reaches into the room with a lampshade suspended from it. Its chunky marble base sits to the side of the sofa, and that's where Bridget heads now, to nose something slumped against it. Joe runs to sit beside her and look back at Caz.

'What is it, Joe?'

She goes to him and gets down on her knees to take a closer look.

It's a handbag. A very good Mulberry handbag.

'Is this why you wanted me to come in here last night?' she asks the dogs as she unzips the main compartment. Inside, neatly stashed in the many organising pockets, she finds three credit cards, Marcy's driving licence, £300 in cash, a bunch of keys and a make-up bag full of expensive-looking products with labels that Caz, not being that sort of girl, doesn't recognise.

'That's odd,' she tells the dogs. 'Why would Marcy leave her handbag behind?'

She takes the bag into the kitchen, where she empties the contents onto the table. Marcy may well have other cards, and no doubt access to any amount of cash, but she wouldn't be without her keys or her make-up, surely?

Caz gets her phone from her own Decathlon own-brand dog-walking bag, and calls Marcy's number. Like when Damian tried, there is no reply. She is annoyed at this. Surely Marcy can see the missed calls? Whatever situation she's in with her parents, it's just rude to ignore them.

'But then that's what we expect of Miss Marcy, isn't it, Bridget?'

Bridget doesn't reply, of course, but Caz is sure she can see a touch of indignation at this slur on her mistress.

'What if I were calling about you?' she argues with the little dog. 'What if it were an emergency and she was just ignoring it? How would you feel then?'

She photographs the bag and its contents and WhatsApps the picture to Marcy.

Just so you know, the dogs found this behind the sofa.

She sits at the table with the make-up bag and studies her unwashed face in the little mirror on Marcy's powder compact. 'Ugh,' she says, looking at her bloodshot eyes with panda rings from the mascara she wore last night in an attempt to look scrubbed up. She usually saves any washing or showering until after her early walk, but then she rarely wears make-up, so her slovenly habits are not usually quite so on display.

She slicks on Marcy's lipstick, which is way too red for her, and the blusher, which is clownishly dark on her skin. She smiles at the dogs, who cower as if they have done something wrong.

'It's only me!' she says.

Head full of questions about the handbag, she's just heading upstairs to find some make-up remover when the doorbell rings.

'Bollocks.'

The person on the other side of the glass will have seen her moving in the hallway, so there's no chance of pretending not to be in. It's probably just the postman or something. Since she's been here, five parcels from high-end clothing companies have arrived for Marcy.

With Bridget and Joe barking furiously behind her, she opens the door, expecting another harried delivery man. Instead it's DS Collins, who appears to be as shocked as she is at the encounter.

What can Marcy have done to bring a policeman to her house? And how amazing that it should be Collins, who is also dealing with Harry's case.

'Please control your dogs,' he says.

As Caz tells Bridget and Joe to sit – which is all they need to hold them back – she remembers the lipstick and blusher, which probably explains a good deal of the look on Collins's face. She puts her hand to her cheek. 'I was just...' she starts, then runs out of steam, because how does she actually explain why she's made up like a clown?

He flashes his warrant card. 'Miss Sessions? I've got a couple of questions to ask you about what happened on Thursday.'

So he's not looking for Marcy.

'It's Caz,' she says.

'It's a client's house.' As she leads him into the kitchen, Caz feels the need to explain her set-up. 'I'm house-sitting while she's up north with her parents.'

'So your mum said.'

'Ah. Of course. You went round there first.' Caz can hear her heart beating, and it's getting faster. 'Did you tell her why you wanted to see me?'

'I didn't. Why do you ask?'

'It's just I haven't mentioned it to her.'

'Interesting.'

'She's a bit delicate.'

Collins raises his eyebrows. 'That's not the impression I got.'

'Would you, um, like a cup of tea?'

'You got coffee?' Collins moves towards the kitchen table,

which, Caz realises with a slight jump, is still strewn with Marcy's things. Make-up, cash, cards and all.

'That's Marcy's stuff – my client's,' she says, again doing battle with the unnecessarily elaborate coffee machine.

'She's very trusting, isn't she?' Collins says, taking a seat with his hands held up, signalling that he's not going to touch a thing.

'I'm very trustworthy,' Caz says. It comes out a little more defensive than she intended. As she attempts to make the coffee, she tries to surreptitiously scrub the blusher from her cheeks, using the shiny chrome of the machine as a mirror.

In the end, she gives up her barista attempt, defeated.

'Are you OK with tea?' she asks him. It means doing battle with Marcy's boiling water tap, which scares her to death, but at least she's managed to make it work a couple of times.

He raises an eyebrow, then, sighing, nods.

He's not happy. And it's clearly not just about the coffee.

ELEVEN

'Where's your client, then?' Collins asks her as she crosses the kitchen with his cup of tea. When she leans in to put it in front of him, she gets that stale sweat whiff she picked up in the station. He's looking around, itemising the objects in the kitchen like that game where you have to memorise everything you see on a tray before a tea towel is thrown over it.

Caz sits at the far end of the table and tells him about Marcy's parents.

'But she left all this?' He gestures at the handbag contents, including, on top of everything, the driving licence, with the photograph clearly visible.

'I just found it,' Caz says. 'Well, the dogs did.'

Collins looks at her like she's a little mad.

'I've left her a message,' she goes on, desperately trying to prove her innocence.

He nods and sips his tea. 'And you're her dog-walker?'

Caz points at the dogs, who are curled on the rug, in every way looking like they are at ease, except for the fact that they are both side-eyeing Collins. 'She asked if I'd stay and look after Bridget and the house while she was away.'

'You do this sort of thing often?'

'It's just a one-off.'

Collins nods again, and Caz feels like she's being inter-rogated.

'How can I help you?' she says. 'It's just I've got to pick up my lunchtime walks in an hour.' It's a lie, but she just wants him to say what he has to say and then go.

'How are you after Thursday?' he asks, sipping his tea and looking across the table at her.

Caz immediately puts up her guard. Is this one of those things she's read about recently, where a policeman will creep on a young women who reports a crime? That's the last thing she needs right now, but unsurprisingly she has got into the habit of leaping to worst-case scenarios.

At least her mum knows he's here, should anything happen.

'I'm still a bit shaken up, but I'll get over it. It's the poor guy I feel sorry for.'

'Harry Turner,' Collins says.

Caz's throat tightens, but she gives nothing away.

'Does the name mean anything to you?'

Under the blusher, she reddens. This is a trap, isn't it? As she places her mug back on the table, she notices her hand is shaking. 'Harry... what did you say?'

'Harry Turner. But perhaps you don't know his surname.'

She looks at him, her eyes wide. He is staring back at her, like he's got her sealed between two glass slides under a micro-scope. There's no escaping this situation. 'Harry...?' she splutters.

He sips his tea again and says nothing.

'I... I was dating a guy called Harry. But he stood me up on Thursday night,' she says.

Collins crosses his arms. 'You went out on Thursday night? The same day you discovered a body?'

'I just wanted to get on with life,' she says quickly, before looking him straight in the eye. 'You're not saying that this guy was *that* Harry?'

'He was reported missing from the primary school where he taught. Out of character, apparently. He didn't have his phone with him, but we went to his home, where his wife – who was angry that he hadn't come home the night before – showed us his laptop.'

Caz flinches like Collins has just struck her. 'His wife? But he wasn't married!'

'Oh, he was. We got into the laptop yesterday and onto his phone backups, and found he was on a dating app called SeeMe.'

'I can't believe this,' Caz says.

'According to the app, you'd been out with him quite a few times.'

'Twice.'

'And you exchanged some quite, shall we say, intimate images.'

How had she thought this wouldn't come back to bite her? Imagining Collins looking at the photos she sent to Harry, she puts her face in her hands. 'It's what you do,' she says. 'When...'

'I'm not here to pass judgement,' he says. 'I'm here to ask you why you didn't tell us you knew him. When you could have saved us a lot of time and energy.'

She casts around desperately. 'I... I didn't look at his face.'

This line of questioning, this attitude, is too much like what happened when she found Ash. She doesn't want to be arrested again. She doesn't want to spend another night in another stinking cell in another police station.

And now she's in too deep with her lies to back-pedal. She has to go on.

'There was so much blood. I kept him in the corner of my eye. I fainted. I...' She breaks down in tears, and Joe plods over to her side to rest his head on her lap.

Collins sits for what seems like an entire lifetime, watching her. Again she gets the sense that she is little more than a biological specimen to him. 'The body wasn't a pretty sight,' he agrees.

'He had a wife...' Caz says. She tries to use her genuine reaction to this shocking discovery to divert Collins from her failure to recognise Harry.

'Sorry to tell you that. And sorry for your loss,' he says.

She glances at him through her fingers. It looks like he's bought it. While she is massively relieved, there's also a part of her that thinks he's a fool for believing her. Him, with his swaggering cop walk and his stupid shiny suit. Is this how easy it would be to get away with murder? No wonder they haven't yet found Ash's killer, and there's clearly no chance whatsoever of poor Harry getting justice.

'We estimate his time of death between ten o'clock on Wednesday night and three on Thursday morning. Where were you at this time?'

She blinks, shocked that he would even ask her this. 'I was asleep!'

He smiles, greasily. 'Can anyone confirm that?'

'No!' She fights back a flash of irritation at the insinuation behind his question. 'I suppose my mum was in the bedroom next door.' She doesn't add that, thanks to her medication, Ruth is usually out cold at night and wouldn't have heard a thing had Caz decided to slip out to do a bit of murdering.

He sniffs and licks his lips. 'It appears, from what we have found from logging on to the leaky, buggy dating app you've been using, that he sent you a message at seven a.m. on Thursday. After he was dead, and shortly before you discovered his body.'

Caz catches her breath. So it wasn't a delay in the app messaging. Of course it wasn't.

'It appears that whoever killed Harry Turner has also been playing you.'

'But how? And why?'

'Are you sure there's nothing else you can tell us, Miss Sessions? There wasn't anything odd when you turned up for the date at the Mesmerist?'

He knows that, too? Perhaps there was. Perhaps if she'd gone, she would have been killed, too, like Harry. Oh God, is there CCTV in the bar? Could Collins find out if she was there or not?

Her ears are getting hot.

Caz looks at Joe and is thankful that he only speaks dog, because she knows a dog wouldn't lie and Collins would now be drawing all kinds of conclusions.

There's no link between the two deaths.

There's no link between the two deaths.

'Nothing,' she says, dizzy with the untruth. 'I can't tell you anything else.'

They'll never find out. The police are terrible at communicating across forces. They'll never join the two deaths up. She was only ever referred to as a dog-walker in the newspaper reports.

'I want you to be very careful from now on. I'd advise deleting that app.'

'Oh, I already have.'

Collins blinks. 'Why?'

Caz could hit herself very hard indeed for that slip-up. 'After Harry stood me up,' she says, frantically. 'I'm done with dating.'

'Good.' He regards her for another uncomfortably long while, and she can't tell if this is a predatory look, or a disbelieving look, or just one that is processing what she has told him and filing it away. 'It's a nasty world out there, Miss Sessions. Do you know how to switch off location services on your phone? Just in case the killer has any interest in you?'

'I don't think he can,' she says. 'I have zero enemies.'

'We all think that.'

She nods dumbly, picks up her phone and, scrolling to her settings, sees with alarm that it is programmed to let all apps know where she is. As she disables it, Collins brushes down his nasty jacket and stretches his wrists out of the cuffs before settling them back.

'Better be off then. But be careful, eh, Miss Sessions? And if anything at all happens to make you feel uncomfortable, let me know, yes? You have my card.'

She gets up and leads him to the front door, but before he steps outside, he turns to her with such purpose that she thinks the game is up.

Instead, he steps forward and shakes her hand. 'I'll be in touch in a week or so, just in case.'

'In case of what?'

'In case there's anything you might have forgotten to tell me today. It's amazing how the mind can unearth details that, with further thought, are actually massively significant.'

She nods. 'I'll have a think.'

'You do that.'

She can't close the door fast enough behind him.

TWELVE

Caz would have leant on the door after she shut it on Collins, but she has the idea that he will be watching her through the glass. So instead she tries to keep it together until she has made it through to the kitchen.

Then she lets out an extravagant but silent scream.

Harry was married. He was cheating on his wife.

Just like Ash.

But those apps, they're a charter for cheaters, aren't they? It could still be a coincidence.

It could.

The message, though...

It was probably sent because Harry's killer wanted to confuse the police, put them off the scent. That's all.

She looks at her reflection in the shiny coffee machine. 'Nothing personal,' she says to herself. 'Nothing to do with you at all.'

She doesn't look convinced. But perhaps that's the curvy stainless steel distorting things.

. . .

Later that evening, she phones Damian and tells him about Collins's visit.

He listens to her justify not telling the police about Ash.

'OK,' he says. 'Because we're still telling ourselves it's all a big coincidence...?'

'That sounds like you're not convinced.'

'I would support you to the end of days.'

'You'd have told him, wouldn't you?'

The pause at the other end says it all.

'I can trust you not to go to them behind my back, can't I?'

'You're joking, right? Me go voluntarily to the feds?'

'True.'

Damian had a run-in with the police after being attacked by homophobes on St James's Street. After refusing to curl up and take a kicking, he narrowly escaped being charged with assault.

She tells him about the handbag. 'I'm a bit worried, tbh,' she says.

Damian roars with laughter. 'You think Marcy's only got one Mulberry? Go into her walk-in wardrobe. Go on!'

Caz does as she is told, all the while listening to him giggling.

'Now open the cupboard to the right of the door as you go in. You're seriously not telling me you've not been through all her clothes yet?'

She's about to explain about how she's only taken a glance and the different sizes thing when she sees what's in the cupboard and gasps.

'There must be forty Mulberrys here,' she says.

'Forty-three, last time I counted.'

'All the same style but different leathers and colours.'

'One for each outfit. She knows what she likes, does our Marcy.'

'OK. So what about the make-up, the credit cards, the cash?'

'Look to your left. See that dressing table over there?

There's a whole Sephora store's worth in the cupboards above and below it, and all the drawers inside it. Again, Marcy mixes it up according to what she wears.'

This concept is so alien to Caz that she has to take a moment to let it settle in. 'But it must cost her thousands of pounds!'

'Doesn't she look fabulous, though?'

'So *that's* what I'm doing wrong.'

'Oh, shut up. You're just a natural beauty. Completely different style. And while we're on the subject of money, look in each of those bags and you'll find wads of notes. You tend to have a bit of cash floating around when you run a shop like hers. You'd be amazed how many of the flash customers buy in used notes. We never question too deeply.'

'What about her credit cards?'

Damian laughs. 'She probably took the shop cards. She'll find a way of making even a mercy dash to her dying parents tax deductible.'

Just before she turns in for the night, Caz counts the bags in Marcy's walk-in wardrobe. Including the one she found downstairs, which she has in her hand, ready to return to the only space left in the cupboard, there are forty-three. So what has Marcy taken with her?

'Perhaps she bought herself yet another one,' she says to Joe.

Before she puts the final bag back in its place, she inspects its beautiful soft red leather, its perfectly stitched lining. She holds it to her nose. It smells expensive. It smells of Marcy. As she slots it back on the shelf, she notices that there's something orange and velvet behind it. Curious, she pulls out the other bags and sees that it is a long box. With some difficulty, she slides it out – it's as wide as the whole shelf and is probably custom-made.

Once it's on the bedroom floor, she lifts the lid. Inside, lined up spine forward as if on a shelf, are fifteen notebooks. Each worn and cracked spine has a year written on it in Sharpie pen, the latest being last year. There is space for another ten or so books.

When they were about fifteen Marcy started to keep a journal. She went on about how it helped her stay sane, how she would never need therapy because she wrote everything out. She bought Caz a notebook so that she could start one, too, but Caz doesn't do routine, so it didn't get filled beyond the third page.

Here they are, then. Marcy's journals.

She shouldn't look.

But there it is: the one from the year Marcy took Mark.

Of course, she pulls it from the orange box.

She opens it and reads.

It appears that Marcy despised Caz in the months leading up to her betrayal.

Caz remembers some of the events, but she doesn't recognise herself in them. The references to her make her cringe. According to Marcy, she didn't value what she had, and was cruel and smug.

Slights are documented in wounded detail. Caz not being able to meet up because she and Mark were having a night in; Caz and Mark deciding they wanted to share a flat alone, without Marcy, when Caz's memory is that Marcy actively chose to live in her amazing warehouse flat.

Even more shocking, Marcy explicitly states that she wanted Caz's life. When, again, in Caz's head, almost the reverse was true. Masochistically, Caz reads on.

She takes him for granted. Poor Mark.

*I'm going to take him from her and then let's see who is the
happiest.*

She reads graphic descriptions of how Marcy seduced him,
of how Mark put up resistance, and how she wore him down.

They were having sex *almost daily* in the run-up to the
party.

Feeling quite sick, Caz reads back through the years.
Marcy's journalling was regular, but brief, so just two hours
later, she has ploughed through the whole period of their
friendship.

She had no idea how much Marcy envied her.

The overriding impression is that Marcy thought Caz was
brought up too cosily by Ruth. She plays it against how difficult
her own home life was, with her submissive mother and tyran-
nical father – Caz remembers him only too well, with his strict
rules and tendency to lash out if defied.

The recurrent theme in the diaries is that Caz needs a good
shaking, a wake-up call, a challenge.

'Well, you certainly gave me that,' she says to Marcy's box of
journals.

Why had Marcy remained friends with her? Was it some
sort of sentimental hangover from the childhood years not
covered by the diaries, when presumably she actually enjoyed
hanging out with Caz?

She can't face the notebooks that cover the M&M years.
Fighting an urge to run out and make a late-night bonfire with
the entire lot, she instead puts them back in order and replaces
the orange box behind its shelter of expensive handbags.

Her entire teenage years have been completely rewritten.

She thought she and Marcy had been equals. If anything,
she had looked up to Marcy. In fact, for Marcy it was all a struggle, a competition, a fight to the top.

If it weren't for Bridget, Caz would pack up and leave right now and never see Marcy again. And she has no idea what she's going to say to her when she gets back. Just letting it go would crush to dust the few crumbs of self-respect she has left after this devastating discovery. But if she says something, it will mean letting on that she had snooped.

Perhaps she'll just back out of Marcy's life again, like before.

But is Marcy right? Is Caz really so glib, so shallow, so unchallenged by life?

Well.

If she was, she certainly isn't any more.

She returns to her own room, turning it all over. The relentless, enveloping, nightmare knowledge of what happened to poor Harry and Ash puts a perspective on the journals.

We're only here for a short while.

There's no point in dwelling on the past.

Cheaters and toxic relationships are a total waste of time.

But how toxic is *she*, reading Marcy's journals?

She wipes away the clownish make-up she has completely forgotten about.

Those words were not intended to be read by anyone, least of all her. And if she had ever got it together to write her own account of their friendship while it was happening, would Marcy have come off any better than Caz has?

She dismisses the thought. She's not going to make excuses for Marcy.

She peels off her Lycra gear in front of her bedroom window. It's a gloriously clear night out there, and with the street lights off – it's gone midnight again; she must start going to bed earlier – she imagines she can see almost every star in the galaxy.

Over in Colette's house next door, a light switches on in the hallway behind the bedroom across from hers. It outlines the unmistakable figure of Jon, standing in the window. She can't see his eyes, but he's not got anything other than her undressing to look at.

She snaps the curtains shut.

She misses her tiny room in Ruth's house, with its view of a wall.

THIRTEEN

'Got your shopping, Mum!' Caz calls as she lugs the two bulging bags for life into Ruth's entrance hall. A strong smell of weed and incense comes from the living room, along with the usual undertones of turmeric, onions and fenugreek.

The scent of home.

There's no reply. She must be in the conservatory, then.

Trying not to dislodge Ruth's canvases, which, having filled every wall in the house, now crowd the narrow hallway, she jostles Joe, Bridget and the shopping past the shoes and coats and the umbrella stand containing various walking sticks.

While the dogs go to greet her mother, Caz slips into the kitchen to dump the shopping. She eyes the dirty dishes piled in the sink and sighs. Her own standards aren't terribly high, but Ruth has never been one for keeping things ordered. 'I'd rather use my time to paint,' she says, which is fair enough, but even so. It's Sunday morning and there's not been any washing-up done since Caz left on Thursday.

She'll have to do it in a bit, but for now she puts the kettle on while she sorts out the daffodils she picked up at the super-market, snipping off the ends and placing them in a favourite vase. When she's made the tea, she sets a tray with the mugs, flowers and the two cardamom buns bought from the eye-wateringly expensive artisanal baker's shop that has just opened up round the corner. Ruth grumbles that this part of town – historically a bohemian enclave of scrappy artists and ramshackle student housing – is rapidly gentrifying and losing its character. But however much she rails against it and how it spits in the face of local young people who will never be able to afford to buy here, she does like the sourdough bread, the cardamom buns and the excellent coffee, 'when I can afford it.'

Caz takes a while making the tray arrangement look nice. She's stalling because she knows she's going to face a grilling.

And sure enough, when she finally walks into the conservatory, sets down the tray, kisses Ruth and pulls up a chair so that they can companionably share the tea, the first words from her mother's lips are:

'Why did that dick of a policeman want to see you, Caroline?'

Caz takes a deep breath. Her mother was never one for dancing around a subject. 'I dropped my wallet and he was bringing it back to me.' This sounds lame even to her ears, and it certainly doesn't wash with Ruth.

'Don't bullshit me. The police don't even turn up if you've got a burglar in the house, let alone hand-deliver lost property. What's up?'

Caz hands Ruth the larger of the two buns – they come up all sorts of sizes, as if this were some kind of proof of them being hand-made. Ruth, who has been smoking her medicinal cannabis, takes a hungry bite, then stares at her daughter, chewing.

Generally Caz no longer notices her facial scarring – it's all she's known, after all; it's just her mum's face. But today, the pull on her lips, her stretched, papery skin, the bulb of her reconstructed nose all demand truth: *I have lived through this. The least you can do is be honest with me.*

'I was a witness to something, and they wanted a bit more detail.'

'So why lie to me about it?'

'I...'

'Witness to what?'

'I found something.'

'Found what? Someone's wallet?' The sarcasm doesn't suit Ruth. Caz knows she's now in too deep and the only way out is to lay everything on the table. Well, almost everything.

'The other day when I was out with the dogs, I found a dead body.'

Ruth drops her bun back onto its plate. 'A *body*? Where?'

'Up by the racecourse.'

'Jesus, Caz. When?'

'Thursday.'

Ruth frowns, counting the days backwards. 'The day you moved out.'

Caz nods.

'Was that why?'

'Eh?'

'Did you move out because of finding the body? Because you didn't want to be here lying to me?'

'It wasn't lying. Just not telling you.'

'Why *not* tell me?'

'Because I didn't want to upset you.'

Ruth snorts. 'You think you need to protect me? After everything I've been through?'

Despite her best intentions, Caz gets frustrated when Ruth talks like this, because it gives her nowhere to go. And sure, it was a horrible crash, and she lost her husband and suffered life-changing injuries. But it was thirty years ago, and still she's using it as a weapon.

Today she is so close to saying all this out loud, but she manages to shut herself up. In any case, it *was* because of Ruth's vulnerability – due to that very crash – that she didn't confide in her.

'I'm sorry,' she says instead. 'It's just I didn't know what to do.'

Ruth leans across the little table between them and takes her hands. 'Caz, I'm your mum. I've brought you up alone and poured all my love into you. We are bound together for life. We have no secrets. We act as one, yes? If you lie to me, if you hide anything from me, where does that leave us? It's a betrayal of everything I've tried to build. And anyway, I'm tough. Much tougher than you think.'

Caz nods.

Joe pads across the conservatory from the spot of sunlight he has been sharing with Bridget and leans against her legs, as if he knows she needs a bit of support.

'So what did this policeman want to know?' Ruth asks.

'He wanted to tell me something.'

'And...?'

'He wanted to tell me that I knew the dead man.'

'And you didn't know this yourself?'

Caz takes a deep breath. 'I did know it. I just didn't want things to get complicated.'

'So you found the body of a man, you recognised him and you didn't tell the police?'

'I told the police about the body. I waited till they came. But I didn't tell them I knew him.'

'It's not someone from when you were at school, is it? Not someone from round here?'

Caz shakes her head. 'It was someone I was seeing.'

'Oh, Caz.' Ruth takes her hand again. 'You were seeing someone? Why didn't you tell me?'

'I'd only been on a couple of dates with him. I met him on an app.'

'Why do you use those things? They're just a front for creeps and rapists.'

'That's not how it is, Mum. You don't understand.'

'And then you meet this guy, and he goes and kills himself up where he knows you'll walk the dogs. What is that? Some sort of sick fantasy.'

'Don't say that. That's a horrible thing to say about a person.'

'People *can* be horrible. He was using you.'

'He wasn't!' Whatever she tells Ruth, she's not going to mention Harry's wife. 'He didn't kill himself. He was murdered.'

Ruth gasps. The influx of breath catches a crumb in her windpipe, and she starts to choke. Caz jumps up and thumps her back until the crumb is dislodged. Grateful for the respite from the questioning, she goes to the kitchen to get her mother a glass of water, and while she's got the tap running, she splashes her face.

'What did you see, Caz?' Ruth asks, once she has taken a sip of water and recovered. She is relentless.

Caz shakes her head. 'It was awful.'

'But if the poor man was murdered, even more reason to tell the police who he was.'

'I didn't think they'd find out I knew him.'

'You didn't think they'd suspect you, did you?'

Caz looks at her. 'Partly that.'

'But anyone could tell you're not capable of doing anything terrible like that.'

Caz closes her eyes. She can't bear the twin searchlights of her mother's eyes. Her compassion is torturing her into a confession.

And then the tears come. Something about telling your mother. It's elemental, goes back to childhood.

The last thing she wants is for Ruth to see her crumble like this. Despite her mother's claim to toughness, for the last fifteen years or so Caz has known that ultimately she is the one who has to be strong. If she caves in, everything will fall apart.

But here it comes. She braces herself. Full disclosure.

'I didn't tell them because I knew what would happen.' She takes a breath. 'My burnout wasn't just stress at teaching.'

Ruth puts her hands together like some kind of counsellor, but everything else in her body language shows that she is prepared for a bomb. 'I'm listening.'

'Eight months before I came back home, Joe and I found another body.'

Ruth gasps. 'Another?'

'Our first body, I mean. The first body. Oh God, I don't know how to say it.'

'Where?'

'In London. Near my flat.'

'What?'

'And I knew him too.'

'Fucking hell, Caz.' Shaking her head, Ruth reaches into her butterfly bag and pulls out three Rizlas.

'I met him on the dating app as well. And he'd also been murdered.'

'Why the hell didn't you tell me?' Ruth licks the papers so angrily Caz thinks she might rip them.

'I didn't think you needed to know.'

'And now this has happened.'

'It didn't happen because I didn't tell you,' Caz says. 'Sometimes, Mum, things occur and they have nothing whatsoever to do with you.' She is properly crying now. Tears and snot and sobs.

Joe does what he always does when she is upset and, despite his size, clambers up onto her lap and rests his head on her shoulder. Even Bridget joins in, taking up his former position beside her.

'Look at those two,' Ruth says, her tone softening. She puts a hand on a part of Caz's leg not occupied by dog. 'I'm sorry. I'm just so upset that you've had to go through all this. It must have been hideous.'

'It was,' Caz says into Joe's neck fur.

Ruth puts down her papers. Her hand is shaking, but then it does sometimes. 'Do the police have any leads on who's doing this?'

'Eh?'

'Oh no, Caz. You've not told them about the other guy, have you?'

Her face still buried in Joe's fur, Caz shakes her head.

'Why the hell not?'

'I just couldn't face it. It was horrible the first time. Because I found him and because I knew him, and because they had nothing else to go on, I was at the top of their list of suspects.'

'How could they think that of you?'

'The questions they asked, really digging into my history – what Ash and I had done...'

'Ash?'

'The first guy. They even got me talking about Mark.'

'Mark?' Ruth says his name like it tastes disgusting. 'What's he got to do with it?'

'Nothing! That's why it was so awful.'

'But don't you think it's important they know there's a pattern here?'

'There is no pattern.'

She snorts. 'You don't really believe that, do you?'

'It's just really bad luck. A really bad coincidence.'

'Impossible.'

'It happens. People get struck by lightning twice. A woman

saw herself in the background of a photograph of her husband-to-be, taken when they were both children. A lost ring got found by its owner years later on a beach...' Caz casts around for more examples but can't come up with any. 'Google it. Strange things happen.'

'But these events... they're like points on a triangle,' Ruth says.

'I don't follow,' Caz says.

Ruth is clearly feeling the effects of her self-medication. It happens, and she comes up with wacky ideas that don't make much sense. But she presses on, drawing a pyramid shape in the air. 'This is you.' She stabs a finger at the apex, then points at the other two points. 'This is the guy you found in London, and this is the one you found on Thursday. There's a link. There has to be.' She runs her finger frantically around the shape, then looks at Caz.

'There's no link. I don't have any enemies. Even Marcy and me are good now.'

Well, they were until Caz found the journals, but she's not going into that.

'Believe me. You never know who your enemies are until it's too late.'

Caz laughs. As if Ruth, who holes herself up in her home, hardly ever stepping out of her safe Brighton neighbourhood, would know about the darker ways of the world.

'And who knows what sort of weirdos you've met up with on this internet dating crap.'

'I'm careful, Mum.'

'But not so careful as to date two men who end up murdered?'

'It's not my fault!'

'There are monsters out there, Caz. Monsters worse than you can possibly imagine.'

'You think I don't know that?'

'You *don't* know that. I hate the idea of you up there on the racecourse so early when there's no one else about.'

'Do you really think anyone's going to get at me with five dogs at my side? No, Mum. It's horrible what happened to those guys, and I wish it hadn't and that I hadn't found them, and I hate the whole thing, but it's done, and it's not going to happen again.'

'How do you know that?'

'It can't, can it?'

'Lightning doesn't strike three times?'

'Look. They're not connected. And the police will never join up the lines between me, Ash and Harry. It's all just too random.'

'You think.'

'Yes.'

Ruth pulls a pouch from her bag and arranges a line of tobacco on the Rizlas.

'You shouldn't be smoking tobacco with your weed, Mum.'

'You shouldn't be telling me what to do.'

'I'm grown-up now.'

'You may be, but you don't know everything.'

'Ha.'

'I'm not happy with you going up on the Downs. Look what's happened. It's horrible. You must be so traumatised by it.'

'I'm fine,' Caz says, though she's not.

'Take the dogs to more populated parts, will you? Don't tempt fate. Look out for yourself. I wish you were back here.'

'It's only a week, and I'm not going to let this stop me living my life. As it is, I've given up on dating.'

'Good.'

'I'll end up all alone.'

'Believe me. There are worse fates.'

Caz looks at her mother when she says this and sees something in her eyes. A new understanding between the two of them.

Or perhaps it's a warning.

'I'm not telling the police about Ash,' she says.

'I think you're wrong.'

'And you're not going to say anything, are you?'

'I'm not going to go behind your back, but I'm not going to give up persuading you.'

'I don't believe you will.'

'And in the meantime, promise me,' Ruth says. 'No more Downs with the dogs.'

FOURTEEN

Her van full of her early-morning dogs, Caz drives up the hill to the Downs.

She has never been much good at doing as she's told. Particularly when the person doing the telling is her mother. Indeed, Ruth forbidding her yesterday is exactly what has brought her back up here for the first time since Thursday.

Monday morning and a fresh start, and all that. Fight your demons.

She parks her van on the verge by the entrance to the racecourse, then jumps out and opens the back doors to greet the dogs pawing at their safety cages, desperate for their morning walk. 'We were getting fed up of the park anyway, weren't we, lads?'

She takes the excitement from within the van as agreement.

Also, she needs to exorcise the sight of poor Harry's body from her mind. She has dreamt about him – embroidered by flashbacks to Ash – every night since she found him.

She's still trying hard to tell herself that this is all coincidence, but she can't get Ruth's triangle shape out of her mind. Is it just a picture drawn by a stoned old hippy, or does she have a point?

Herself, the dating app, the two men, the killers. She has to think that it's two killers, because for both Harry and Ash to be killed by the same person is a coincidence too far, even for her. And unthinkably frightening.

One of the undeniable similarities is that both men were liars. They both had partners and hadn't told Caz about them – appalling, almost psychopathic behaviour from both of them. It's not a big leap to supposing that men who lie like that surely have other shit going on in their lives. Potentially shit that might get them murdered.

She clips leads onto harnesses, slips her dog-walking bag over her shoulder, bips the van lock and sets off. It's a bright, blue-skied dawn, much like when she found Harry. Everything is the same, in fact: the light, the smells, the sea the same silvery satin shimmer. As they go through the underpass – which still smells as if ten men took a piss here the night before – Mungo the Dalmatian even puts up a fuss again, this time about a length of bramble he has somehow got attached to his spotty back.

'You expensive dogs, eh?' Caz says as she untangles him. She lets Joe off his lead, but thankfully he doesn't race on ahead like he did the other day.

No fresh corpse smell in the air today, then.

'Shut up, ghoul,' she tells herself for even thinking that. She twitches on the leads and she and the dogs set off.

But then a heady perfume hits her nostrils. The sweetness reminds her of what she smelled on Thursday, though perhaps that's just memory kicking in. Whatever it is, the dogs get it too; there's a general twitching at the end of the leads.

She may be kidding herself, but she thinks they too feel apprehensive.

As they reach the bend in the footpath that leads to where

she found Harry, she closes her eyes and holds her breath. Half of her expects to still find him there.

The smell is stronger here.

She turns the curve and opens her eyes.

He's not there, of course. Instead, marking the spot is a tatter of blue-and-white police tape and a mound of bouquets. All sorts of flowers: from seasonal daffodils to exotic lilies.

There are balloons, too. Heart-shaped balloons.

Caz didn't expect this. Her survival instinct was well on the way to demonising Harry the cheater. She was framing him as someone hated by everyone who knew him. Even his wife, she imagined, would have turned her back on him for his infidelity.

She bends to read one of the cards attached to the flowers.

We will always love you, Mr Turner.

It's signed by twenty-eight children from Year 6. He told her he was a primary school teacher, and it appears he was telling the truth.

She moves on to a luscious, extravagant arrangement of lilies. It's this bouquet that is scenting the air so strongly. She squats and reads the card.

Dear Harry, you are greatly missed. With love, Marcy and all at Fox & Hunter.

She doesn't know why this card from Marcy's shop shocks her so much. There are plenty of explanations. Perhaps Damian managed to get in touch with her and told her about Harry. Or perhaps he arranged these flowers on her behalf.

She reaches across and opens another, with an angel drawn by a child on its front.

I miss you, Daddy, love you, Jess.

'Jesus,' Caz says.

Here was a man who had a life. Was loved. Had a *child*, for God's sake. However much he wronged Caz, his wife and child – or children – by lying, he did not deserve to end up here. He was loved. All of this shows he was loved.

She stands and thumps herself on the side of the head.

There she was, castigating her mother for making it all about her. When in fact she was doing exactly the same thing.

Poor me, finding a dead body.

Poor me, finding another dead body.

She was so concerned about the effect on *her*, about whether she should tell the police, that she completely forgot the main point, which is that the lives of two flawed but charming and loved men have been violently taken.

'I'm so sorry this happened to you,' she mutters to the spot where she found him. Whatever kind of two-timing shit he was, he didn't earn that death.

She throws some treats down for the dogs, to give herself a bit more time, and closes her eyes.

How was he killed?

Can she feel it? Can she feel the evil? Was he taken by surprise, or was he threatened, knew what was coming his way? Did he know his murderer, or was it a total stranger?

What would be worse?

She tries to imagine it unfolding, as if that can somehow explain it to her, reassure her that it was a random horror. That, like Ash, Harry was just purely unlucky. An unlucky man in the wrong place at the wrong time.

She gets nothing. Just the sound of a flock of seagulls passing over the death spot, heading off towards the ocean.

She wishes she could join them.

'Come on.' She tugs the dogs' leashes and leads them away. At first she walks, but soon, to the delight of the hounds, and barely noticing it herself, she is running, as fast as she can, tears streaming down her face at the cruelty and horror of it all.

She didn't need to come back here.

She should have looked after herself better.

Back at Marcy's, she sits by the pool, smoking a rare cigarette, unable to think about anything but the horror of it all. She would call Damian and ask him to come round and keep her company, explain about the lilies, help her work out what she went through today up at the racecourse. But he'll be busy in the shop. She misses her old Marcy, the one she thought she knew in her teenage years, the friend she confided in about everything. Ever since Marcy did the dirty on her, she's not trusted other women, holding them all at arm's length.

Indeed, knowing what she now knows from the journals, Caz wonders if Marcy ever did anything but use her. And isn't she still using her? She hasn't returned any of her calls or messages. She probably sees her as nothing more than a safe bet for house-sitting. Handy. Convenient. Two grand is just loose change for Marcy, the equivalent of tossing Caz a few coins to make her as loyal as Bridget Jones, running around for her, fetching things, rolling over when she tells her to.

She knows she's touching the edge of the same spiral that took her down when she burnt out after Ash. There's a lunchtime walk and the afternoon gang to take out, but all she feels like doing is curling up under a duvet and shutting the world away.

When she came back to Brighton and started her dog-walking business, the freedom and exercise, the fresh air and the simple pleasure of spending the largest part of her time with the animals she loves meant that she could gradually wean herself off the pills that helped her out of the trough of her lowest point. But right now she feels like renewing her prescription, grabbing fistfuls of them, stuffing them into her mouth and washing them down with half a bottle of Marcy's designer gin.

'And there you are again, Caz. Making it all about you,' she says out loud. 'You've got to stop this. Have some compassion. Get over yourself!'

This last part, perhaps unwisely, she shouts into the sky. She hauls herself off the sunlounger and heads for where Joe's ball lies on the far side of the lawn. Perhaps something simple like playing with the dogs will bring her back to herself, reverse the spiral.

But because she doesn't have her mind fully on what she's doing, she walks right into a branch hanging low from the big apple tree at the back of the garden.

'Ow!' she yells, putting everything into the cry.

'Hello?' A hoarse male voice calls from the other side of the gate to the back alley. 'Are you all right?'

Caz freezes.

The gate rattles, and she realises that somehow the lock has been disengaged.

It opens.

FIFTEEN

A tall man stands in the twitten, his face hidden in the shade cast by the tree.

Bridget and Joe run in front of Caz and bark and snarl, ready to do whatever it takes to protect her.

'Are you OK?' The man's voice is croaky, grating.

Caz stands, hand clamped across the bump already forming on her forehead, heart racing.

The man holds his own hand up in greeting. 'Sorry. It's Peter. From Colette's the other night?'

'Oh God, sorry.' Caz lets go of her breath. She calls the dogs off and he bends to let them sniff his hand. 'Your voice sounds so different.'

'Damn cough,' he says. 'Caught it from June. I think I'm losing my voice. Anyway,' he goes on, 'I was just on my way to the Tesco Metro to pick up some milk for a cuppa and I heard you shout. Is everything all right?'

Caz nods. 'I just hit my head, but I'll live. I overreacted. Sorry.'

'No problem.' He makes to leave, but Caz, desperate for company right now, calls out.

'Would you like that cup of tea here?'

'Well, that would be grand,' he says.

'Are you sure you're OK?' he says as she struggles with Marcy's fancy boiling water tap. Just hearing a kind voice has got her back on the verge of tears, and she's having difficulty hiding it from him.

'It's this bloody tap thing. I still haven't got the hang of it, and now I can't make it work and she doesn't have a kettle.' Her eyes hurt and she feels so tired she might just keel over right where she's standing.

He looks around at the high-tech white and stainless-steel kitchen. 'She likes it new and shiny, doesn't she, your friend?'

'Certainly does. Oh, bloody, bloody thing,' she says to the tap. Any minute now she's not going to be able to control herself.

'Tell you what, why don't you bring some milk round to mine,' he says. 'I've just made some cookies, too. And I can show you Uncle Ezra's studio.'

'Sounds great.' Caz had forgotten about the sculptor uncle. Perhaps this is the thing to take her out of herself.

She leaves the dogs behind and, clutching a two-litre bottle of milk, walks round the front way with Peter to Ezra's house. As they pass Colette's place, she sees Jon watching them from an upstairs window. She nudges Peter.

'Don't look now, but Colette's Jon is watching us.'

Peter makes a face.

'He was looking at me the other night when I was getting changed for bed,' she tells him.

'How horrible for you.'

'I drew the curtains.'

'If it happens again, let me know.'

'Why do men do that?'

'In his case, he's probably not seen many women the past few years.'

'What do you mean?'

'Ex-con.'

'No!'

'She met him when she was a prison visitor.'

'No!' Caz's mouth is wide open. She can't imagine the fragrant Colette ever falling for a jailbird. 'How do you know?'

'Strangely enough, I was on the team that nicked him, up north. And when I recognised him, I did a bit of asking around. Don't let him or Colette know I told you.'

'You're a policeman?'

'Was. I had enough, though. I'm a diversity trainer now.'

'Wow. That's a bit of a swerve.'

'I couldn't bear all the misogyny, homophobia and racism in the force, so I decided to do something about it. Now I go in and sort out the police and the army, pushing back the tide of ignorance. Bit of a thankless task, but I like to think I make a small difference.'

'Didn't he recognise you?'

Peter shakes his head and smiles. 'It was twenty years ago. I'd just signed up on the graduate path. Very junior. Invisible.'

Caz does the sums in her head. Her initial estimate of Peter being mid forties was a little out. He must be slightly younger than that.

'What did he do?' she asks.

Peter winces. 'You don't want to know. It'd colour your view of him.'

In fact, Caz's imagination, fed by her recent experiences, is running riot on what Jon's crimes might have been. Cocaine-smuggling serial-killing gangster-rapist?

Peter leads her up the overgrown path to Ezra's house. Where Marcy's has been pimped to the max, this place looks as if it hasn't even been painted since the original builders attached half-timbering and pebble-dash to the front. The dull and warped front door takes a bit of nudging before Peter can get it open.

'Uncle Ezra had his mind on higher things than house maintenance,' he says as he shows her in. 'I've made a bit of a start, but as you can see, I've got my work cut out.'

The hallway is lined with neat piles of old *Guardian* newspapers.

'There's a logic to it,' he says. 'Each string-tied bundle is a month's worth, and they're arranged in chronological order, starting at the bottom of the stairs.'

'That's reassuring.' Caz peers in on the front room as they pass. It's crammed with canvases lined up sideways-on like giant books, and a tangle of stone sculptures.

She can imagine Ruth going this way if she's not careful.

Peter sees her looking and laughs. 'It's a miracle the floor hasn't given way, the weight of some of those things.'

'He was a painter, too?'

He shakes his head. 'He took payment in canvases for his sculptures. There's work by some pretty famous artists in there. I don't know much about it, but Google is my friend.'

'So, as Jon said, there could be some treasures in there.'

'Undoubtedly, and I want Ezra's gallerist to catalogue it all before Colette's bad boy gets his paws on them.'

He leads her through to a ramshackle kitchen made up of various free-standing dressers, a gas stove that looks like it should have been decommissioned decades ago, and a fridge so ancient that it has come round to being fashionable again. The air is full of the smell of baking.

'Took me a while to scrub it clean in here,' he says. 'But then we all have different standards, don't we?'

He fills a little whistling kettle at the Belfast sink, reaches down a yellow trigger lighter from a hook on the wall and ignites one of the old cooker rings. The blue flame appears with a pop, making Caz jump.

'Take a seat,' he says, putting the kettle on and pointing to some worn vinyl chairs set around a faded Formica table. 'And help yourself.' He pushes a plate of chocolate chip cookies towards her.

'Yum,' she says, chewing far too greedily. 'I'd ask you for the recipe, but I don't think I've baked anything since I was a kid.'

A memory surfaces from when she was aged about six, standing on a chair not unlike the one she is sitting on now while her mother helped her stir a bowl full of lumpy cake batter. Ruth has never been a baker either, but Caz remembers insisting. The fairy cakes they made were close to inedible, but they both pretended they were the most delicious things in the world.

This memory, this kind man, this kitchen: so safe, so cosy, so unthreatening. She tries to smile and make small talk about her favourite cookie flavour, but the corners of her mouth keep turning down until she is powerless to suppress the sob that escapes from the depth of her belly.

Peter fetches a dusty box of man-sized tissues and sits opposite her.

'Can I help in any way, Caz?' he asks, his voice so gentle beneath the virus croak it brings on another great heaving sob.

She shouldn't be confiding in a virtual stranger like this. But she needs to tell someone *something*, face-to-face. Now.

So she does. She tells him about finding Harry, and about how she knew him, and how she doesn't like DS Collins.

'That's a terrible thing to happen,' he says. 'And that Collins sounds like he's a prime example of what I'm trying to fix. I'm sorry that on top of all the horror, you had to deal with someone like that.' He offers her another cookie. 'Even though things look shinier from the outside, it's still very *Life on Mars* among the ranks. I'm fighting an uphill battle. Does he have any leads on who might have killed the poor guy?'

'I don't think so. He was married, though.'

'The DS?'

'No, Harry. The guy. I didn't know that, of course. I'm not like that. Wouldn't date a married man.'

'Perhaps the wife knew he was playing away and had had enough.'

'Do you think?'

'Hell hath no fury like a woman scorned.'

This gives Caz an almost unreasonable surge of hope. Because if that happened to Harry, then it could possibly be what happened to Ash, too. Because, thinking about Ruth's diagram, there was a wronged wife or long-term partner on one of the points of both men's pyramids. *That* could be the common denominator, not Caz.

Of course!

'But it was a brutal murder,' she says.

'Tell me what you saw.'

She tells him about the blood and the flies.

'Horrible,' he says. 'I'm sorry you had to witness that.'

'A woman couldn't do that, could she?'

'You'd be surprised. I worked on a case where the wronged wife hired a contract killer. She even told them to make the murder look like the work of a serial killer we were searching for. Really confused us for a while.'

'Well, this certainly looked like it could have been the work of a serial killer. Looked like it was done by someone who enjoyed what they were doing.'

'I'm so sorry. There are things I've seen I wish I could forget about. You've been through it once, but it doesn't get any easier, believe me.'

'I know exactly what you mean,' she says, and they smile at each other, in their new-found witness-of-horror kinship. She's on the verge of telling him about Ash, too, but he speaks before she has decided whether to go ahead.

'Hey. Bring your tea out to the garden and I'll show you Uncle Ezra's studio and his prepper larder.'

'Prepper larder?'

'Ezra was always ready for the end of the world, but sadly he beat the world to it.'

'Unbelievable,' Caz says, as she stands in the metal shed lined with shelves of tinned food. 'There's enough here to keep him going for thirty years.'

'And he was eighty!' Peter says.

'What a waste. What else could he have done with all that time, money and energy?'

'And I'm now stuck with a conundrum. A lot of this is past its sell-by date, so I can't give it away to food banks or anything. I don't want to throw it all away, though. I opened a can of beans that was five years out of date, and it was fine.'

'You could just work your way through it all.'

He laughs. 'I don't aim to be here quite that long.' He picks a can from the shelves. 'And tinned carrots? Really?'

Ezra's studio is in another, much larger outhouse at the bottom of the garden. Just outside the entrance, a home-made crane contraption stands by a big block of stone, a giant rusty hook dangling from it on a metal chain with links as thick as a man's arm. Acquainted as she is at the moment with horror, Caz tries not to visualise the harm it could do swinging into a person's head.

'For hauling his stone blocks into place,' Peter says.

Inside, it is every bit as crammed with stuff as the rest of the house, but there is a greater sense of arrangement here. Mallets, drills, chisels and giant mechanical instruments that look that they might have come from a nightmare dental treatment room hang from the walls and from rafters.

Angular, squared-off carvings of human forms stand on plinths around the flagstoned space – some nearly completed, others barely emerged from the block of stone. One, on a trestle table, is just the beginning of a person: only the muscular leg and foot have appeared, but so clearly that it's hard not to imagine the rest of the body is there, waiting to be released. A mallet and chisel sit next to it, beside a scummy mug of tea.

'It's like he's just taken a break,' Caz says.

'I know. Sad, isn't it? This is where they found him. Massive coronary. I haven't had the heart even to tidy away his mug yet.'

'At least he died doing what he loved.'

'There is that.'

Caz runs her fingers over the edges of the stone foot. 'I can't picture my mum in this sort of environment, though she worked in stone. Her stuff was curvier, though. More female, I suppose.'

'Be careful there about gender stereotyping.'

She laughs and salutes. 'Sorry, Mr Diversity Trainer.' Her Fitbit buzzes. 'Damn. Better get going. I've got four lively dogs to wear out.'

'Fun job.'

'It has its upsides.'

They head on up through the scrappy overgrown garden towards the house. Where Marcy has manicured lawns and cobble borders, Ezra has a clutch of ancient fruit trees, all in blossom. The long grass is uneven, hummocky, like it has been laid over the remains of a church.

'Does he have a bunker?' Caz asks.

'Eh?' Peter says, as he holds aside a bramble for her to pass.

'You know, an underground shelter where he can take refuge from, I don't know, zombies or whatever. Preppers always have them in the movies.'

'I've not seen anything.'

'Though it would be well hidden.'

He smiles. 'I'll report back if anything turns up.'

He holds open the back door for her – a curiously old-fashioned gesture that she finds rather touching. 'I do feel for you,' he says as they go into the kitchen and towards the front door. '"Dog-walker finds body" is a bit of a tabloid cliché, isn't it? But it actually happens a lot – dogs like the smell of death.'

Caz shudders. 'Joey certainly seems to.'

'Each of those corny headlines is only the beginning of the story for the dog-walker, though, isn't it?'

Caz nods. At last, someone who gets it.

'Believe me,' Peter goes on as he leads her to the front door, 'I've worked with many, many witnesses like you, and I know the questions that'll be keeping you awake at night: Why me? What if I'd been five minutes earlier? Will I ever forget what I saw? And yes, you're not the first person to find the body of someone they know, and that only makes it worse, of course – particularly if, you know, there was a relationship there.'

'That's exactly what I've been thinking.'

'And these thoughts don't disappear quickly. You worry, too. To witness the product of murder is frightening. You see the world through different eyes.'

Caz pauses on the doorstep. 'It *is* frightening.'

'But let me tell you this. From my own experience in the force, these events are extremely rare. And usually, in well over ninety-five per cent of all cases of homicide, the victim knows the perpetrator. And in eighty per cent of those cases, it's someone very close. It's likely that your Harry died because someone he knew had it in for him.'

Caz nods, desperate to tell him about Ash. But if she doesn't go now, she's going to be late for her clients.

'Believe me,' he says as they shake hands, 'you shouldn't give a thought to worrying about who did it and whether they might come after you. I'd put money on it being the wife. Or someone employed by her.'

His words nagging at her, she hurries back to Marcy's place.

He was only trying to be reassuring, but until he said it, she hadn't even thought about the murderer coming after her. As she turns into Marcy's driveway, she looks over her shoulder to see if anyone is following her.

She's being ridiculous. Of course no one's following her. And anyway, why would anyone want to harm her? She has no enemies.

As far as she knows.

She puts the key into Marcy's front door.

But what kind of judge is she of what other people think of her? She thought she and Marcy had been best friends. When in fact, as she now knows, from Marcy's point of view almost the reverse appears to have been true.

From Marcy's point of view, they were something like worst enemies.

She shakes the thought from her head. Marcy is many things, but she's not a killer!

As she lets herself into the house, she repeats the thought that has become something of a mantra to her now.

It's all a coincidence.

It's all a coincidence.

But there's the start of an echo around her certainty.

The chant is beginning to sound a little hollow.

SIXTEEN

Exhausted after the last walk of the day, Caz ushers Bridget and Joe across Marcy's threshold and dumps her shopping bag full of ready meals on the kitchen work surface. As she's deciding which it is to be tonight, Joe runs through from the hallway with an envelope in his mouth.

It's addressed to her in uppercase handwriting, but it has no stamp, so it must have been hand-delivered, which is weird, because the only people who know she is here are not letter-writers.

As she picks it up and feels the weight of it, she knows chillingly and exactly who it's from. She rips it open, and yes, inside is a card, almost identical to the one she received back in London. Like with the first, the sender has spent some art-and-craft time on it, cutting it into a heart shape and painting it a dark red that's less hearts-and-roses and more wounds-and-scabs. On the other side, once more, he has written in backward slanted capital letters, again like the earlier note: I LOVE YOU XXX

She shudders. Edwin Rourke.

A major upside of leaving her job at the school was getting

away from that man, an older maths department colleague. And now it seems he's found out she's staying at Marcy's. But how? He could have got Ruth's address from the notoriously indiscreet school secretary, who had it to forward any loose ends to Caz. And Ruth told Collins that she was here, so perhaps she helped Edwin out, too.

She shudders again. It doesn't seem likely. But then he *is* persistent...

When she started at the school, Rourke, a man with breath that could start a war and who could never, ever look her in the eye, approached her in the empty staffroom. Standing right there in her personal space, pecking at a packet of crisps, his gaze fixed on her left ear, he asked her out for a drink. He added that he too came from Brighton, and they could compare notes on growing up there.

'Although my youth somewhat pre-dates yours,' he said, laughing and showering her with bits of crisp.

She backed away, mumbling her excuses.

Nothing more was said, but she would often catch him staring at her, and every now and then she would find a single red rose on top of her locker.

After she left work, he sent her the first card. And now this.

Don't say she's got herself a stalker.

And then it hits her. The first card came after Ash. And now, *right after Harry*, here's a second. Collins talked about the killer potentially having an interest in her. Harry and Ash aside, no one in the past couple of years has shown any interest in her apart from Edwin.

Shuddering again, she tries to picture him doing all those horrors to Harry. She can't. Edwin is tiny – shorter than her and a good twenty pounds lighter, not to mention at least a couple of decades older. Harry was fit, strong, over six feet tall, beautifully muscled. Edwin looks like he is made of wrinkled paper, as if one puff from her could blow him away.

Even so, he's annoyingly dogged.

She runs out of the front door and into the street. It is empty but for a fox, who stares at her until she feels like she should apologise.

He slinks away and she hurries back indoors, locking and bolting the door. She pulls out her phone and, as with the first card, photographs this one. A long time ago she read that with stalkers it's important to keep a log of the evidence, in case things escalate.

Even so, she tears the actual card up and buries it in the recycling box.

Wired, scared, hungry and tired, she grabs a lasagne from her haul and stuffs it in the microwave. She turns the dial, sets the timer going and almost instantly there is a puff and a crackle and a smell of electrical burning. She yanks the plug out of the wall and lets out a roar of frustration.

Swearing, she switches on the oven. She's going to have to wait forty minutes now.

She calls Damian, tells him about the card. He already knows about Edwin.

'That creep. Want me to sit on him?'

'You'd kill him. He's a puny little man.'

'It would be my very great pleasure.'

Despite herself, she laughs. She takes a breath. 'Hey, Dame, did you send those flowers for Harry?'

'You haven't been up there again, have you? You should keep well away.'

'Did you send them, though?'

'Of course.'

'Have you been in touch with Marcy, then?'

He sighs. 'Not heard a word. I messaged her about Harry, but she didn't get back. I sent them on behalf of her and the shop because I know that's what she would have wanted.'

'Really?'

'She did the same thing when another of our customers fell down in the North Laine from a heart attack. Did they look nice?'

'Beautiful. There are loads of bunches up there, from his school, other people. There's a drawing from his kid.'

'So sad.'

'Awful.'

The oven pings. It's hot enough for her lasagne.

'Marcy, Marcy, Marcy, where the hell are you?'

While she airs her walk-weary toes and washes down her single-girl ready-meal supper with a large glass of wine, Caz scrolls through the stream of messages she has sent Marcy. Four nights and not a whisper of contact from her.

And now she has WhatsApped her about what happened to the microwave and how it wasn't her fault. The least Marcy could do is absolve her. She knows how Caz hates being in the wrong.

But bearing in mind her journals, she's probably enjoying thinking about her stewing away here. And anyway, this is typical of her. She never bothers about anything unless it directly affects her. When they were growing up, Caz had to really dress up texts, make them appear super-urgent or scandalous before she'd get a response. She kicks out her own path, does Marcy. Caz supposes that is what drew Mark to her. Caz is rather more conventional. Rather more keen to please.

Yes. Caz is the boring one.

And now, according to the journals, she can add the *smug* boring one.

That taste of vitriol from Marcy's journals still lingers, tainting her food. For one brief second she forms the maddest of theories that Marcy might somehow be behind the deaths of

Ash and Harry. That for some reason she still despises her so much that she would commit murder just to mess up her life.

'But that's just ridiculous,' she says to her boring lasagne, which she's eating on her boring own, and washing down with a boring tumbler of boring Merlot.

Marcy wouldn't bother to go to such lengths with someone she considers to be so dull.

She wonders what kind of supper is normally eaten in this house. Cooked from scratch, no doubt, using one of the many books on her shelves. Or perhaps not, as they all look way too pristine to have been actually used. No, she would eat out, or have friends round for fresh pasta and pan-fried scallops from a little fancy deli in the North Laine, and they'd have fancy wine from the pretentious wine cellar thing, but they'd drink it from jam jars because they're just too cool to worry about proper glasses.

Perhaps that's it. Perhaps her texts just bore Marcy.

Caz tries to go further into Marcy's motivation. She hasn't actually ever apologised face-to-face for what she did. But it must have cost her an unaccustomed dose of cap-in-hand to send that first message about meeting up. After all, for what was possibly the first time in their relationship, it made Caz queen of the castle. Perhaps this not replying is her way of redressing that, of reasserting herself at the top of the hill.

Thinking like this makes Caz even crosser. Over the years, since Marcy stole Mark, Caz has increasingly viewed her as an imperious princess, trampling over anyone to get what she wants. Since she rekindled their relationship, she has softened that view, but now she doesn't know...

Perhaps this is some kind of test.

If so, how does she pass?

Or fail?

She scrapes the last bit of dreary lasagne from the tray she hasn't even bothered to decant it from and licks it off her knife.

'Throw me a bone here,' she says to Bridget, who must have some idea what goes on in her mistress's mind.

Bridget sits on her expensive purple velvet doggie divan, which throws serious shade on Joe's neighbouring beige fake-fur doughnut bed. She eyes Caz. She knows exactly who should be bone-throwing in this relationship.

And then, as if summoned by all of Caz's turning it over, a message from Marcy pings up on her phone.

Oh no, poor you, Cazzer. I don't ever use the microwave. It irradiates your gonads. So take care. But if you must, buy another the same brand and I'll put the money in your account.

Irradiates your gonads? What is Marcy going on about? Does she even know what gonads are?

And not an explanation or apology for not responding to all her earlier messages.

Yeah, that's it.

Marcy and Caz are done.

She is just doing the washing-up – never having lived in a house with a dishwasher, she can't justify using it just for herself – when the doorbell rings. The dogs kick off like it's the devil himself come for all the pets, and Caz drops a glass so it hits the tile floor and smashes.

'Fuck!' she says, then, stupidly, given her bare feet, sets off across the kitchen to see who it is on the doorbell camera screen.

Of course her foot finds a jagged piece of glass.

Of course she starts bleeding all over the floor.

Framed by the screen, the man on the doorstep looks up at the camera, because he knows exactly where it is.

'Oh no,' Caz says. 'Oh bloody hell.'

SEVENTEEN

She has no idea whether it is horror or delight on his face as she opens the door to him. Or just plain shock.

'Caz? What the hell—'

Mark is cut off by Bridget Jones, who has brought him one of Caz's shoes and is crawling around his feet, her extreme excitement getting in the way of her attempts to roll onto her back.

It's the first time Caz has seen him since he left their student flat with his possessions in a battered rucksack.

'Daddy's back,' she tells Bridget, attempting to calm her by putting a hand on her head. She looks up at Mark. 'Well, hello. I suppose you'd better come in.'

'As it's technically my house.'

Limping, she leads him through the kitchen, pulling a 'we're in trouble' face at Joe, who isn't quite as welcoming as Bridget to this male stranger. He stands just inside the kitchen door, still judging the situation, his ears and tail held stiffly.

'It's OK, Joey. Mark's a friend,' Caz says. Although she's not completely sure on that point.

'Where's Marcy?'

'Away,' Caz says. 'I'm house-sitting for her and looking after Bridget.'

'I could have looked after Bridget.'

'She asked me.'

'Oh yeah, you're a dog-walker now, aren't you?'

Caz wonders how he knows that.

'Don't tell me she's paying you to walk Bridget? Ha!' He strolls over to the stupid wine cellar and selects a red. 'Since when did you two patch things up?' He lifts two fine wine glasses down from where they are suspended under the bottles. 'Oh. Let me guess. When she and I split up.'

'It's not all about you, Mark.'

He laughs like he doesn't quite believe that and moves over to the kitchen drawer where the corkscrew lives. 'Blood down here,' he says, pointing at the floor.

'That's my foot.'

'Ouch. Want me to kiss it better?'

Ignoring him, Caz pulls the dustpan and brush from under the sink and sweeps up the broken glass.

'And what's up with the face?' He motions at the bump on her forehead.

'I walked into a tree.'

'That's what they all say. Where's madam anyway?'

The lie is out before she can stop herself. 'Off on a romantic getaway with Charlie.'

'Charlie?'

'Her new guy?'

Mark frowns. 'I don't know any Charlie.'

'Oh no.' Caz puts her hand over her mouth. 'Perhaps I wasn't meant to say anything.'

'Damn right.' He pops the cork and, without even asking her, pours two glasses of wine. 'So, she's putting it about with yet another man. Poor bloke.'

'Wow. No love lost between you two, then,' Caz says.

'It's hardly an amicable split. For example, this bottle is worth fifty quid. It's mine, but she's still got it, and all its cellar mates, as well as every piece of art I ever bought. Go figure.' He hands her a glass. 'You look exactly the same. I like that fringe.'

'Stops my hair getting in my eyes.'

'No. It's cute. Covers up the bump, too, mostly.'

Caz sits at the kitchen table, trying really hard not to blush.

'Didn't you see it all on her Instagram? About what a dick I am? About how heartbroken she was? All such bollocks, designed to look edgy and get her more followers so she can shift more stuff at the shop. Pity purchases.'

Hearing him talk so bitterly about Marcy feels like karma on steroids, and Caz loves it. 'I don't look at her social media,' she lies. 'After... you know. I didn't want to have anything to do with either of you.'

'Really?' He eyes her like he really doesn't believe her.

'Really.'

'I look at yours.'

'Do you?' She's shocked, because the privacy settings on her genuine Facebook account are pretty good. 'How?'

'I have my ways,' Mark says.

'Of course. Mr IT Guy. Mr Developer. Mr Hacker.'

He takes a bow. 'Meet Miss Sonia White.'

'Sonia White? From when we were at school?'

'One and the same. I found her account and just made a little clone...'

Caz smiles, at once repulsed and flattered. That is so typically Mark. 'You devil.'

'I *am* a devil. Anyway, I hated the way we parted. I wish we could have remained friends.'

'Ha!'

'Yeah. I know. I was a shit. But over the years I just couldn't get you out of my mind. Wanted to see what you were up to.'

Caz sips the red wine. It's thick and velvety and tastes like plums and jam and tobacco.

'And then your profile picture. You with Ruth's Mother sculpture. Brought it all back. When I went round to yours for supper the first time to meet her, and I saw that in the conservatory. I knew I had to fall in love with the girl who grew up in a place like that, with an extraordinary mother like that, who made a sculpture like that.'

'Hmm.'

He strolls over to another kitchen cupboard and grabs a bag of crisps. Taking Caz's oranges out of a hand-made bowl on the table, he replaces them with the crisps. 'This is the snack bowl, Caroline, not the fruit bowl.'

She smiles. 'Sorry, sir.'

He offers her the crisps. 'Leaving you was the biggest mistake of my life.'

'Why'd you do it, then?'

He sighs. 'Marcy was very persuasive. She had me by the balls. But I see her rotten side now. My God, she's rotten. And greedy. She cheated on me and now she wants to bleed me dry.'

Caz blinks. Her glee at hearing him bitch about Marcy has soured, and she finds herself in the strange position of wanting to defend her former friend against the man who allowed himself to be seduced by her. Even now, when she knows Marcy wrote so disparagingly about her in her journals.

He sits opposite her, Bridget leaning against his leg looking wooingly up at him. As he leans back in the chair, his lopsided smile, his warm brown eyes and craggy face and those finely muscled forearms do things to Caz she would rather they didn't.

'So how did she get back into your good books, then?' he asks, throwing a crisp into his mouth.

Caz tells him about the meeting, about her choice of pub. She feels a shiver of pleasure at the laugh this elicits from him.

'She's pretty short of friends,' he says. 'She let all that slide in her quest to earn as much money as me.'

'Was it really like that?'

He laughs. 'She's probably the most competitive woman in the world – as you know only too well. Sees what you've got and wants it herself. I gave her the money to start up the shop, but it barely turns a profit. It's more of a vanity project. Which is why she needs a good settlement from me. I mean, look at this place. All to her very expensive taste, and I hear there's an extension in the offing.'

'I believe so.'

'What does she need even more space for, eh? For what's his name? Charlie?'

Caz shrugs and grabs some more crisps, just for something to do with her hands.

'What's he like?'

'Charlie? No idea.'

'Where'd she meet him?'

She smiles. She's really got to him with the Charlie thing. 'I don't know.'

'I'm sorry,' he says, suddenly. 'I was a shit to you.'

'You were. But it was a long time ago.' She holds up her hands, waves her fingers in the air. 'I'm over it.'

He looks at her, his eyes unreadable. 'Lucky you.'

'Anyway,' she says, taking another mouthful of the insanely delicious wine. 'What can I do for you?'

'Eh?'

'What are you here for? Can I help?'

'I came for the Banksy.'

'The what?'

'In the garden room? The painting of the kid with the Union Jack?' He stands, and gestures to her to get up.

Joe growls.

'Shh, Joey,' Caz says.

'Here.' Mark takes her by the hand, a gesture she finds alarming and confusing – should she shake herself free, or allow herself to be led? But her fingers remember exactly how they fit into his.

He leads her through to what she thinks of as the living room, and points to the picture over the fireplace, which she assumed was a print.

'I bought that at auction six years ago.' He lets go of her and moves so he is standing in front of it. 'And I want it in my new house.'

'You have a new house?'

'Yep. Lewes Crescent.'

'A whole house?' Caz whistles through her teeth. That's the grand Regency square at the far end of Kemp Town, where oligarchs, rock stars and movie stars live.

'Used to belong to Cate Blanchett. You should come and visit.'

He reaches up and takes down the painting. The wallpaper around it has faded, leaving a darker rectangle to highlight its absence.

'Shouldn't you wait until Marcy's here?'

'It's mine.'

'Perhaps she thinks differently.'

'Undoubtedly she will.'

'But what will I say to her?'

'Just put her in touch with me.'

Caz puffs out her cheeks. In this situation, as with most in her life, it seems, she is powerless.

'Gotta fly,' Mark says, the Banksy tucked under his arm. The artist's daughter in Caz worries for the fate of a painting given such treatment. 'Zoom with LA at ten.'

'Business going well?' she asks as she follows him through to the hallway.

'Swingingly.' He opens the door. A shiny Ferrari sits on the driveway like a big red basking shark.

He kisses her goodbye. Once on each cheek. He smells exactly the same. Eau Sauvage.

'Oh,' he says, as he bleeps the car open. Its lights flash, making it appear even more predatory. 'I've got two VIP comps for Nick Cave at the Dome tomorrow night. It's a try-out before his tour. Home crowd. I was going to take Ginny – remember what a Nick Cave nut my little sis is? But she's got that flu everyone's going down with. Wanna come?'

Caz pauses a beat. Partly because she's not all that into maudlin goth punk, but mostly because she's wondering if it's a great idea to go on a night out with Mark.

But Jesus. She's living like a nun at the moment. The least she deserves is a bit of music and a couple of drinks. Let her hair down. Forget the horrors.

'That'd be great.'

'Cool. I'll swing by about six, yeah? We could get a bite to eat beforehand.'

Again she hesitates, but then remembers her grim solo lasagne. 'OK.'

He jumps in the car without a backward glance and is off with a stomach-churning roar of engine and spew of raw petrol smell.

'Was that Mark?' a voice says from the street, beyond Marcy's front hedge.

Caz catches her breath. 'Who's that?'

'Only me!' Clive steps forward into the drive, and she shrinks back into the doorway. 'You haven't seen Meatloaf, have you?'

'Meatloaf?'

'Our cat. He's not come in tonight yet.'

'It's early, though, isn't it?'

'Not for him. *Was* that Mark?'

'He just dropped by to pick something up.'

Clive laughs. 'Stripping the place while she's away?'

'No.'

'Anyway, glad I caught you. I just wanted to ask: which school did you teach in when you were in London?'

Caz frowns. 'Why do you want to know?'

Clive hesitates for a beat. 'My niece goes to school in London.'

'What area?'

'South.'

Caz sighs and tells him. It can't do any harm, can it?

She finishes the wine. It would be madness not to. Would she have taken such fine things for granted had life turned out differently? From all the stuff in this house, and how much energy it must take keeping everything together, being rich seems like an awful lot of effort.

Her phone pings. It's a message from her bank. Marcy has sent her £500 for the microwave, which is a bit excessive. *Blood money*, Caz thinks.

Glass in hand, she gets her laptop out to find a new microwave. Stalled by too many choices, she gets to thinking back to what Peter said about Jon. Now fully distracted from her task, she googles him, curious to find out what his unspeakable crime was. She tries all sorts of searches around Jon and Jonathan Ashdown, including words like arrested, crime, imprisoned. But nothing comes up. He appears to have no digital footprint whatsoever. She broadens it to include Colette, whose Facebook account is unguarded, meaning that Caz can get right in.

There is no mention of Jon.

Not even a photograph.

It's late, and Joe is making the sounds that tell her he wants a last pee. She lets both dogs out and, remembering that the back gate somehow opened itself yesterday, goes down to the bottom of the garden to make sure it is securely locked.

It's nearly a full moon tonight and she doesn't need her usual torch to see where the dogs are. They quietly do their business, then she follows them as they head back towards the house.

But there's a noise coming from next door, on Colette's side.

She tiptoes towards the fence and stands completely still, all ears.

On the other side, Colette is sobbing her heart out.

Like it's the end of the world.

Caz pauses for a moment, wondering if she should call out, see if she's OK. But then she decides against it.

The last thing she wants right now is to get caught up in another drama.

EIGHTEEN

'He's quite a performer, isn't he?'

Caz and Mark are strolling back along a moonlit Brighton beach. Despite her reservations, the gig was astounding, one of the best she has ever seen. Onstage, Nick Cave is like some sort of god. At one word from him, the entire audience would have readily drunk poison-laced Kool-Aid.

She is so glad she decided to come out. It was a close-run thing. She was exhausted when she got home after the day's last dog-walk. Thirty thousand steps is enough of a strain, but combining that with the effort of not thinking too much about either her situation or what lay ahead of her tonight completely poleaxed her. She picked up her phone ready to cancel with Mark, but something – the thought that she couldn't let all this stop her living her life – made her put it down again.

'Kind of see why Ginny's so fixated now,' she tells Mark. 'He's so watchable. Sort of ugly, but also sort of beautiful.'

'I envy him his power.' Mark stops and skims a flattish stone across the water, which is eerily still tonight. There's no wind, no waves, no noise other than the faintest tap of the sea on the shingle and the traffic a few hundred metres away up on the coast road.

'You have more than enough power. Which is exactly what you wanted me to say, isn't it?'

'I would never be so shallow.'

'Ha.'

They walk on in silence, past the remains of the old pier, wrecked by storm then fire then storm, and on towards the Peace Statue. Caz hasn't been down this way since she got back to Brighton. She had forgotten how much she loves it.

'It all stops at the sea, doesn't it?' she says. 'City, city, city, ahh. And then, out there, endless possibilities, all the way to the horizon and beyond. I can't believe I spent so many years away in London.'

'What were you doing there?'

'Teaching maths in a state secondary school. You'll know that from my Facebook.'

'Yeah.' He laughs. 'I do.' He reaches into his jacket pocket. 'Look what I've got.' He has a hip flask in his hand. 'Some very fine twenty-five-year-old single malt. Wanna sit and take in a wee dram?'

They crunch down on the stones towards the water's edge. Mark takes off his linen jacket and lays it, lining side down, on the stones.

'Oh, don't worry about me.' Caz sits on the shingle. She's wearing jeans that aren't anywhere near as lovely as Mark's jacket.

'You know,' he says as they both watch the lights of the wind farm twinkling through turning blades, 'I sometimes wish Marcy had never existed.'

Three seagulls sail quietly over them, heading out to sea like pale ghosts.

'Well, she does, and we can't turn the clock back.'

He leans against her and passes her the hip flask. 'Is that what you'd like, if it were possible?'

'What? For Marcy not to exist?'

'No, to turn the clock back.'

She takes the whisky and shifts slightly away from him. 'We can't, so I've never thought about it.'

'Hmm.' He lies back and props himself up on his elbows. 'Tell me about dog-walking. It's a sharp curve away from maths teaching.'

Caz nods. 'I make about the same, though, once I take into account how much I spent on commuting and so on.'

'Make or turn over?'

'OK, turn over, Mr Business Brain, but it's early days.'

'Why'd you do it?'

She looks sharply at him. 'Do what?'

'Come back here.'

She answers by gesturing at the sea, glittering under the moonlight, the wind farm, looking like it might be a Greek island in the distance.

He lowers an eyebrow in her direction. 'Yeah, you said. But what else?'

'Ruth's getting older.'

'Sixty's hardly ancient.'

'It's different when your body's as damaged as hers.'

'So, dutiful daughter, yes?'

Caz nods. Her stomach feels empty, despite the tapas they ate before the gig. The hollow swells inside her, stretching like a slowly blown-up balloon.

'You stopped posting,' he says, looking out to sea. 'About a year ago, you stopped posting on Facebook.'

'Eight months.'

'What?'

'It was eight months ago. Eight months, three weeks, two days.'

The sea shifts. The tide is quite far out now; the sands that lie beyond the pebbles are starting to show.

He turns to face her, and in doing so, his hand finds hers. 'What happened, Caz?'

She takes a deep breath, and, in one long, tight sentence, tells him.

Perhaps she shouldn't have.

Or at least, perhaps she shouldn't have told him everything.

He's sitting up, his head in his hands. 'Twice?'

She nods. 'Lightning, striking twice.'

'Twice, guys you knew? Guys you were dating?'

'It was just a horrible, awful coincidence.'

'What makes you so sure?'

'Why would anyone bother to do something like that to me? I've got no enemies. I've never even put anyone's back up.' She tries not to think of Edwin, his pathetic little love letters, his weaselly face when she turned him down. She knows he hasn't got it in him to do what happened to Ash and Harry. 'And one was in Hackney, and one was down here. And...'

'And what?'

She closes her eyes but opens them immediately to stop the pictures forming. 'They were both killed in very different ways.'

'Oh God.'

'Yes.'

She shivers, a great shudder that runs through to her very core.

He turns to her and puts his arms around her. She leans into him.

'Poor Caz,' he whispers into her hair. 'My poor Caz.'

His touch makes her feel hungrier, emptier. She needs warmth, closeness, connection. She thought she could do without it, but she can't. She reaches up for his hair, her fingers finding a familiar hold in his dark curls. Before she kisses him, he draws away.

'Are you sure this is what you want?'

She nods and pulls him to her.

The beach is dark, and quiet.

'What was that?' she says, as he strokes the hollow of her back.

'What?'

She sits up and looks behind her. 'I heard footsteps. On the stones.'

He shines his phone torch over the deserted beach behind them. 'No one there, see?'

'Perhaps it was a dog.'

'Damn dogs. Now. Where were we?'

Afterwards, they lie propped up on the shingle bank, sharing the whisky and listening to the waves.

She holds up her phone and takes a photo, the two of them smiling up at the camera, like they have been together for ever.

He still fits her like no one else ever has. After he went off with Marcy, she went through a rebound, sleeping-around phase. It was a sort of exorcism, but each of those lovers felt wrong, like jigsaw pieces that almost went together but not quite. The closest was Max, one of the older men, who appealed to the absent daddy issues even Ruth's ardent mothering failed to eradicate. But despite what happened joyfully under the duvet, in the shower, on the living room floor, their lack of shared cultural references – and the sense that she had become something of a walking cliché – put paid to that fling.

'You know,' Mark turns to her, smiling, 'perhaps I shouldn't get involved with you again, given what happened to the last two guys you were seeing.'

A shimmer of what she thinks is anger passes through her,

but her whole body is confused right now, so she can't fully read it. She flips onto her side and faces him. 'Neither had anything to do with me, OK?'

If she says it often enough, she will continue to believe it.

He touches her hair. 'In any case, it's a price worth paying.'

'It's not a joke.'

'Sorry.'

'Those poor men.'

'What were they like?'

'I don't want to talk about it.' She doesn't want to tell him that, like him, Ash and Harry turned out to be massive cheats. In any case, it does no good to speak ill of the dead.

He rolls onto his stomach and kisses her on the nose.

'And I will respect your wishes.'

'Will you?'

He nods, serious. 'I don't think I've ever stopped loving you, Caz.'

She looks into his eyes, those brown, swirly eyes, and her stomach flips, although she's just had him, she wants him again.

And there's Ruth, in her head, an eyebrow raised.

Be careful, Caz.

Eight years ago, when the betrayal happened, when this man she thought she was going to spend the rest of her life with went off with her best friend, she ran back home to her mother's arms.

'Once a cheat, always a cheat,' Ruth told her, holding her tight for the long hours she wailed and railed.

It's funny how she never fully blamed Mark for what happened. The betrayal by Marcy was the worst thing. Women don't do that to each other. Not normal women. Men, at a certain point, they're like dogs, they just can't help themselves. And even though she kept the thought deeply hidden, Caz always naturally assumed that all men, Mark included, would find Marcy more attractive, more interesting – more everything, in fact – than her.

But now she can't help feeling grateful to the double-crossing Marcy. If she hadn't reached out to her, then she would never have asked her to house-sit and Caz wouldn't have been there to open the door to Mark and this – *this!* – wouldn't have happened. She's so glad Marcy's poor mother fell over. So glad Marcy has gone away.

Be careful, the Ruth inside her head tells her again.

Guilty or not, Mark broke her heart. But that's mended now, strengthened by scars. This won't kill her. She will take him for now. See how things go.

Something in the sea catches her eye. It was almost completely still, but now the surface is boiling, spurting flashes into the night sky.

'What's that?' She sits up.

They get up and, hand in hand, hurry down to the water's edge.

'Careful,' he says.

Underfoot, the line between sea and sand is strewn with tiny dead fish no bigger than Caz's little finger. More are leaping frantically out of the water to join them.

A couple of metres beyond them, out to sea, bigger fish leap and turn like silvery daggers, chasing and catching their prey, driving those they don't devour to their deaths.

'Mackerel chasing whitebait. It's the wrong time of year for that,' he says.

He's right. It's unseasonal.

And it is carnage.

NINETEEN

The doorbell buzzes right into Caz's dreams and she climbs into consciousness, glad to be released from yet another rerun of turning from dead Harry to dead Ash, the mutilations and distortions increasing with each frantic whirl of her head.

She gropes across the duvet to her phone and sees, with a shock, that it is 6.45. She slept through her alarm. No. It's switched off. She must have done that before falling asleep last night.

She needs to have picked up the dogs by 7.15. Although thankfully, because she is at Marcy's and the dogs all live nearby, it's still just about possible.

But she switched her alarm off! That's hardly professional.

She throws back the duvet and swings her feet to the ground.

And realises she is in Marcy's room.

Standing on the rug beside the bed, Joe and Bridget look up at her like she has failed them in some way.

Last night... what happened? Raking her fingers through her hair, she tries to arrange the hangover-disordered rooms in her mind.

A rustle on the bed behind her makes her jump and Joe snarl.

She turns, her heart pounding in her ears.

Mark's gym-honed back is turned towards her. He's on his side of the bed – or at least it was his side when he was with her. Glaring at her like it's spotlit is a tattoo on his shoulder blade of a heart with the letter M wound around it. She curbs a sudden urge to claw it out.

She winds last night back. On the way back from the beach, they stopped off at a little cocktail bar up by the Floral Clock for a couple of ironic Sex on the Beach cocktails, which they followed up with Tuaca shots. Then it starts to get blurry. She can remember that, back at the house, Mark opened a bottle of champagne – worth, he informed her, over £300 – and then they headed out to the pool, where they threw off their clothes and jumped in.

They made a lot of noise. Too much noise, Caz remembers now, groaning and covering her face with the shame of it.

Was there something with Jon saying something to her?

Or did she see him watching?

Or is that just a flashback?

She shifts the images. Will Colette complain today?

The doorbell – which she had forgotten about – rings again.

'Fuck, fuck, fuck, fuck,' she mutters, quickly jumping out of bed and grabbing the doorbell monitor from Marcy's dressing table. It's Peter, and he's smiling into the camera. 'Won't be a sec,' she says breathlessly through the speaker.

She struggles into her dog-walking leggings, which she left strewn on the floor last night while she was changing for the gig. Changing – she remembers with a tiny stain of shame – into some of Marcy's black, silky and slightly, sexily, too-tight lingerie.

But they worked, didn't they, the sexy undies?

And she doesn't think Mark recognised them.

Better that than her usual big pants.

Mark stirs, lifts his head from the duvet and smiles at her. 'Hello, Cazzer,' he says, sleepily, his hair all tousled in that way that has always made her think of Juliette Binoche.

'Gotta do the early dogs,' she says. 'Hang around and I'll bring back some bacon butties.'

'I like big butties and I cannot lie.'

Pulling on her hoodie, trailed by the eager dogs, she hurries down the stairs.

On the other side of the glass, a man coughs.

'Sorry,' Peter says as she gingerly opens the door. Freshly shaven, he looks younger than he did before. 'Are you OK?'

Caz licks her finger and rubs it under her eyes. She made free with Marcy's mascara and eyeliner again last night. What with the swim and the sex, she probably looks like a panda right now. 'Overslept,' she groans. 'Just as well you called!'

'Glad to be of service,' he says. He's holding up a beautiful velvet dog collar. 'I'm just on my way down for a swim and then on to the shops. I wanted to catch you before you left – I imagine your working day starts early.'

'Left?'

'Didn't you say Marcy was coming back today?'

'Oh. Yes!' Caz's face flushes. Jesus, yes. It's Wednesday. What with Mark and everything, it had completely slipped her mind. She has to get Mark out, clear up her stuff, move out. Thankfully a woman calling herself Lena the Cleaner came for five hours yesterday. Lena had no idea Marcy was away, and her comment when she saw the state of the living room was 'For once I get job satisfaction, yes?' While Caz tried to hide away from her, she gave the place a proper polishing.

'I found this yesterday and I wondered whether you'd like it for Joe. It was Roop's. I asked the lady who took him on, but she's already got him a new one.'

'That's really kind,' she says. 'Thank you so much.'

'My absolute pleasure. It was great to meet you, Caz.'

'You too, Peter.' She shakes the hand he offers. 'And thank you for listening to me.'

'If you ever need any help, you know where I am,' he says, then focuses on something over her shoulder. 'Oh, hello.'

Caz turns and, to her horror, sees Mark padding barefoot down the hallway towards them. Thankfully he has thought to put on Marcy's waffle dressing gown.

'Hi.' He beams at Peter and holds out his hand. 'Mark Jones.' But there is a question in his greeting.

'This is Peter. He's clearing out his uncle Ezra's house.'

'Ezra on the corner? What happened?' Mark says.

'Heart attack,' Peter says. 'Swift and brutal. How he always said he wanted to go.'

'Oh, man,' Mark says.

'Did you know him?'

'Of course.'

'Um, Mark used to live here.'

'Ah.' Peter nods.

'I liked the guy,' Mark said. 'Great sculptor, too. What's happening to his work?'

'I'm trying to sort that out. I've got his gallerist coming to take a look.'

'Well, once you know ballpark prices, let me know. I'd love to come and take a look. You can contact me through Caz here. Or Marcy.'

Caz is astounded by Mark's audacity. He clearly didn't get rich by letting opportunities fly past.

He touches her on the shoulder in a way that makes it clear that they are not just friends. 'Coffee?'

'I've got to dash,' she says. 'Dogs.'

'See you later, then.' He kisses her on the top of the head and heads off to the kitchen.

'That's Mark, Marcy's ex-husband?' Peter whispers, lifting an eyebrow as if he's enjoying a bit of potential gossip.

'It's complicated,' Caz says.

'Nice guy.'

'He is.'

'Nice wheels, too.' Peter's eyes twinkle with mischief.

'Eh?'

He turns to show her Mark's flash red Ferrari, parked conspicuously on Marcy's driveway. Caz closes her eyes and takes a deep breath. He arrived in it last night, then suggested that they walk down to the Dome because he wanted to have a couple of drinks. A couple!

'I'm more of a jeep man myself,' Peter says.

'I've seen you driving it down the close,' Caz says, but her mind is somewhere else.

He nods again towards Mark's car. 'Mud would show up too much on one of those.'

She laughs, weakly.

Was Mark intending to walk her back and stay the night? And there could be no finer signal to the neighbours that Caz is shagging Marcy's ex than his highly recognisable and prominent car staked out here like a flag claiming the moon.

Is he hoping that the street gossip will get back to Marcy?

'He's solvent then, this Mark?'

Is he just playing her?

She smiles, weakly. 'You could say that.'

And then he was the one who suggested they go out to the pool, and if she remembers rightly, it was him leading the noise, firstly by beaming music through some hidden poolside speakers Caz had no idea about, then making her laugh and exciting her to the point of crying out. Colette and Jon at least will have lots to say to Marcy when she returns.

Oh God.

She's just not cut out for the adult world.

'Well, good on you. Let him spoil you rotten. You deserve a good time after everything you've been through.'

Caz leans forward and, without thinking, hugs Peter tightly. 'Thank you so much, Peter.'

He steps away, blushing. 'It's been good knowing you, Caz.'

He sounds a little sad to be saying goodbye. Confused about what she feels about this, she closes the door behind him, puts the beautiful collar on Joe, then grabs her dog kit bag and heads on out for the morning walk.

Perhaps she'll take them down to the beach, see if the dead fish are still there.

'Great butty,' Mark says in an entirely suggestive way. They're outside by the pool again. He eyes the water, where, he has informed her, he has swum the hundred lengths he used to do daily when he lived here. 'I've got my energy back. Can you think of a way of burning it off?'

He leans towards her, and she laughs.

'Sorry, matey. You've got to go. Marcy's back today, and in between clients I've got to clear up her bedroom, wash all the bedding, sort out the kitchen...'

'Oh, we mustn't upset Marcy.'

'I fear we're going to upset Marcy a great deal.'

'Ha.' He stands. 'She won't care. She doesn't give a shit about me.'

'I can't imagine that,' Caz says.

'She's no doubt full of this new bloke, this Charlie wanker.'

For one second, Caz feels guilty for the lie she has told Mark. But, in the scheme of things, it's a small sin. 'Rebound. Believe me, I know about that.'

'Sorry.'

'Please stop apologising. She's going to think this is all some sort of revenge plot.'

He stops smiling and looks sharply at her. 'Is it?'

She stands, puts her arms around him and kisses him, aware that she is mud-splattered from the diversion she took onto Hove Lawns on the way home, and that she has not yet cleaned her teeth – or any other part of her body. 'Nothing could be further from the truth.'

He puts his hands on her hips. 'Can't I just stay for an hour or two?'

'No! I don't know when she's due back. She could be here any minute.'

'That would mean an early start. Marcy doesn't do early starts.'

Mark's phone buzzes. He picks it up and squints at the screen. 'Oh Jesus.'

'What is it?'

'Something's kicking off in our Netherlands office.'

'Not too serious, I hope?' Caz knows that Mark develops apps and sold his firm for a great deal of money, but beyond that she has very little notion of what his business involves and can't imagine how it might lead to things 'kicking off'.

He picks up his leather jacket, which is draped across the back of a kitchen chair. 'I'm going to have to go hop on a Zoom.' He turns back to her and kisses her. 'So sorry.'

'You go.'

He's forgotten that before his phone message, she was actually trying to hurry him away.

TWENTY

After she gets back from the mid-morning walk, Caz texts Marcy, asking her what time she can expect her back. She gets no reply. Annoyed, she starts straightening out the house. Mark used to be a neat freak, but it's clear that he has been seriously spoiled by his wealth. He's no doubt got a whole clutch of people now to take care of the more mundane aspects of his life.

As she removes the blobs of toothpaste from the en suite basin, she wonders if she could get used to living in a house in Lewes Crescent, with housekeepers and gardeners and people to clean up her own toothpaste blobs.

Very possibly.

Would she keep the dog-walking business going? Perhaps Ruth could move in with her and Mark. Those Regency seafront houses are enormous. But then in a few years' time she's going to have problems with stairs, and there are loads of floors – some must be six storeys or more, great sweeping stone staircases. They could install a lift. There could even be a self-contained granny flat for her in the basement...

She eyes herself in the mirror. 'Shut *up*, Caz.'

It has been just one night with Mark this time round. And

she's not even sure she wants to properly get back together with him. Would she ever be able to trust him again? And even if she could get over the journals, it would be the kiss of death to any hope of rekindling her relationship with Marcy.

Again, the sense that she might be being played returns to her.

Is it some sort of weird thing they are both doing to her? Is she a little mouse being batted about by two giant egotistical cats?

Shaking the thoughts from her head, she strips the bed and takes the linen down to the laundry room, where she selects, from the range of products available, an organic washing liquid scented with pure lavender essential oils. Anything to get the sex off those sheets.

Later, she's walking the dogs in one of the more populated parts of Stanmer Park, a country estate bequeathed to the people of Brighton, all woodland and bucolic fields full of sheep, with its own manor house and sweet village of knapped flint cottages. As she reaches a spot where she can let the dogs off their leads, she picks up a text. It's from Mark.

I love you. I have never stopped loving you.

She gasps, puts her hand to her mouth. Something lifts from her shoulders.

She restrains herself from replying, from diving in. She's not sure what she thinks, but her abiding feeling right now is one of victory: she has got Mark back from Marcy's clutches. It doesn't make her proud, but it does make her smile.

Safely off lead in the great expanse of grass at the back of the big house, the hounds – reddish brown, piebald and dusty cream – stream over the shaggy lawn, snuffling, tumbling, meeting the other dogs out for their afternoon walks, then returning to her for treats and reassurance. A group of dog owners stand around chatting in the sunshine, leads slung over mud-stained waterproofs, pockets bulging with treats and poo bags. They beam love and pride at their charges in the exact same way a parent might at a child.

Caz stands apart from the others. For one thing, the last thing she wants to do is engage in small talk. But also, she has learned that these amateurs tend to see professional dog-walkers as a different breed to themselves – like parents might view nannies in a playground. Plus, with Bridget tagging along, she has one more dog in her posse than is strictly legally allowed, so she doesn't want to face any awkward questions.

Buoyed by Mark's text, she is also sore from his attentions to the degree that she couldn't stop thinking about him even if she wanted to. Anything and everything seems possible right now. She will go back to Ruth's house this evening and a new life will open up for her. The life she had stolen from her. The life – she whispers the thought – she deserves.

No. Say it loud and proud. She's owed some luck and easy times, after what she's gone through. She imagines herself in the grand hall of Mark's house. Trying to make it sophisticated, she puts herself in a glamorous evening dress – something Marcy might wear – high heels, hair all smooth, make-up beautifully applied. She's standing beside Mark, greeting guests as they arrive for dinner.

She can't keep it going. The vision of stately adulthood is smashed by a frankly more realistic kids' movie version of herself and Joe sweatily rushing through the front door from the beach, haring along the corridor, running up the stairs, tumbling onto a big bed.

Just because she's moving into a large and glorious house doesn't mean she has to change. She *will* keep the dog-walking going. And perhaps she'll open a home for strays...

'STOP!' she yells. Her pack of dogs freeze and look at her like they've been doing something wrong without realising it. Every single one of the amateurs glares at her. Feeling their judgement, she smiles and mouths, 'Sorry!'

In fact, she'd really like to tell them all to get lost.

That would be the great advantage of being Mrs Rich Caz. She wouldn't have to worry about anyone's approval any more.

Is she going mad? Have the horrors unhinged her?

The dogs returned to their empty homes, Caz rolls the van into Marcy's driveway. The house stands still and silent. It doesn't look like she's got back yet.

'Hello?' she calls out as she lets herself, Joe and Bridget in through the front door.

But the house is empty, and Bridget, who is concentrating on trying to nibble Joe's ear, is not showing any signs whatsoever of a dog detecting her owner's presence.

For what feels like the fortieth time, Caz checks her phone for any contact from Marcy. And still nothing. A whole week now with not a word, except the weird thing about gonads and microwaves. Marcy lives in the present, she knows that, but this is taking the piss. She texts her again.

Let me know your ETA.

Then she types:

I could pick you up from the station if you're coming by train.

But before she sends it, she deletes it, because it shows that she has been snooping and seen Marcy's car. And perhaps Marcy has a car and driver and would laugh at Caz's assumption that she would take the train like a common person.

And anyway, Caz thinks, her irritation growing, Marcy doesn't deserve a pickup at the station. It's really rude, keeping her hanging on like this.

She might as well get packed, though.

The dogs look worried as she starts carrying her stuff out to the driveway. They stick beside her, brushing up against her legs, and when Caz opens the van to load her bag, Joe melts down onto the ground and rolls over, trying to distract her by demanding a tummy rub.

She hears a man cough over by the magnolia. Peering out from behind her van doors, she sees Peter standing at the front gates.

'Still here?' he says.

'She's not back yet.'

'When's she due?'

'She hasn't said.'

'So you've got to hang around and wait for her?'

Caz shrugs. 'I don't know. It doesn't feel fair on Bridget just to leave. I mean, she said she'd be back today, but that could be any time up to midnight.'

'I guess. Oh, doesn't he look a smart boy?'

'Eh?'

She follows Peter's gaze. He's looking at Joe in his new blue velvet collar.

'It's a really good one,' she says. 'Thank you so much.'

'I'm sure Ezra would approve.' Peter smiles and beckons to Joe to come to him, but Joe stays where he is.

'He thinks I'm going to take him by surprise, jump in the van and make a dash for it,' Caz says.

'He likes it here?'

'He does.'

'And you?'

'It's a beautiful house,' Caz says.

'Perhaps she won't come back, and you can stay for ever!'

Caz laughs. 'I'd like that!'

But as midnight approaches with no sign of Marcy, and aware
that she has to be up early tomorrow morning, Caz is not so sure
that she does like that. She's had another Deliveroo burger for
supper because she didn't want to mess up the kitchen she
spent an hour polishing to a minimalist gleam. She has phoned
Ruth and explained the situation, and she's tried calling, texting
and emailing Marcy. She's even tried direct messaging her on
her Instagram, which she notices hasn't seen any updating over
the past week. But then grim northern hospitals and ailing
elderly parents aren't exactly consistent with Marcy's brand.

She's sitting on the sofa working her way through season
four of *Friends* – the one where Rachel and Ross get back
together. The bottle of red she bought at the Tesco Metro to
welcome Marcy home stares at her from the coffee table. If she
opens it, she's going to have more than just one glass, which
means she won't be able to drive back to Ruth's tonight.

Her eyes are dry and heavy and her legs ache. Dog-walking
may be easier on the brain than teaching, but physically it wears
you out. She reaches for the bottle.

As she unscrews the top, it briefly passes through her mind
that she should perhaps be worried about Marcy not coming
home.

But no, she tells herself. If anyone can look after themselves,
it's Marcy. She would rather die than be thought of as a victim.

She watches TV and drinks one glass, then another.

As Ross accidentally says Rachel's name at the altar instead
of Emily's, Caz stretches out on the sofa with a final glass of
wine. She covers herself with one of Marcy's pure alpaca
throws and with the dogs on the floor beside her, falls fast
asleep.

TWENTY-ONE

'Come on, come out with me.'

Harry smiles and reaches one hand out towards her. 'It doesn't matter that I'm married now.' His other hand scoops up his guts and tries to push them all back inside the gaping hole in his stomach.

She backs away, her hands up.

But she bumps into Marcy. 'He's mine,' she says, shining a torch into Caz's eyes, blinding her...

The pale light leaching through the open curtains coaxes her eyelids open.

Grateful to be free from the nightmare, she squints at her phone. It's 6 a.m.

The dogs are asleep on the floor beside her.

Everything – even the half-empty wine glass on the coffee table – is exactly as it was last night. *Friends* is still playing, now deep into season five. Caz rolls off the sofa. Out in the entrance hall, the coat hooks are bare but for her dog-walking bag and jacket, hanging where she left them last night so that she wouldn't forget them when she headed home.

There's no bag, no shoes, nothing dumped on the backs of any of the kitchen or dining room chairs.

'Marcy?' she calls up the stairs.

She knows she's not there, though. Marcy's not the type of person to come in without announcing her arrival. She absolutely would have woken Caz up, and anyway, the dogs – who are just sleepily padding through to the hall, wondering why they have to wake up so early – would have reacted in some way to someone even tiptoeing into the house while Caz was asleep.

She checks all the bedrooms, and they are as untouched and unoccupied as she imagined.

Her phone has no notifications, but she checks her messages anyway. There is no sign of Marcy. She even checks her calendar to make sure she has the day right.

She does.

More cross than worried, she takes advantage of her early start to have a shower and wash her hair, using Marcy's lovely expensive products. Then, while she's standing wet in the shower, she remembers that all her clothes, everything, are packed in the van.

While she's dripping and wondering what to do, her phone rings.

'At last,' she says, nearly slipping as she hurries out of the shower. She reaches for her phone, which is sitting on top of the vanity unit.

It's Ruth, though.

'Are you OK?' Her voice comes out like she's being strangled by panic. 'You didn't come home!'

Caz talks her nearly hyperventilating mother down with a little lie. 'It's OK, Marcy can't get away yet.'

'But why didn't she tell you earlier? I'd made a lentil lasagne for you and got your hottie all ready in your bed.' Ruth means Caz's hot-water bottle, but an image crosses her mind of Mark splayed out in her teenage bedroom, like he was so many times when they were younger.

'Her mum's still in hospital so she's got to stay with her dad a bit longer.'

'You're lying to me.'

'I'm not!'

'I don't need your protection, Caz.'

'I know you don't.'

'If anything odd's going on...'

'What, other than my mother ringing me at six in the morning, you mean?'

'Seriously, Caz, I—'

'Everything is just fine, Mum. Marcy's going to be away for at least the next couple of days and I'll give you due warning before I come home. I'll drop by with your shopping tomorrow.'

'I can get a Sainsbury's delivery.'

Caz sighs. This is Ruth telling her that she doesn't need her help or protection, which is also her saying that she doesn't believe what she's telling her. 'Fine, then. I'll call you when I'm due home. Gotta dash now. Dogs.'

'Just take care—'

But Caz finishes the call. She actually does have dogs to deal with.

She's out on Hove seafront, wrestling the dogs away from the corpse of a gannet strangled by fishing wire, when her phone pings.

It's a message from Marcy. Finally.

Cazzer, so so sorry. Mum still bad, poor dear Dad still needs looking after. Gonna b a while yet. U can stay, can u? More ££ coming thru.

Instantly Caz gets a bank alert that her account has received £1,000 from Mrs M. Jones.

'Well, that's that, then.' Another grand in the bank slightly takes away her irritation. Something's niggling in the back of her mind, though, and it takes her a while to realise what it is. Two things, in fact. The first is that in all her life, Caz has never known Marcy to apologise for anything. Secondly, in the past Marcy would refer to her father as a number of things, but *poor dear* was never one of them.

Perhaps she's changed. Perhaps she's softened – after all, she did reach out to Caz when she arrived in Brighton. But it all feels a bit laid on with a trowel, and Caz is beginning to wonder what Marcy is actually playing at.

Do you have any idea when you might be back? she texts.

There is no reply, which is a real pain. Does she have to be ever ready for Marcy to walk back in?

She decides to run the message past Damian to see what he thinks, but as shop manager, he doesn't allow personal calls for assistants so refuses to take any himself. So when she gets back to the house, she leaves Joe and Bridget snoozing in the sun at the back of the house and jumps on a City Hire bike to pedal down to the shop.

The wind is against her all the way, blustering up the hill, away from the sea. 'Stiff offshore breeze,' Ruth used to tell her on the many seafront walks she dragged her out on when she was small. 'Blows away the cobwebs.'

She docks the bike in the stands by Churchill Square shopping centre.

Crowds of marauding seagulls hover over the street waste bins, pulling out half-eaten burgers, kebabs and fried chicken, squabbling over the remains and strewing them around the pavement. The clock tower, where she used to meet her mates for a Saturday afternoon mooch round Topshop and Gap – all gone – is a colony of the dispossessed and homeless, a crowd of desperate-looking people wrapped in bundles of dirty old duvets and sleeping bags, sharing bottles of cheap cider and fag-end roll-ups.

A young woman with grey skin breaks out of the group and stands in front of her. 'Got the price of a cup of tea, love?'

Caz remembers how when she was younger, she had the feeling that everything was going to get better. But it hasn't. It's all got worse. And that's just in the outside world. What happened to Ash and Harry has stained her own life for ever. She will never be rid of that.

At least she has a roof over her head. And she suffers no major addictions or mental health problems that stop her living a comfortable life.

She fishes in her pocket and finds a pound coin for the woman, who looks at it disdainfully. Of course you can't buy a cup of tea for that round here.

'Sorry, it's all I've got,' she says, truthfully.

She carries on down the hill, into the pedestrianised part where Marcy has her shop. Here, the cluster of independent boutiques and cafés are thriving, and the area looks like some effort has been put into it. The street is fairly busy with shoppers and browsers: funky middle-aged Brighton art women, wealthy-looking students, young mothers with buggies the size of small cars, a man in heels and a leopard-print dress.

Clever Marcy, choosing this spot.

The smell of baking from the fresh cookie shop on the corner reminds Caz of Peter, and her mood lifts a little. A world that has such a kind man in it can't be all bad. Perhaps she'll call him tonight, invite him over for a drink.

If Mark doesn't come round.

She wonders again if this isn't all some kind of trick. Perhaps Marcy's just using her to get a favourable settlement from Mark. She pauses outside a café where once, when they were nineteen, Marcy didn't turn up because she was in bed with some boy she'd picked up. She didn't even bother to let Caz know, so she sat there like a lemon for over an hour.

It has always been a toxic friendship.

And the café is now all boarded up.

When Marcy returns, Caz is definitely going to back away. Cancel her as a client. Ghost her if necessary. She will miss Bridget, but hey.

It is with this resolve that she steps up to the heavy door of Fox & Hunter. As she pushes it open, a retro brass bell tinkles, and she is greeted by the tobacco and patchouli scent of a row of expensive candles burning on a high shelf. Her first impression of the long, deep shop is of dark wood, leather and polish. It's clean and clear, like Marcy's house, but darker and more masculine.

Dealing with a client who is buying a five hundred quid parka, Damian gives her a tiny wave and half a smile. She knows better than to interfere, so she hangs back and browses the racks in the rear part of the shop.

She's drawn to these men's clothes – thick cotton jersey T-shirts, hand-finished Breton shirts – she has a thing for stripes – lightweight denim shirts with large patch pockets at breast and hip. And the quality is fantastic. But the cost!

Then she remembers the extra grand from Marcy. She pulls out one of the denim shirts and holds it up against herself, checking her reflection in a full-length antique mirror on the wall.

Buying here would just be recycling the money so it goes back to line Marcy's pockets. She doesn't put the shirt back on the rack, though.

'Byeee,' Damian sings to his customer, who bundles out with his giant branded paper carrier bag, looking excessively pleased with himself. Then he swoops over to Caz and gives her one of his hugs. 'Lovely to see you, hun.' He steps back and tucks a strand of her hair behind her ear. 'What's this?' He pushes aside her fringe and points to the bump on her forehead.

'Marcy has too many trees in her garden.'

He tuts. 'How you doing?' He's still thinking about Harry and Ash.

For her part, the events of the past couple of days mean that, although they still take a starring role in her nightmares, her two murdered boyfriends have receded to the back of her conscious thought.

She wrinkles her nose. 'I'm fine, Dame. It's just Marcy's not back yet and then I got this weird text from her. Have you heard anything?'

Damian shakes his head. 'It's odd, because she's not exactly what you would call hands off with the shop. Entre nous, I've really enjoyed not having her constantly sticking her oar in, and I'm sure we've made more sales because of it. She puts customers off, I think. A bit too much in their faces.'

'I can imagine.'

'Hold on and I'll ask Wayne and Ness if they've heard anything and not told me; it's unlikely.'

He goes and speaks to the two junior shop assistants, who look up from rearranging the front window display and shake their heads. They glance apologetically over at Caz.

'Show us the text, then.'

Caz gets out her phone and hands it over.

Damian frowns as he reads it.

'That doesn't sound like her, does it?' Caz says.

'Nope. Not the words nor the money-flinging.'

'She's been doing quite a bit of that. Look at the one she sent before.'

Damian scrolls to the irradiating gonads text. 'You what?' he says.

'Exactly. Just weird.'

'What the hell's she playing at?' He hands the phone back

to Caz. 'Whoops.' Grabbing her arm, he pulls her behind the curtain of the changing cubicle. 'Perhaps that person just stepping in over there might be able to help?'

'What?'

'Mark,' he whispers.

TWENTY-TWO

They peek out from behind the curtain and watch Mark stride into the shop, heading for a rack of canvas jackets. Behind him, Wayne and Ness pull faces.

Normally, Caz and Damian share all their dating stories, but she has had neither the opportunity nor the desire to tell him about this new development. She knows what he would say, and how forcefully, and she can't face that right now.

Has Mark followed her into the shop? He always liked a bit of drama, a bit of trouble.

He pulls out a rust-coloured fitted jacket and holds it up. 'Damian!' he calls out.

'You stay here,' Damian whispers. He wheels out towards Mark, who, without greeting him, asks him if he has the jacket in the next size up.

'I'll just go and check for you, Mark.' Damian is decidedly snippy with him. It must be a tricky relationship, with Mark now being Marcy's ex. Not that there was ever any love lost between them. They went to the same secondary school – different to the one Caz and Marcy attended. When they all met at sixth-form college and Caz started going out with Mark,

Damian tried to warn her off him. He's never fully explained why he dislikes him so much. Caz has always suspected it had something to do with unrequited love.

But if Damian ever felt anything like that, it's certainly long disappeared. His face as he passes her on his way to the stock-room looks like he's just tasted a rotten blueberry.

Caz doesn't know whether to show herself or to remain hidden. In the end, the dilemma is taken from her by Mark, who sees her in the angled mirror opposite the changing cubicle.

'Hey!' he says, his face lighting up with delight. 'What are you doing here?'

'What are *you* doing here?' she says, stepping out with the denim shirt, as if she has just been trying it on.

'Only place in town for quality menswear. Besides, I get cost price, don't I, Dame?'

'You do, Mark.' Returning from the stockroom, Damian takes in the situation and ever so slightly purses his lips.

'I do.' Mark inspects the larger jacket. 'Because I own half the company.'

'Oh,' Caz says.

'Yes. It's a little awkward for Damian.' Mark smiles.

Damian looks from Caz to Mark and back again, frowning slightly. As far as he knows, she and Mark haven't met since Mark left her for Marcy. But here they are, relaxed with each other, as if continuing a conversation.

Mark puts the jacket on and turns to Caz. 'What do you think?'

'Nice.'

It is. It suits him very well. Emphasises the triangle of his broad shoulders and narrow hips, without looking sleazy or overworked.

Damian turns pointedly to Mark. 'Caz is in because she's wondering what Marcy's up to, because she's not back yet and is sending her weird messages.'

'Really?' Mark sounds nonchalant, but his jaw tightens, a sign Caz knows from way back means that all is not as calm as it seems on the surface. And then she remembers the story she told him about Marcy going off with a lover. He takes off the jacket and hands it to Damian. 'I'll have this.'

'And she hasn't checked in here for over a week now.' Without making eye contact, Damian straightens out the jacket on the counter and crisply folds the sleeves in.

It's almost as if he is accusing Mark of something.

Mark examines his nails. 'She's probably too busy shagging Charlie.'

Damian blinks. 'Charlie?'

'That creep she's swanned off with. I'm sure you know all about it. It's sweet of you to try to spare my feelings, Dame...'

'What?'

'... but there's no need.'

Damian snaps the jacket into a carrier bag. 'Actually, Marcy has gone up north to care for her father while her mother is in hospital.'

Mark laughs. 'Is that what she told you?'

Caz stands behind Mark, mouthing, 'I didn't tell you that,' at Damian and shaking her head, silently pleading with him not to dump her in the shit.

'Yes,' Damian says, and she wants to leap across the counter and hug him.

Mark slips his platinum credit card out of his wallet. 'My friend, you have been lied to.'

'I don't think I have.'

'Marcy's parents cut off all contact seven years ago when they moved back to Montego Bay, where her dad was originally from. They didn't even come to our wedding.'

'Montego Bay? Where's that?' Caz wonders if perhaps it's near Morecambe Bay, somewhere she knows is up north.

'Jamaica.'

To hide her dismay – and her discomfort – she gets out her phone and fires up Google Maps.

Damian prickles. 'Things can change.'

Mark nods. 'I wish that were the truth. But she told Caz she was off with this man, and I don't see Marcy as a mercy-recon-ciliation-dash-across-the-world type of girl. Do you?'

Tight-lipped, Damian hands Mark his receipt.

'She's just too busy shagging to bother with anyone but herself and the dick in question.' Mark turns to Caz. 'Fancy a spot of lunch across the road?'

'I've got to get back for the afternoon dogs,' Caz says.

'I'll call you later, then.'

'Great.'

He kisses her on the cheek, says goodbye to Damian, Wayne and Ness, and hurries out with his carrier bag. Despite the fact that he clearly had time for lunch with Caz, he's acting like he has something pressing to do.

As the door swings shut behind him, the air in the shop turns mint cold. Caz wants to curl up into a ball and roll away behind the velvet curtain of the changing cubicle.

Damian folds his arms and fixes her with a stare. 'Where do I start?'

Caz holds up her hands.

'Have you no self-respect, girl?'

'It's not what it seems... I know what I'm doing.' Caz doesn't even convince herself.

'I'm not going to go into that right now, but you'll have a good idea what I think. Which is that you are being a fucking idiot. But more importantly, what is the truth, Caroline? Is Marcy in bed with a lover, or the other thing?'

'She told me she was going up north to look after her dad while her mum was in hospital.'

'Not Jamaica.'

'She went of her own accord.'

Damian doesn't even raise a ghost of a smile. 'Caroline.'

'No, not Jamaica. Perhaps she meant north of Jamaica?' Eyebrows raised, Caz holds up her phone, which shows that Montego Bay is indeed on the north side of the island.

He looks even less impressed than he was at her joke.

'Well, perhaps not, then.' She pockets her phone.

'So why did you tell Mark a lie?' Damian takes the denim shirt from her and goes to put it back on the rack.

'I'm going to get that,' she says, following him.

'I don't think you deserve a nice new shirt,' Damian says. 'Not till you tell me why.'

Caz looks at her feet. 'I wanted to make him jealous. He told me she cheated on him and I wanted to capitalise on that.'

Damian holds the shirt and faces her. 'All such bloody liars.'

Wayne and Ness are now leaning against a rack of corduroy trousers pretending to share a bag of popcorn. 'Shall we do some work here, perhaps, ladies?' Damian says very pointedly to them. They turn and busy themselves straightening the clothes.

He fixes Caz with a raised eyebrow. 'Do you want to know how it actually finished between those two? Mark went off – not for the first time, might I add – with some twenty-one-year-old intern and Marcy finally had enough. After she kicked him out, he wanted to crawl back to her, but she wasn't having any of it.'

Caz looks at her feet. 'Oh.'

'So Mr Moneybags is lying to you. Again.'

She bites her lip. She can understand why Mark painted the picture of the break-up the way he did. It was not entirely unlike what she had done by lying to him about where Marcy was. When you want something enough, you shape the truth so you get it.

'I'm sorry, Damian.'

'But the big question now,' he goes on, 'is where Marcy actually is. She's not up north, she can't be in Jamaica, and she's sending you weird messages and excessive amounts of cash. If I didn't know this Charlie thing was made up, I'd be half imagining that Mark had tracked her down in a jealous rage and tied her and lover boy to the bed, leaving them to die a slow and horrible death.'

Caz shudders. 'Don't.'

'Why not? He's got it in him. Remember I saw the worst of him when I was growing up.'

She looks up at him. 'What was that about? You've never told me.'

'I never told you because I believe people can change. Plus for some reason you fell in love with him, and despite everything, all I want is for you to be happy. But he made my life hell from when I was eleven until I was fifteen and finally grew taller than him.'

'Why?'

'I've never been what you'd call a rugby player, have I? He found my softness offensive for some reason, bullied me mercilessly.'

'You mean he got at you because you're gay?'

'He did.'

'I'm sorry.'

'I've had worse since.'

'But he changed in sixth form, didn't he?'

'Only because you were friends with me and he wanted to get into your knickers.'

'Or perhaps he grew up and saw how idiotic he'd been. Like with me. He's really sorry for what he did to me.'

'Well, *I've* never had an apology. And has he *really* changed? What about him cheating on Marcy?'

'Perhaps Marcy deserved it.'

Instantly Caz wishes she could suck the words back into her mouth and swallow them down. What a stupid, awful thing to say.

Damian looks at her and sighs. 'Unbelievable.'

'I'm sorry.'

'And now,' he says, 'we don't know where Marcy is. She's disappeared just at the point where she's got to make urgent decisions on stock for the autumn collection. That is not Marcy.'

'No.'

'Did she tell you face-to-face where she was going?'

'She texted. She'd gone when I got to her house.'

'And she left the place in a mess, and all her things in her bag, and her car... I'm worried, Caz. Now we know she's not with her parents, all those out-of-character bits turn into cause for concern.'

'Yes.'

'And Mark lying to you doesn't make me happy. It smells of stinky fish to me.'

'But—'

He waves his hands at her. 'Shut up, Caz. Go and walk your dogs or whatever. I'm going to phone round everyone who knows Marcy and see if they've any idea where she might be. And then, once I've got over this and forgiven you for being such a fucking imbecile, I'll let you know if I hear anything.'

Caz nods.

He picks up the shirt. 'So do you want this?'

She looks at it. 'You're right. I don't deserve it.'

'He didn't do that, did he?' He points at her head bump.

'No! I promise, I literally walked into a tree.'

'Hmm.' He puts the lovely shirt back on the rail and guides her to the exit, where he kisses her like a father on top of her head. 'Be careful. Mark is the worst of all possible news for you. Everything he does is for one person only: Mark. He's fucked you over once in your life. Don't let him get away with it again.'

TWENTY-THREE

A sea gale roars outside. Caz has walked fifteen dogs twenty thousand steps since she left Fox & Hunter, and yet she is still shuddering at the whole situation. Mark has texted her and tried to call her and, Marcy style, she's not answering.

Indeed, she was relieved not to find him waiting for her when she got back to the house, because presumably, as it is still technically his, he could just let himself in.

Now, at nearly midnight, she lies on Marcy's sofa, the remains of tonight's takeaway – chicken tikka masala and Peshwari naan with a whole tub of Ben & Jerry's Cookie Dough – on the table in front of her, watching comforting reruns of early *Simpsons* episodes.

Even this third glass of Shiraz can't banish the awfulness of what happened in the shop.

She has disappointed Damian, and she is mortified.

And since she got back to the house, the final nail has been driven into the coffin of her flimsy north-of-Jamaica theory. Searching for a charger for her head torch – she forgot to pack her own – she found Marcy's passport in a folder of ID documents hidden in a drawer in the utility room.

So where *is* Marcy? Perhaps Caz has somehow magicked the entirely fictional stud Charlie into existence. So many strange things have happened this week that she wouldn't put it past the universe to pull something like that on her.

She thought that when she came back to Brighton, she was going to have a quiet, even boring couple of years slowly recovering from Ash.

But in the last week she has seen more drama than in her entire life. Even the possible high point of getting back together with Mark is tainted with fear, uncertainty and a feeling of being used that borders on paranoia.

The TV screen blurs on Bart's face and for a moment she thinks the telly is on the blink. But then she realises that she is crying.

'Stop feeling sorry for yourself, Caroline,' she says.

But she can't.

Joe shuffles across the sofa and snuggles into her, tucking his nose under her chin and placing a paw on her hand. Bridget crawls under her leg, placing her chin on her knee.

Then, just as she is beginning to find a sort of equilibrium, both dogs snap their heads up and start barking.

They jump off her and head to the door.

Caz puts her wine glass down on the table, stumbles to her feet and heads off after them. She doesn't put the light on in the hall. Doesn't want anyone outside to see her through the glass door. Outside, the security light has snapped on. Is that a shadow of a man she can see? Or is it just the magnolia tree, blowing in the wind? Her head reeling, all her nerves right up against the inside of her skin, she tiptoes towards the front door.

Nearly pushing her over, Joe rushes towards something squatting on the doormat and grabs it. This is unusually bad behaviour from him. Ever since an unfortunate incident with a cardboard pack of Parma ham Caz ordered online, he has been taught to leave post alone. Bridget tussles with him, keen to get it from him.

Joe tries to get past Caz with the package, but she stops him and, reluctantly, he lets go. It's one of those brown cardboard envelopes, the kind Amazon send when you order a paperback. But it has no bar codes. It hasn't come from Amazon. She half glimpses the backward slanting upper case handwriting on the front, and even though it's bigger than the past two envelopes she has received, she knows exactly who this is from.

Clutching the package, she flings open the front door. The security light is still on, but there is only a white plastic carrier bag, dancing wildly in the wind.

'Edwin!' she shouts as she runs out in the post-midnight darkness to the end of the driveway. 'I know you're there.'

There is no reply. Not a soul in sight.

Every single one of the beautiful flowers on Marcy's magnolia has succumbed to the wind. They lie on the brick pavers of the drive like fallen soldiers.

Parts of gored Harry, pieces of strangled Ash flash up in front of her, like the dead rising. A scream scratches at her throat, before she sees it is just the wind-driven Scots pine waving its blood-red cones at her.

She tries to talk herself down, but she turns and sees the dogs standing silently in the doorway, the hairs on their spines standing up, their teeth showing.

Something is definitely up.

Better to be inside, though, than a sitting target out here.

'Come on, chaps,' she says, hurrying them back indoors.

Reluctantly they obey.

She takes the package through to the kitchen and puts it on the table as gingerly as if it were a bomb. She can feel something hard and lumpy inside.

'Down!' she commands the dogs, who are still trying to grab it.

She tears it open and draws out another home-made heart-shaped card. With shaking hands, she opens it. Once again, the message is all backward-slanting upper case.

I LOVE YOU

YOU DESERVE THIS PLACE

EVERYTHING THAT'S HAPPENING IS GOING TO BE

GOOD FOR YOU.

I AM MAKING SURE OF THAT.

LET'S MAKE THIS OUR LITTLE SECRET.

RELAX.

TRUST ME.

DON'T DISAPPOINT ME.

THAT WAY EVERYONE STAYS SAFE.

XXX

This doesn't sound like Edwin.

And *everyone stays safe*? What does that mean? Is it a threat? The capitals certainly make it feel that way.

She turns her attention to the final item in the envelope, a small parcel wrapped in heart-patterned paper, tied with a red ribbon.

Carefully, thinking about anthrax powder and Novichok, she unwraps it.

Inside are two action figures, each about the size of her thumb: Batman and Robin. Frozen in time, capes flying, fists ready.

So is this from Mark, then?

Why so cloak-and-dagger? Why this sinister, oblique message?

And if it *is* from Mark, then the other cards must have been from him, too.

She just doesn't see him cutting out heart shapes, sticking them down on card...

Without thinking, she grabs her phone and calls Damian. As she does so, a text message pings through for her. But he answers before she can look at it.

'Yup.' He sounds like she has woken him up, which is likely, as it's now heading to one in the morning.

'Dame?' Her voice is that of someone whose spirit has been put through a grinder.

'It's Mark, isn't it?' he says. She can hear the anger in his tone. 'What has he done? I warned you, didn't I?'

'It's not that. It's just...' She has the card in her hands. She is just about to ask him to come over when she reads it again, this time more carefully.

... OUR LITTLE SECRET...

... EVERYONE STAYS SAFE.

She can't tell him. 'I'm sorry, sorry, sorry,' she says, trying to swerve away from her shock, from the impulse that made her automatically call him. 'You were right earlier. I'm such a fucking imbecile.'

'I didn't mean it. I was angry.'

'I found Marcy's passport, so she can't have gone to Jamaica.'

'No shit, Sherlock.'

'Did you manage to find anything out?'

'Nope. No one even knew she'd gone away.'

'Oh.'

'So, Caz?'

'So what?'

'So why'd you call me at this time on a school night?'

She breathes out. A short, sharp exhale. 'I just wanted to hear a friendly voice. It's weird, not knowing where she is.'

'Let's give her another couple of days, see what happens. Then we'll call the police.'

Caz winces.

'Although,' he goes on, 'I know they're not all that bothered if an adult goes missing and there's no sign of anything untoward.'

She flashes back to the blood on the bed, the handbag, the mess the house was in, the spilled fragrance, the estranged parents in Jamaica, the passport... Just one of those would have meant nothing. But all together? The very definition of untoward.

She turns the Batman and Robin over in her hand. Could they be from Marcy?

She feels dizzy. 'I've got to go,' she says, suddenly. Her enormous supper is sitting uneasily in her stomach.

'Fancy a drink? Proper kiss and make up?'

'I'll message you.'

'Play hard to get, then. See if I care.'

'Bye.' She stabs the call shut and rushes to the downstairs toilet, where she empties everything into the pan. She hates throwing up, but it lightens her a little. Or at least it does until she staggers back to the kitchen and sees the card, the little figures turned on their sides. She picks up her phone and photographs them, just in case.

Just in case of *what*?

Shivering, she turns the heating up.

'I have no idea what to do,' she tells Joe, who looks levelly at her.

'You're right,' she says. 'I need a clear head. We'll sleep on it then, shall we?'

Her phone pings. It's a text from Mark.

Well?

It's a follow up to the text she didn't look at because she was speaking to Damian:

*I need to see you, for a drink, a meal, a film, a walk, a shag.
Anything! When and where??*

The card can't have been from him, can it?
She is exhausted.

She switches on the outdoor lights and checks through the
bifold doors that the garden is free of intruders, then lets the
dogs out for one last pee. They come back in and sit while she
locks up and sets the burglar alarms, then, with them both at her
side – she might be imagining it, but since the package arrived,
they seem to be on guard dog duty – she heads upstairs and
cleans her teeth to get rid of the taste of vomit.

While she dutifully brushes for two minutes, she looks at
herself in the mirror.

'You're being played,' she tells herself, through a mouthful
of wine-red foam. 'You're just too damn gullible.'

She climbs into bed – fully dressed, because she can't be
bothered to take off the clothes that she is going to have to put
back on again in four hours' time – and flicks through the photos
on her phone, trying to see if she can pick up any clues about
what the hell is going on. It's mostly pictures of the dogs that
she takes and texts to their owners to show them what a good
time she's giving them. But then she sees the photo of herself
and Mark on the beach after the Nick Cave gig. If there's something else in those brown eyes of his, she can't see it.

If it *is* him sending the cards, then he has set up this whole
situation, her being at Marcy's place, him dropping round. He
would have had it in mind a long while. But why did he need to
do that? He could easily have wooed her the conventional way,
asked her out for a pizza, a movie, and she would definitely have
said yes and gone back to his palatial home afterwards.

She scrolls back through the years to find pictures of herself and Mark when they were together – photos she only looks at in moments of extreme masochism. She slides forward in time again, and there's Marcy, dressed up for that fateful end-of-uni party. In character as Wonder Woman, looking all sorts of fierce and aiming a high, brutal kick at the camera.

So. Batman and Robin. 'Is it you?' Caz asks the grinning Marcy of eight years ago. 'But why? To get rid of Mark? To punish me? Or are you trying to put things right by getting us back together?'

But Marcy has so much going for her. Why would she absent herself from her home and business for Caz, who until recently she hasn't seen for the best part of a decade? It's just too selfless.

Scrolling forward towards the photos she took this morning of three dogs leaping for a red ball against the green of Hove Park, she comes across herself and Damian by Marcy's swimming pool.

Could it be *him*? She looks at his open, bearded face, his laughing eyes, his vulnerably bald head, like a bird's egg, his arm protectively around her.

No. There's no way it's Damian. What would be in it for him?

She puts down the phone. It's nearly three now. She really needs to sleep. But first, she picks up her phone once more and downloads the app that controls Marcy's doorbell. She doesn't want ever again to be creeping round in that hallway, hiding from the front door glass. She signs in and takes a quick look on the camera by the front door at what is going on outside. Nothing, she is pleased to see, but trees blowing in the wind.

She goes to switch out her bedside light, but Bridget and Joe, who are lying on either side of her like sphinxes, are panting. She realises that she too is hot. Sweating, in fact. She's left the heating on high.

She throws back the duvet, grabs the smart home controller

from the dressing table and turns the thermostat down. Then she goes to open the window to let in some cool night air. As she does so, she notices movement in Colette's garden.

Right there, at the far end, underneath an old beech tree, Jon is standing alone, looking up at Marcy's house.

She is standing fully lit in her bedroom.

He sees her.

He smiles, and waves.

She snaps the curtains shut and runs back to the bed.

It's just as she is falling asleep that she realises that for a short, merciful time, she forgot about Ash and Harry. Could they somehow be connected to the cards, and to Marcy's disappearance?

But that would be madness.

She closes her eyes and sees three islands. The first is the cards and Marcy and Mark. The other two, bloodier and more trashed, are Ash and Harry. She sees herself laying down threads to connect them, like a cork board in a TV police incident room.

Like Ruth's pyramid.

She should go to the police.

But she needs to keep it quiet to keep everyone safe. And she'd be wasting police time.

Around the islands, the muddy waters swirl, picking up the threads, tangling them.

'There's no connection,' says the TV Caz in her head, wearing a senior police officer's uniform, addressing a room of TV coppers. She uses a baton to point at photographs of Wonder Woman Marcy and Batman Mark pinned on her TV cork board. 'Both these suspects have a motive to kill the victim's potential boyfriends...'

Real Caz opens her eyes. Hold on. She's the victim? What does that make Harry and Ash?

But TV Caz just rumbles on regardless.

'Marcy, because everyone – except, until recently, the victim – knows she hates her; Mark, either because he is in Marcy's thrall or because he wants the victim to himself. But to think they would act on these impulses and commit murder is completely insane. Therefore, to draw any link between this card' – TV Caz points her baton at today's heart-shaped message, also pinned on her cork board – 'the mystery of Marcy's disappearance and the two bloody murders' – TV Caz indicates graphic photos of Harry and Ash's bodies – 'is, again, completely and utterly cuckoo bananas.'

Her assembled TV police force – including a literally slimy DS Collins – all nod and agree. Indeed, they take it one stage further and give her a TV standing ovation. Then she's asleep.

And once more there is no respite from the bloody nightmares.

TWENTY-FOUR

She wakes a couple of hours later from a state that barely qualified as sleep. At some point in the night, a fox screaming like a distraught baby jolted her wide awake. In her dream she thought it was Marcy being overpowered. The fox stopped and the silence of the otherwise empty house pressed down on her, making it hard to breathe, despite the open window.

This morning her mouth feels like it is coated with fungus, her brain like all its cushioning fluids have been drained off.

Thankful for the balm of routine, she heads downstairs, flanked by the dogs. She harnesses Bridget and Joe into her van and sets off. There are just three pickups this morning from the close – lucky Henna is off with his owners in their French house.

After picking up her charges, she drives down to the seafront and parks up in the King Alfred swimming pool car park. She and the dogs stumble over the pebbles to the low-tide sands, where she lets them off their leads.

In counterpoint to her mood, it's another bright day, little clouds scudding through a blue sky, blown by a fresh westerly breeze that whisks her hair back from her face as she walks straight into it.

Her phone pings. Irritated by the intrusion, she glances at it. It's Mark.

And? So?

She remembers the texts he sent her last night.

She silences and pockets her phone, then pulls out four balls and what she calls the flinger, a plastic cup with a long handle on it that sends the balls hundreds of feet across the glittering wet sand. It feels good. It feels like she's getting rid of something, even if it's only a series of balls.

The dogs stream after them, splashing through the puddles left by the retreating sea.

The sight of their uncomplicated joy almost manages to lift her again. But she keeps getting drawn back to the big question of who sent her the package, and what it actually means, and where Marcy actually is.

Too many strange things are happening to her.

The dogs crowd around something on the sand, and she runs over just in time to stop them tucking in to the stinking, rotting corpse of a seagull.

Her brain lurches right back to Ash and Harry.

'There's no link,' she says into the cool breeze. 'They're islands on the pyramid. No connection to the cards, no connection to me, no connection to Marcy disappearing.'

If she says it enough, she might believe it.

She runs ahead of the dogs to draw them further along the beach, towards the row of houses at the very end of Hove Lagoon where the pop stars live and you're not supposed to go on the beach above the high-water line.

While the dogs chase a flock of bold seagulls, she crunches up the beach, sits where the pebbles are dry and tries to banish all thought by concentrating on the horizon. This was something she did when she was a child, when she was worried about her mother, or unsure of herself. The emptiness, the hint of infinity, gave her small concerns a comforting perspective.

It doesn't work today.

Perhaps it's the wind farm, which now studs the blue-grey line with real, tangible turbines, or perhaps it's because there is no perspective to be found.

Joe has followed her up and is sitting next to her, leaning against her. Her faithful friend. Her guardian.

'Why is all this happening to me?' she asks him.

She should keep her eye on the dogs, but instead she buries her face in her hands.

Joe leans harder against her.

She doesn't want to see anything, doesn't want to look at anything.

The wind whistles. The other dogs bark at the seagulls. Caz just wants to disappear.

The hand lands on her shoulder as if out of nowhere. She jumps and lets out a stupid, girlish yelp.

'God, I'm sorry,' the male voice behind her says. 'I just saw you down here, and you looked so sad.'

Her adrenaline stands down. It's Peter, in a fluorescent running jacket, shorts and running shoes. He pulls the AirPods from his ears.

She smiles up at him, absurdly pleased to see him. 'No, I'm sorry. I was miles away.'

'Mind if I...?' He gestures at the pebbles beside her.

'Be my guest.'

He sits, sending a not-unpleasant waft of fresh sweat her way.

'These your charges?' He nods at the dogs. 'They're having fun.'

Caz nods. She is on the verge of tears, which would make it the second time she's cried in his presence. He's going to think she's such a weak, girlie type, when she has always prided herself on being quite the opposite.

'So you're back with your mum, then?' he says.

She shakes her head. If she speaks, that will be it.

'What? Marcy's not back yet?'

'No.'

'That's a bit much on you, isn't it?'

'I don't mind,' Caz says. She's trying to keep it light, because she's going to have to explain her continuing presence to him. 'It's a lovely house.'

'It is indeed. Her mum's not any better, then? It can be so hard with older people. My mum hung on for weeks, rallying then falling back again. So cruel.'

Caz nods.

'What's that film? *They Shoot Horses, Don't They?* Poor old Ezra didn't want to die, but at least it came on suddenly for him. So I guess we were lucky in that respect. I miss him, though.'

That's it for Caz. The sob she can no longer contain escapes in a great rasping hiccup. She turns away and presses her fingers against her eyes.

'What is it?' Peter asks, touching her gently on the shoulder. 'Oh God, sorry. I shouldn't go ranting on about death and dying. Not after what you've been through. What a bloody idiot.'

'It's not that,' Caz says.

'Is it anything I can help with?'

She turns to look at him through tear-blurred eyes. He is all kindness. She can't stop herself. 'It's just that Marcy's not with her parents. I don't know where she is. And since I got to her house – well, before, really – all these weird things have been happening to me.'

She tells him about last night's package, about the two earlier envelopes, about how she found the place when she first arrived: the bloodstains, the bag, the disarray.

'Do you have any idea who might be sending these cards?' he asks her when she's finished.

Her back prickles. A sudden, shivering sense that someone is watching them makes her turn suddenly.

'What is it?'

'I thought I...' The promenade behind them is deserted. She's being paranoid. Shaking her head, she turns back to him. 'There's this ex-colleague of mine, but I don't know how he could know where I'm staying, and anyway, there's no way he could know about Batman and Robin.'

'Batman and Robin?'

'Long story. But what if I have a stalker?'

'Would you like me to take a look at the notes? I worked on some stalker cases back on the force.'

'I threw away the first two. I didn't want them anywhere near me. The other's back at Marcy's. I'm supposed to keep it secret, but I can't see how whoever sent it is going to find out if I tell you.'

'I'll certainly not tell anyone.'

'Thank you.' Bored, the dogs are beginning to bicker with each other. 'I've really got to get these guys back,' she says.

They start to walk towards the car park.

'Can I give you a lift home?' she asks him.

'I'll run. Got to get three more kilometres in today. I have a plan, and this damn cough has set me back a couple of days.'

'Plan?'

'I'm training for the Brighton Marathon.'

'I'd love to do that.'

'Why don't you?'

'If I started running on top of all the steps I put in with the dogs, I might wear myself away.'

He laughs. 'We don't want that!'

They climb up onto the wide promenade between the car park and the beach. The bright day is drawing out dog-walkers, cyclists and runners.

'I'll see you at Marcy's in about an hour, then?' he says.

She takes his hand and leans in to kiss him on the cheek. 'Thank you, Peter.'

Is that a blush on his face?

No. She's kidding herself. He just wants to help.

She watches him lope off along the tarmac, a tall, athletic figure. He could be a teenager, viewed from behind.

She's just reading him wrong, isn't she? He's just a kind man.

A kind man who was once a policeman.

They sit in the sunshine by the pool with coffees – she has finally mastered the machine. Bridget and Joe lie sunning themselves on the concrete flagstones, although Joe still has one eye open. There's no stopping him looking out for his mistress at the moment.

Caz cuts into a cake she picked up after dropping off the dogs. On the table beside it lie the card, Marcy's passport and handbag, and the Batman and Robin.

'"I love you. You deserve this place",' Peter reads. 'Do you have any idea what it could mean?'

Caz shrugs. 'I suppose it's a thought I sometimes had, because of Mark.'

'Ah. That guy who was here on Wednesday morning. With the flash car? There's a story there, isn't there?'

'Afraid so.' She tells him about Marcy and Mark and how they did the dirty on her.

'So that explains these two,' he says, pointing at the two action figures.

She nods. 'And so I sometimes feel that I should have shared in Mark's good fortune instead of Marcy. It doesn't make me proud.'

'It's only natural,' he says. 'He was yours in the first place.'

'And now I've slept with him again.'

Peter shrugs. 'All's fair in love and war.'

'But is it, though?'

'They're divorced, right?'

'Divorcing.'

'So you're not doing anything wrong. In fact, in one way it's sort of natural justice.' He frowns. 'Could it be that Marcy is behind all this? Believe me, I saw stranger things on the force.'

'I have had that thought. But...'

'But what?'

'OK. I need your professional opinion.'

He smiles. 'It's been a while since anyone asked that. People usually want to run a mile from diversity consultants.'

'It's the ex-copper bit I want to appeal to.'

He salutes. 'Evening, all.'

'What?'

'Generational blip there. Sorry. Go on.'

'Do you think there could be a connection between the cards, Marcy disappearing and the murders?'

'Murders?'

And then Caz realises with a rush of horror that she hasn't told Peter about Ash.

'OK. So I need to tell you something else...'

'Keeping all this to yourself must have been an awful burden,' he says when she's finished.

'It was horrible, being arrested when what I really needed was someone to look after me after finding him like that. I'll never forget the smell of that cell. I even began to question myself, wonder if I *was* guilty. I can't go through that again. So I haven't told the Brighton police about the first time.'

'I see your point, but...'

She looks at him quickly. 'You believe me when I say I have nothing to do with it, don't you?'

'Of course.'

'But do you think there's a connection?'

She so wants him to say no.

'It seems quite unlikely, doesn't it? But for you to be the meeting point of both events is also not usual.'

'That's kind of what Mum said.'

'Most people go through their entire lives never going near anything this disturbing.'

'And then there's all the card stuff, and Marcy disappearing...'

'You should tell the police.'

'But there's a fairly clear threat in this card about not telling anyone.'

'That's true.'

'So what do I do?'

He thinks for a moment. Takes a bite of cake. 'In view of the threat in the card, I would advise you to wait, see what happens. Marcy could come back any moment. There may not be anything sinister at all about her being away. Have you heard from her?'

'I've had a couple of texts, but they're weird, like they're not in her voice.'

'Show me.'

She hands over her phone and explains about the gonads comment and Marcy calling her father a poor dear. 'And we know she's not with her parents,' she says. 'So either she's lying, or...'

'Or she could just want a bit of time to herself. Tell you

what. Give it a couple of days. If she isn't back by then, let's talk about it.'

'Good plan. I wouldn't want to waste police time.'

The doorbell rings. The dogs stir, start barking. Caz pulls up the app she downloaded onto her phone.

DS Collins stands on Marcy's doorstep, chewing gum and looking up at the camera like he wants to arrest it.

If Peter weren't here, and if the dogs hadn't given her presence away with their barking, she would scuttle through the back gate and hide in the alley.

'Speak of the devil,' she says.

TWENTY-FIVE

Caz shows Peter the video of Collins waiting on the doorstep.

'Who's that?'

'The policeman in charge of the Harry case. I really don't like him.'

'Can I?' Peter takes the phone and squints at the screen. 'Oh. Him.'

'What do you mean?'

'He was on one of my courses. Or should I say he was sent on one of my courses. Turned out he didn't want to learn anything. Misogynist doesn't even go halfway to describing him. A total creep.'

Caz shivers. 'What should I do, then?'

'Just act normal. Don't give him anything he doesn't ask you for. I'll stay out here. Don't let him know about me, but if you get any trouble, just call my name. I'll slip behind the pool shed.'

She nods, gratefully.

. . .

Taking a deep in-breath, she opens the door. Collins stands and looks at her, frowning.

'Good afternoon, Miss Sessions.'

'Hello.' She doesn't tell him to call her Caz this time. Not now she knows about him. Keeping her distance, and very glad indeed that Peter is out in the back garden, she leads him through to the kitchen.

'May I?' He points to one of the chairs.

She nods. His body language is more formal than it has been in the past, and she wants to react in a similarly stiff way. But, remembering Peter's instruction to act normal, she offers him a cup of tea.

'No thank you,' he says. He points to the chair opposite him. 'Would you take a seat?'

And with that instruction, he has turned Caz's kitchen – well, Marcy's kitchen – into his interview room.

Caz obeys.

He sighs. 'You haven't been entirely honest with us, have you, Caz?'

'Wh-what do you mean?' She wishes she had something to hold on to, to stop her hands moving like Lady Macbeth trying to wash off all the blood.

'What do you think I mean?'

This is torture. She wants to say 'no comment', like they do on TV, but it always makes the suspects look so guilty.

'I told you that I knew Harry,' she says.

'But you didn't tell us about something else, did you?'

The thought of Peter out in the garden gives her strength. She pulls herself up tall in her chair. 'Please don't play games with me, DS Collins.'

He sits back. He's waiting for her to crumble. She looks at him silently, her face as neutral as possible. In the end, he is the first to speak, which he does with a weary sigh that reminds her of a disappointed teacher waiting for one of his class to own up to a misdemeanour. 'What does the name Ashley MacDonald mean to you, Caz?'

'Ah.'

'Yes. You see, computers allow us to make all sorts of links these days.'

She looks at her hands. 'I'm sorry I didn't tell you about that.'

'Didn't you think we might be interested in the fact that Mr Turner wasn't the first murdered body you'd found? The first murdered *lover*, I should say, shouldn't I?'

'I wouldn't say lover,' Caz says. She doesn't see herself as the kind of woman who would have a *lover*.

'What would you say?'

'Person I was seeing?'

He shoots her a look that is a cocktail of contempt and frustration.

'I didn't think you needed to know. I—'

'What would you say were the odds on this happening to you twice and it being unrelated?' DS Collins says.

'I haven't thought about it.'

'*You haven't thought about it?*' His look could wither a cactus. 'I should imagine it's been the only thing on your mind since you found Mr Turner.'

He's right. Except now, of course, she is also thinking about what the hell has happened to Marcy and who is putting weird stuff through her door.

He leans forward and makes a good stab at sounding reasonable. 'Why didn't you tell me?'

'I... I...'

He sits back, folds his arms and smiles. 'You didn't want to be treated like a suspect, did you?'

Caz's shoulders are up by her ears. She blinks.

'I spoke to my colleague in the Met. DS Chowdhary. Do you remember her?'

Caz nods. She remembers DS Meera Chowdhary very well indeed. The iron fist in a velvet glove who, despite no evidence whatsoever, for a horrible day and night until confirmation of the time of death came through, was completely convinced that Caz killed Ash.

The thing Caz hates most in the world is people thinking ill of her. And now it looks like it's happening all over again. Her toes clench like she is trying to burrow a hole in the floor, to disappear herself away.

'Not telling us is effectively obstructing our investigation, and I could nick you for that.'

'Please don't,' Caz says.

'But let me go back to that thing about the chances of it being a coincidence that on two separate occasions, you discover the bodies of men you have met through the same dating app. What do you think the odds are there?'

She shakes her head, shrugs.

'The answer is: massively stacked against. Now, if I were a gambling man – which I'm not...'

In her nervous state, Caz tries not to giggle at this TV cop cliché. It's a reaction arising purely from the seriousness of the situation and her powerlessness, but if she gives in to it, she runs the danger of looking flippant, or even psychopathic.

'... I'd place a year's wages on the two dead certs that a) this is not a coincidence and b) whoever has done this has done it because of you.'

Hearing it put so baldly makes Caz gasp.

It's what Ruth was trying to say, but the truth is much easier to ignore when it's your mother telling it to you.

Collins plants his elbows on the table between them, steeples his fingers and rests his chin on top of them. This is something Mark does when he's flirting with her, but from Collins it makes her feel ill. 'Now, Caz. You have already failed to tell me two really important things about your involvement with these crimes.'

She gulps audibly. *Involvement!*

'I want you to think really, really hard. Are you sure there's nothing else you haven't told either me or DS Chowdhary?' A string of hair flops across his forehead from the greased-back slick on top.

Is this another trap? Should she mention the cards? The Marcy mystery? Her heart thumping so hard that she swears it is moving the wicking fabric front of her T-shirt, she shakes her head.

'Is that "no, you're not sure there's nothing else"?'

Caz shakes her head. 'It's "no, there's nothing else".' Her voice doesn't sound like it's hers.

There's lots else, though, and part of her wants to break down and tell him everything. But then what? He'd only look at her with renewed suspicion, and in any case, if she says something, it could all go horribly wrong. She needs to keep everyone safe, doesn't she?

Yes.

Peter's right. She should wait for a couple of days, see if Marcy turns up.

Given the threat in the card...

She will say nothing.

He looks at her as if he is trying to see inside her head. She wants to pick up the tea towel drying on the radiator to her left and drape it over her face.

'Good,' he says at last, although he doesn't sound entirely convinced.

Is she really that transparent?

'And do you have a... Sorry, I mean, are you *seeing anyone* at the moment?'

She frowns at him. OK, right, here we go. Is this the start of him hitting on her? 'Why do you want to know?'

Just for one second, his eyes roll upwards, a hint of exasperation, before his face takes on a more neutral expression. 'We're not sure the link is that these men were in a relationship with you. The common denominator could have been the dating app, or perhaps there's some other mutual link. But we can't rule it out, so you need to let me know: are you seeing anyone at present?'

'Not exactly *seeing* quite yet,' she says. Because she isn't really, not yet. She's not even sure if she wants to take Mark to seeing level. Not if it could be him sending the cards.

He shakes his head and picks at something at the back of his teeth. 'Let me spell it out, then. Are you currently having a sexual relationship with someone?'

Her face now the colour of a tomato, Caz looks at her feet and nods.

'Does he know about the murders?'

'Yes.'

'So you told him, but not me?'

She takes a deep breath and puts her hands on the table. 'I haven't been myself since I found Ash. I had a bit of a breakdown and was sacked from my teaching job.'

'You resigned.'

Again the scarlet rushes to her face. 'Technically, yes. I resigned. I moved back down here to live with my mum and started dog-walking. Finding Harry has brought all the horror back, and I don't think I'm coping all that well. I needed to confide in someone, so I spoke to Mark – the guy I'm seeing.'

'And he didn't run a mile?'

Caz twitches at this unprofessional question. 'He doesn't think they can be connected.'

The subtext of the snort Collins gives at this is clearly that he reckons Mark is mad. He quickly gathers himself and his face turns grave. 'I'm afraid he's wrong.'

'Have you got anywhere with finding out who's responsible?'

'It helps that we now have more to go on with the London murder.' He looks accusingly at her. 'And we're putting that SeeMe app under the microscope. But we have no concrete leads whatsoever. Have you upset anyone, or do you have any enemies that you know of?'

She shakes her head.

'Any stalker behaviour or weirdness?'

'There is someone.' Jumping on something she *can* speak about, she tells him about Edwin. He notes down everything she says.

'We'll get him checked out.'

'He wouldn't have killed anyone. He's not the type.'

He shoots her a look. 'What *is* the type?'

Caz recoils. Again, she feels like she is being accused.

'Have you told anyone else about these... um... finds?' Collins says.

'My friend Damian Folds. He works in Marcy's shop.'

'Marcy?'

'The client I'm house-sitting for. I've told you all this.'

'Oh yes, the client who left her cards and keys behind.'

'She's got other cards...'

'We'll have to have a chat with Marcy, and Damian, too.'

'Oh, it won't have been Damian. I'd trust him with my life.'

Collins raises an eyebrow. 'It's only the people we trust who can betray us.'

'But why would Damian even think about killing men I'm dating? He's gay!'

'It may not be a sexual jealousy thing.'

Caz feels dirty having Collins even refer to her in that way.

'So do you trust Marcy?'

'Yes!' But her cheeks grow hot.

'And when is she due back?'

Caz shrugs. 'It's not entirely clear.' She has her fingers crossed behind her back, although this isn't a lie.

'I'll need a number for her. And anyone else you come into regular contact with.'

'Not my clients? Please don't talk to them. I don't know what they'd think about their pets being there when I found a dead body.'

'Just a list of names and numbers, so we can check if there's anyone interesting. And we'll need to speak to your mother. Ruth, isn't it?'

'No. You can't. I don't want to worry her. She's... fragile.'

'You said that last time. She honestly seemed quite robust to me.'

Despite her disabilities, Ruth often has this effect on strangers. Something to do with her constant state of alert. 'Well, she is fragile,' Caz says. 'And none of this has anything whatsoever to do with her.'

'Nevertheless, I would like a number for her. You see, Miss Sessions,' he says, reverting to the formal, 'what you're forgetting is that we have two young men who have been brutally murdered. This is extremely serious.'

'Yes. Sorry.'

'And I am also extremely concerned for your safety.'

She gulps. 'Really?'

'I'd like to offer you protection. We can put a car outside, keep an eye on you.'

Caz quickly shakes her head. 'I really don't want that.'

He looks at her for a long moment with his pale blue eyes. He is sizing her up.

'OK. I'll do it when we have real cause for concern.'

'*If* you have cause for concern.'

'If. So I want you to promise me that if anything happens that worries you, you *must* contact me. Any time, night or day. You have my card, right?'

Caz nods.

Collins's phone buzzes. He squints at the screen. 'I'm needed at the station.' He stands. 'So is that all the people you've told about the two murders?'

'Yes,' she says, a little too quickly.

'Are you sure?'

'Of course.'

It would be unwise to tell him about Peter. Not with the whole diversity awareness course stuff.

'And there's no other information you can give me right now?'

'Nothing.'

On their way out of the kitchen, Collins clocks the recycling box, which is full of wine bottles. He throws her a glance, and she knows he is reframing her as a woman with a drink problem.

'I had a few friends round...' she tells him.

'Of course you did,' he says.

After she has shut the door on him, she runs out to the back garden and just about stops herself from flying into Peter's arms, sobbing. Instead, she holds herself tight, to stop herself from shaking.

The sun has gone behind a cloud, and the air reveals how chilly it actually is.

'He's certain there's a connection between Ash and Harry,' she tells Peter.

'I'm afraid he may be right,' he says.

'He's worried for my safety.'

'That's where he's wrong.'

She frowns. 'What do you mean?'

'Don't you think that if the person who did that to those two boys was interested in physically harming you, they would have done so already?'

Caz thinks about this. 'Of course! But it hurt me in here.'
She taps her head.

'It's really tough, I know, and you're doing amazingly. If
there's anything I can do, just tell me.' He gestures at the house,
the dogs, her. 'And after all you've been through, at least you've
got this lovely space to recover in.'

'That's what he said.'

'Who?'

'The note writer. He said, "You deserve this place."'

At bedtime, she stands exhausted in the back garden waiting for
the dogs to do their night-time pees. Her head is reeling from all
the information she is having to process. All she wanted was a
simpler life, and now it feels like she is in the middle of the
tangle from hell.

It's chilly tonight, and again the sky is clear and full of stars.
The thought of all the endless space out there makes her throat
ache.

'Where are you, Marcy?' she whispers.

She could be anywhere. Anywhere at all. Caz just wants
her back, safe, and that mystery solved.

The trees stand silently in the darkness, not moving even a
hair's breadth, so still is the night. Their presence is comforting,
like they are guarding her, the house and the dogs.

She closes her eyes and imagines violence, fighting, blood.
Marcy being taken forcibly away.

Her mind spools onwards, unravelling. She thinks she has to
call it off with Mark. It complicates everything, and she's so
unsure about what's actually happening, what his game is, if
Marcy's involved...

She turns and looks back at the house. While she has every
light blazing on the ground floor, Colette's next door stands
dark, dead and silent. She shudders to think of Colette know-

ingly cuddling up to a man whose crimes are unspeakable. Presumably she knows. Does she find it a turn-on?

Might Jon be responsible for the cards?

For the deaths, even? But why? Who is he? What is his connection to her?

And if Marcy has been forcibly abducted, might it have been by him?

TWENTY-SIX

Late Saturday afternoon, Caz is out in the driveway giving her van a sorely needed deep clean. In the past ten days, this is one of the tasks she has neglected. She has also failed to do any of her paperwork and is horribly aware of it piling up.

The truth is that since finding Harry, she just hasn't had the heart to do anything but the basics. Another sign of slippage is that the dogs have been returned to their owners without their usual hosing-down. This has drawn comments from the owner of Percy and Rusty, two Jack Russells who love nothing more than rolling in anything disgusting. She suspects her daily outings with the pair are the only time they get a proper run outside – which in her view is criminal with a terrier – so until now their owner has forgotten how mucky they can get.

And she is further distracted by Collins's concern for her safety. If a toughened copper – however much of a sleazeball he is – is worried enough to suggest assigning protection to her, then she probably really is in danger.

Exhausted when she came in after the final Saturday dog walk, she tried flopping down on the sofa and having a rest, but the house roared its emptiness at her.

So instead of lying there turning over every single ingredient of the pickle she is in, she hauled herself up and gave Bridget and Joe the shower they should have had when she came in with them. Now, with them flat out asleep in the house, she is outside tackling the van.

Better to keep busy, chase away the demons.

She has the cages out and is sluicing them down when a car turns into the driveway in an awfully big hurry and nearly crashes into her.

The driver slams on the brakes, spinning gravel up against her clean van. It's Mark, in his stupid red Ferrari.

The last person she wants to see today.

'Sorry!' He swings his long legs out of the car and almost leaps towards her. 'I tried your mum's, but she said you were up here. Marcy still off shagging, then?'

She's cross. So cross she has to stop herself from turning the power-washer hose onto him. 'It's twenty miles per hour round here. What if I'd had the dogs loose?'

He holds up his hands. 'What can I say? I'm a total arse. Sorry.'

She turns off the spray and rubs her forehead. 'I don't have much patience at the moment.'

He goes to kiss her, but she backs away.

'What?' he says, looking genuinely hurt.

'Did you send me a card?'

'What?'

'A card, Thursday, put through my door?'

He laughs. 'Of course not. The last card I sent anyone was probably that Valentine I gave you when we started going out.'

'Huh.'

'What card, anyway?'

Caz gives him a long look. She believes him, and she doesn't think she's being gullible. She shakes her head and lifts one of the cages. 'Nothing.'

'So do I get a kiss now?'

Ignoring him, she hauls the cage back into the van. He offers to help, but she refuses. Once it's in, she turns to him again, hands on hips. 'Damian told me the truth about how you and Marcy split up.'

Mark looks at his feet.

'You went off with someone else. Again.'

'I didn't...' But he can't meet her eye.

'Why should I believe you when you did the exact same thing to me?'

He grabs her hand. 'Please believe me. Marcy did the dirty on me. Damian's lying. He's always had it in for me.'

'He also told me about how you treated him when you were at school.'

'Eh?'

'How you bullied him for being gay.'

'That's not true either.'

'Why would he lie? You bullied Damian, and you betrayed Marcy just like you betrayed me.'

'Damian's just saying that because he doesn't want to share you.'

This again. Like from Collins. It's ridiculous, because she's so not the kind of woman men fight over.

'He's in love with you.'

'He's gay!'

'But he still wants you to himself.' He moves towards her, but she backs away, still holding the hose. 'I love you, Caz. I have never stopped loving you.'

'I don't want to see you again.'

He looks as shocked as you'd expect from a man who has never had to deal with rejection. However, he quickly wipes it from his face with a bright white smile. 'You can't mean that.'

'It's no good for either of us. Especially not me. I'm doing fine as I am. And who's to say that, however Marcy and you split up, you wouldn't go back to her at some point.'

She turns her back on him and lugs the pressure washer towards the garage, where it is plugged in.

He grabs her shoulder and turns her to face him. 'Look, Caz. Marcy and I are over. We split up because we were terrible for each other. We had awful fights.'

She recoils. 'You hit her?'

'No! It was the reverse, in fact.' He lifts the hair from his forehead and shows her a slim scar about three centimetres long, a white thread through his tanned skin. 'She did this to me with a lamp stand.'

Despite herself, Caz reaches up to touch the scar. A piece of concrete evidence in a world where everything has become a mystery. 'Ouch.'

'Yes.' He presses her hand to his cheek. 'Please forgive me for everything you need to forgive me for. I promise I will never, ever lie to you again.'

He looks at her with those soft brown Robert Downey Jr eyes, and she nearly caves in. Chemistry is a harsh mistress. Her hand buzzes where it touches his skin. It takes everything she has, but she gently pulls away and continues towards the garage.

He follows, but stops on the threshold. 'Whoa,' he says.

'What?' She unplugs the pressure washer and coils the cable.

'Marcy's not taken her car.' He peers through the windows of the silver Mini, as if there might be clues inside. 'So she allows Charlie to drive her, then?'

'I guess.' Her voice strangles through the lie.

'Odd. She always said she got sick in the passenger seat.'

'Perhaps it's being in the Ferrari makes her ill.'

He bites his lip.

She doesn't know how long she can go on with the Charlie thing. It's so clearly cutting him up.

He sighs, and looks deep into her eyes, and suddenly he's the boy she knew when they first got together. Not the bully of Damian's experience – and what if Mark is right and he *is* lying? – but a troubled soul for whom her practical nature and ability to love without complication were once as necessary as breathing.

She softens enough to invite him in for a glass of wine. The sun's nearly over the yardarm.

And she has made up her mind. She has a confession to make to him.

'There is no Charlie,' she tells him once, wine in hand, they are sitting on the sofa that looks out over the back garden. Joe and Bridget lie together on the purple doggy divan. It took quite a while to settle them, because when Mark walked in, Joe started barking and snapping so furiously at the unexpected guest that Bridget forgot all her loyalty to her former owner and joined in.

The bright day has given way to one of those dusks that feel like a dark curtain is being drawn over the sky. With the shadow come early spits of rain. They threaten something grander – a storm, even. Filtered through this cloud, the sunset has been demoted from fiery orange to a dull yellow, giving the room a sickly glow.

'I made him up.'

'Ah.' His face shows nothing. She waits for him to speak. He doesn't.

'Please say something.'

'I thought something was off.'

'Did you?'

'When I was in the shop. The way Damian glanced over my

shoulder. I knew you were behind me. You were signalling something to him, weren't you?'

Caz looks into her glass, ashamed.

'Were you both trying to make me look like an idiot?'

'No! Damian was just being kind, not letting on that I'd lied to you.'

'But he thought she'd gone to her parents, and that was a lie.'

'It wasn't!'

'But it's not true.'

'I know that now.'

'So where is she, if not with some man?'

'I don't know! She told me she was with her parents, and that's what I told Damian.'

'So it's Marcy that's lying.'

'I think so.'

He takes her hand – she puts up no resistance – and frowns. 'Why did you make up this Charlie, then?'

'I wanted you to be angry with Marcy.'

'Marcy achieved that all by herself.' He smiles and steeples his fingers. 'Why did you want me angry with her?'

She drinks her wine and blushes.

He leans towards her and puts his hand on her cheek. Again, that spark, that flash. 'I should be flattered, shouldn't I?'

'I'm an idiot.'

'I'm afraid you are. But that's what I love about you.'

She thinks about pulling away, but it's as if she is stuck to him by a magnetic force.

'So,' he goes on, casually moving his thigh so it just touches hers, 'if there is no Charlie and she's definitely not with her folks, where *is* she?'

Caz frowns. 'I guess only she knows.'

'She'll come back when she's ready. She's such a player.'

And that brings her back to the thought that Marcy has set

all this up. Or, much worse, that someone has cleared her out of the way so that it can happen. And if that is the case, then who could it be but Mark?

He moves so his face is close to hers. 'Let's hope she doesn't burst in on us.'

So much of her is telling her not to kiss him. But her monkey brain is in charge right now. She has no idea what it is – something to do with pheromones, or cell memory, or old times' sake – but she reaches forward, puts her hand on the nape of his neck – so warm, so smooth – and pulls his mouth towards hers.

An electric flash lights up the room, followed almost instantly by a deafening crack of thunder. Whining, the dogs run across to Caz and push her away from Mark, burrowing in on either side of her, partitioning her from him.

TWENTY-SEVEN

'Your gang,' Mark says. 'Not so ballsy now!'

'They don't like storms.'

'Perhaps we should go upstairs.'

But the dogs have brought her to her senses, and she realises that there is something that Mark can help her with.

The rain is tipping down now, thundering on the living room roof, clattering on the windows. She can barely hear what he's saying.

She turns to face him. 'I've got something to ask you,' she says in a low voice.

He smiles. 'Go on.'

She drains her glass. Then she lifts the bottle and refills them both. 'You know how when we were on the beach I told you about Joe finding those two bodies when we were out walking?'

'I could hardly forget.'

'And how I said they couldn't be linked?'

He nods.

'The police found out about me finding Ash, the first one.'

'Oops.'

'The guy dealing with the case came round. He was actually quite OK about it. Understood why I didn't mention it, I think.' Even though she knows DS Collins is a creep, she has to give him that.

'That's a relief.'

'Anyway' – she takes a deep breath – 'he thinks they *are* linked.'

'No shit, Sherlock.'

'What?'

'Well, it's pretty obvious, isn't it? I just didn't want to worry you by arguing against your coincidence theory.'

She narrows her eyes at him. Is he being deliberately patronising?

He catches her look, and shrugs. 'It gave you some comfort, didn't it?'

'It did.'

'So what do you want to ask me?'

'There's something else that connects Harry and Ash. And perhaps you can help, what with you being an IT specialist and all.'

He takes a swig from his wine glass. 'Oh yes?'

'I met them both through a dating app.'

He leans forward, interested. 'Which one?'

'SeeMe.'

'Oh.'

'I was wondering if someone might have hacked it.'

'Impossible. Those sorts of apps have the highest-level encryption. Their whole reputation relies on their security.'

'But then how did the murderer know they were dating me? And presumably knew where they lived?'

'Some other way. Perhaps in real life, you know? Like an old-fashioned stalker?'

She sizes up the thought. It's possible. 'But—'

'SeeMe is completely safe.'

Another flash of lighting zaps the room, and five seconds later – she always counts – thunder rocks the house. The dogs hunker in closer to her.

'I'm sorry,' Mark says, holding out his glass to her. 'I've had a shit day. Do you mind if we don't talk about apps tonight? I just need to be off-duty right now.' His eyes are glittering, and she realises he is nearly crying.

She pours them both another glass of wine, then edges closer to him. 'What is it?'

'I'm just so tired. Work is exhausting. And really, I just want to enjoy life after...'

'After what?' she asks, gently.

'I've not been well,' he says.

Hardly surprisingly, given the situations she has found herself in over the past week, her mind jumps straight to all the worst-case scenarios. Cancer? Heart? One of those awful slow wasting diseases?

'I mean in here.' He taps his head. 'Too much, far too young. You know me. I've always been a bit of a solitary nerd. Like you.'

'Thanks!'

'You know what I mean. I like my own company, a quieter life, noodling around with code.'

It's true. When they were together, if anyone had said he would be a multimillionaire with dozens of employees, a red Ferrari and a Regency pile in Kemp Town, she would have laughed in their face. Because that was the late noughties, right back at the very birth of app development, when nobody knew how limitless the possibilities were going to be.

She had viewed with devoted amusement his obsessive work on developing his first app – a puzzle game inspired by the machines they used to play in the student union bar. Later – a couple of years after the Wonder Woman debacle – she found out on one of her many Google trawls that he had sold it for twenty million dollars. It was a great game. She downloaded it and was so caught up in it that she once missed her bus stop on the way to work.

'I ended up in a place I didn't ever ask for. It was never about the money or the big business,' he says. 'I'm not great at handling people, and I have to manage a team and take a lot of responsibility.'

'Did Marcy push you into it?' The question is out of Caz's mouth before she thinks. It surprises her as much as it does him.

'Marcy is an ambitious person. She likes the nicer things. So when I came to her to talk over whether I should sign this or that deal or option...'

She screws up her face to stop herself picturing Mark and Marcy functioning so well as a couple that he turned to her for advice.

'... she always egged me on. Perhaps those decisions were wrong. Perhaps I should have been more modest.'

Caz gestures at the room. 'But all this. Your car, your two houses—'

'Four. Got one in Spain and another in Wales.'

'Wow. OK, four. You can't say you regret having them.'

'It's all just stuff, isn't it? For a while, I lost sight of what's important. And then I looked at my actual life. You know, how I spent my days, whether I was happy or fulfilled, and yes, how my marriage was turning out, and I came to the conclusion that it was all worthless. I could go out and buy whatever Marcy or I – usually Marcy – wanted. But inside, I was deeply, deeply unhappy. I'll be honest and say it wasn't the only thing that was wrong, but I missed you, Caz. I missed what we had. Leaving you was the biggest mistake of my entire life.'

Cue, almost as if an outside source were directing the scene, another flash of lightning, then – seven seconds later this time – a clap of thunder.

She closes her eyes. This is bewildering. She thinks back

fifteen minutes to the kiss they shared. Something about the stress she's under, his revelations, the proximity to death and danger, makes her want to just fuck. Grab that closeness, that life-affirming connection with someone else. She is very much on the verge of dragging him upstairs and throwing him on the bed.

'And then,' he goes on, 'Marcy told me she wanted out, that she was seeing someone else, and instead of realising that it was absolutely the best thing for both of us, I kind of cracked in half and burned out. I swear smoke started coming out of the top of my skull.'

'Poor you.' She knows exactly what that feels like because it happened to her after Ash. But now is not the time to share her own pain.

'I was drinking too much, I was on pills to get up in the morning, to see me through the day, to sleep at night. In the end, I checked myself into this clinic in Switzerland for four weeks of intense therapy. Everything crystallised for me there, and I realised I had to sell up, move on, try to work something out. And then when I called round the other day and you were there, it was like fate, Caz. Bringing us back together.'

She catches her breath.

'It's like fate,' he says again.

She knocks back the remains of her wine. She's not eaten any supper and she's feeling quite drunk, quite reckless.

She stands and holds out her hand, which he takes. She pulls him up. Joe lifts his head from where he was nestled into her and growls.

'Jealous boy,' Mark says.

'Quiet, Joe,' she says.

Shutting the living room door behind them so that no dogs can interfere, she leads Mark upstairs.

She briefly considers setting the burglar alarm, but the dogs moving around in the living room would set it off. In any case, an intruder wouldn't get very far with Joe's guarding instinct. So she allows herself the luxury of forgoing the chore.

She shows Mark to the room she has been sleeping in.

'The bed's nicer in the other room,' he says. He means the bedroom he shared with Marcy, which he and Caz used the last time they had sex.

Made love.

Shagged.

Whatever.

'No. We'll be in here,' she says. With the question marks around Marcy, she's feeling squeamish about using that bed now.

'So soft all over,' he says as he runs his hands over her body, peeling off her leggings and T-shirt and sports bra and big knickers.

And she tries not to think of Marcy, whose body is not soft but firm and toned, clad in that silk underwear Caz has not had the chance to borrow this time.

It's only after they are done, and she is feeling sore and turned inside out, and he is fast asleep, breathing as regularly and deeply as a man who has had all he wants should, that she realises the rain has stopped and a full moon has slipped out from behind the storm clouds. She hadn't thought to draw the curtains, and the room is lit up in silver.

She doesn't know when that happened, but if Jon were watching from Colette's house, he would have seen everything. Shame at the idea creeps over her body, makes her leap up, retrieve her T-shirt and pull it over her head. Her nakedness covered, she steps towards the window to draw the curtains. But her hand stops, half raised.

Thankfully, he is not at the window, but her eye is drawn by a movement at the far end of Colette's garden. Underneath an old beech tree, by the strong beam of a builder's work light, Jon is digging a hole.

A big hole.

The size, in fact, of a grave.

Shuddering, she tugs the curtains shut.

TWENTY-EIGHT

Woken at dawn with the sense of a question hanging over her that she can't quite form words around, Caz picks up her phone and tiptoes out to the en suite. While she blearily sits on the loo peeing, she composes a message to her Sunday morning client telling them she has a terrible cough and a fever, so to be on the safe side she is cancelling today's walk. They don't rely on her because of work – they're just lazy. It will do them good to bond with their pet on a weekend walk.

That's what she tells herself anyway. Another part of herself tells her she is being irresponsible, that this is not the start, but the second stage of a slippery slope, and she needs to be careful or she's going to start losing clients.

But perhaps she doesn't need to worry too much about her business. It's not like she's going to need money any more.

Shocked by this thought springing itself on her again, she flicks back to her home screen and notices with a touch of annoyance that SeeMe has automatically reloaded itself onto her phone.

And then, like a lightning flash, the question comes to her fully formed.

She tiptoes back into the bedroom and looks at Mark, his dark curls spread over the linen pillow, his smooth brown chest showing her that he still spends time at the gym. He probably has a gym in his house, in fact. And possibly a swimming pool.

She likes swimming.

But there's something about his face, about the curve of lip and eyebrow, that she realises she *doesn't* like. It's like he knows just how very beautiful he is.

She started off last night trying to finish with him, and yet here she is waking up – after a night of undeniably brilliant sex – next to him.

He claims to love her. She absolutely fancies him. And the practical side of going back to him makes sense.

Does it matter that she might not actually like him all that much?

She needs to ask him the question, now. She coughs.

'Hey, gorgeous,' he says, sleepily coming to. He pulls aside the duvet, inviting her in for a little morning delight.

Instead, she perches on the side of the bed and faces him.

'You know you didn't want to talk about SeeMe last night?'

'What's this about?'

'SeeMe is one of yours, isn't it?'

He says nothing

'It is, isn't it?' She stands and moves away from the bed. The belief in coincidence she was trying to uphold has now been roundly trashed. The Ash/Harry/Caz pyramid has exploded into another dimension with a new thread added to the web; it's almost visibly here in her bedroom, attached to Mark.

'I developed it, but I sold it a couple of years ago,' he says. 'We still have the development and maintenance contract. Believe me, Caz, those poor men dying is not SeeMe's fault. I put my entire being into developing my apps, and the whole point is that they are watertight. Otherwise, I am worth nothing.'

'Nothing but four houses, a red Ferrari and a half-stake in Fox & Hunter.'

'I meant in here.' He thumps his chest.

He reminds Caz of certain of her clients who can't believe her when she reports that their little darling has turned on another dog. They always say that it must have been something the other animal did, and did Caz actually see what happened? – the implication being that she must be mistaken.

'I stake my reputation on the functionality of what I create,' he says.

She knows this. She knows how passionate he is about his work. Even back when they were students at Manchester, he spent inordinate hours coding, testing, user testing, learning about hacking so he knew his enemy. In their second year, they shared an attic bedsit in Fallowfield and, skint students, would stay in and eat pasta and drink cheap wine while she slogged diligently away at her maths coursework and he went rogue, developing the products that would see him become a millionaire before the age of twenty-five.

'Perhaps it was human error with the app,' she says. 'People cock up, don't they?'

He shakes his head. 'It can't be. There are checks built in.'

'Or perhaps it's someone who works at the company that bought it?'

'But why?'

And then she gets it, and the fear rises in her throat. If the app is so watertight, it could only be him spying on her through it. She doesn't know a lot about it, but surely the creator must know how to get into an app, however strict its security settings.

Is Mark a killer?

She looks at his hands – soft, keyboard-worker hands with long, tapering fingers; hands that have touched every part of her; hands that look like they have never even stroked something rough, let alone committed a violent act.

But then... But then...

As if he can read her mind, he says, 'I'm not involved, Caz. You have to believe me. I've not touched that app for years. My team in India do the maintenance. I'm hands-off.'

But she's backing out of the bedroom, muttering about needing to let the dogs out.

'I'm going back to sleep,' he says, turning over crossly and pulling the duvet over his head.

He's acting as if he owns the place.

'Hey, guys,' she says as brightly as she can as she opens the living room door.

But Joe and Bridget don't run to greet her.

She cruises round the room, expecting to find them curled up somewhere behind one of the chairs, or snugly tangled into a curtain.

The empty bottles and wine glasses from last night sit like crime-scene evidence on the coffee table, but there are no dogs.

The bifold doors to the garden are closed, but when she tries the catch, they slide open.

Her heart thumps and she closes her eyes. How can she have been so stupid?

Stupid, horny girl. Just thinking about one thing. No burglar alarm *and* she left the doors to the back garden unlocked!

She is just telling herself that the dogs must have somehow got out of the living room and are probably in the dining room when she sees what looks like a bloody mess of bone and flesh and fur on the terrace.

Her belly hollowed with fear, she steps outside onto the cool stone and, not really wanting to look, walks sideways towards the carnage. Out here, the stink of death and meat undercuts the fresh smell of the storm-wetted grass.

This is all too reminiscent of her other bloody discoveries. Even though those were human deaths, if this is what she fears it is, it will be the worst of the lot.

Because even though they didn't deserve to die, those men were cheats.

The dogs are innocents.

The dogs only want to please.

She stands above the bloody tangle, viewing it through the corner of her eye, imagining the full horror.

But there is no Joe-style black-and-white fur. Just creamy curls – too many for it to be Bridget, surely? She's only small.

Cautiously she squats to examine it.

It's the back quarter of a sheep – horrible, but nowhere near as bad as she feared. Someone has put it here, though, and why would they do that except to lure the dogs away from the house? Looks like it was successful, too. Gnawed and chewed, it has been dragged bloodily along the ground.

Her face hot despite the damp chill of the morning, she straightens up. 'Joe?' she calls out. 'Bridget?'

She checks the gate to the front garden. It's locked. But once again, the gate to the back lane is on the latch. It's probably been that way since Peter left through it yesterday. She is such an idiot. There is blood on the gatepost. Whoever placed that sheep up by the house must have got it in this way.

She works her way around the garden, looking behind bushes, lifting the wheelbarrow propped against the wall. Because what if that mess back there is poisoned? Will she still find Joe and Bridget dead somewhere?

She tries the pool house. It's unlocked, but there's no one in there, just a stack of towels on a wooden stand and the delicious scent of cedar wood, which goes some way to clearing her nostrils of the taint from the meat.

The pool is thankfully empty of anything but water, a few leaves gathered at the bottom and a couple of drowned spiders.

Finally she checks the DJ shed, which she knows is locked because she tried the door when she first arrived. She has no idea where the key is. But when she pushes the handle, the door opens easily and Joe runs out, nearly bowling her over. Relieved, she kneels and holds him in a tight hug, letting him lick her face. He puts his paws on her shoulders and tips her backwards onto the wet grass.

Someone must have lured him out to the garden with the meat, then got hold of him and led him in here, where, thanks to the soundproofing, his barking wouldn't be heard.

But why?

She sits up, still holding onto him, checking him over to make sure he hasn't been injured in any way. Thankfully, he has no wounds, his eyes are clear, his gums pink.

He's troubled, though. Now that he's greeted her, he's watchful and alert, sniffing the grass, searching.

'Where's Bridget, Joey?'

He sets off. His nose leads him to the back gate.

'She went through there, didn't she?'

He looks up at her as if he really wants to nod.

Caz steps out into the twitten. Of course there's no sign of Bridget. Just the usual litter and weeds, and now, thanks to the rain, mud, which is scarred with too many footprints to give any meaningful clues.

Joe runs up the narrow footpath, sniffing, but she calls him back. She knows what to do when a dog gets lost out on a walk – thankfully not a situation she has yet had to deal with. But who do you call when you think a dog goes missing from home?

She googles, and the answer is the council. Though perhaps she should call the police, because the sheep is evidence that it's theft. But why take Bridget and not Joe as well? Because she's a Maltipoo and Joe's a mutt? Dog theft is a thing – she dealt with it during her accreditation training, and pedigrees are obviously more valuable to the thief.

Or is it because Bridget is Marcy's dog?

Of course it's because Bridget is Marcy's dog. Caz can no longer put her faith in coincidence. This is clearly not just a regular dog theft. whoever has taken Bridget must have Marcy's keys for the DJ studio and the back gate.

And possibly the house itself.

So perhaps it's Marcy?

She needs to speak to Peter.

Thank God he is an early riser. If she acts quickly, she can catch him before he goes out for his run.

With Joe firmly at her heels, she hurries back to the house, kicking the sheep remains under a shrub. She'll deal with that later. She locks the bifold doors behind her and, grabbing her keys, heads for the front door.

But in the hallway, she stops so suddenly that Joe slams into her heels.

There's another buff-coloured envelope rammed through the letter box. It's too early for the postman or any parcel delivery company, so this must have been hand-delivered.

As she pulls it out to examine the writing on the front, Joe pushes at her hand, his nostrils busy.

All it says on the outside is *CAZ*. But even with this few letters, the writing is clearly the same as on the previous envelopes.

In the kitchen, she carefully pulls out the contents: a small box like you get when you buy jewellery, and another card. Like the others, it's home-made, but the crafting activity this time has involved sticking a computer printout of an image on the front.

She takes it to the window and holds it to the light to get a better look.

It's a reproduction of an old painting. In it, a beautifully dressed woman sits with her left arm around a man with a long beard and tangled hair. He is wearing nothing but a loincloth, and his arms are shackled to the wall. It looks innocent enough until you see what the two subjects are doing. Her right hand holds out her naked breast, offering it to the man.

And he is feeding from her.

Caz flinches and drops the card. It is horrible – weird and disturbing.

Mouth-breathing, as if the thing stinks – which it doesn't – she picks it up and opens it. Inside, the handwriting is a little less careful than before, the capital letters rushed and badly formed.

I TOLD YOU TO KEEP IT SECRET.

YOU TOLD THE OLD PIG.

YOU'RE SPOILING IT, CAZ.

STOP SPOILING IT.

The old pig? That throws her for a moment until she realises it means Peter, because he used to be a policeman. How does the sender of this grotesque card know that she has spoken to him?

She thinks back to Friday, when she met him on the beach, and that feeling she had of being watched, which she so easily brushed off.

She photographs the card, both inside and out and files the pictures away with the others. Then she looks at the box. It's black, anonymous, looks harmless. Taking a breath, she lifts the lid. Inside, a layer of wadding hides the contents. She pokes at it and realises that it's not the synthetic polyester she thought. It's too coarse, too creamy for that. Too curly.

Joe whimpers, trying to nudge at her hand.

'Oh Bridget,' Caz says, rubbing the clip of fur between her fingertips.

She lifts it slightly. There is no blood, so perhaps that's a good thing.

And then she sees what's underneath.

TWENTY-NINE

Quickly she snaps the box shut and clasps her hand over her mouth.

'Joey, come.'

She can't do this on her own.

She runs out of the house and along the pavement to Peter's house, where she hammers on the door.

There is no reply. Has he left already for his run? She leans on the doorbell, her heart pounding, her stomach threatening to empty itself on old Ezra's worn doorstep.

'Coming, coming.' She presses her ear to the door and hears Peter running down the stairs. 'What do you want?' he says crossly as he opens the door. Then he sees her. 'Oh! Caz!'

He is wearing pyjamas and a dressing gown – possibly Ezra's, because it looks so odd on him, the type an old man would wear, woollen with a twisted cord tie and matching piping. It's only then that she realises that although it feels like the day has lasted a whole lifetime, it's only just gone 6 a.m.

'What is it?' he asks her. 'You look like you've seen a ghost.'

'Can you come to Marcy's, please?' Her voice seems to be

coming out of the top of her head, which feels as if it has been blasted right off.

'I'll just get dressed,' he says.

'No, can you come now. Marcy hasn't taken herself off. She's been kidnapped.'

They hurry back to Marcy's house and Caz takes him to the kitchen table and shows him the jewellery box.

'Open it,' she tells him.

Peter opens the box. Caz can't bear to watch.

'My God,' he says.

Inside, nestled like a brown snail with the remnants of a blue shell on its back, is the tip of a little finger, complete with a nail that still bears what looks like an expensive blue gel manicure.

'This is Marcy's?' Peter says.

Caz nods. 'And this' – she lifts the tuft of fur – 'is Bridget's.'

'What?' Peter says.

'Her dog.' Caz would cry, but she is beyond that now. It's like she's in a surreal and savage alternative reality, living in a movie she would only normally watch from behind her fingers.

'What's this?' Peter prises something from the bottom of the box. It's a note, the size of a business card, slightly bloodstained. He holds it up and reads it – '"Remember Ash and Harry. We don't want a repeat, do we?"' – then turns it for Caz to see. Her heart has sunk to the soles of her feet. The room whirls.

'So they *are* connected,' she says. 'The murders and Marcy and Bridget.'

'This is a dangerous person.'

She tries to push the thought away, because she's not the one who is physically suffering or dead, but it is there, pressing against the inside of her skull.

Why me?

Why is all this happening to me?

She shows him the card with the horrible breastfeeding picture on the front. He reads it, his face darkening.

'I need to tell the police,' she says, pulling her phone out of her pocket.

'Of course. But hold on. Look what the card says. Somehow they know you told me about that last one. They really don't want you to tell anyone else—' Suddenly struck by something, he stops speaking and nods to a corner of the room. 'Cameras,' he mouths to her.

'What?'

He carries on, whispering. 'See that box on the wall there? Just glance, don't look.'

Caz blinks. She's never noticed it before.

Peter steers her outside into the back garden.

'It's part of a burglar alarm system,' he says, once they are at the bottom of the garden. 'I noticed the boxes on the wall outside – old habit. There's going to be cameras with microphones in every room in the house. And if I'm not very much mistaken, this set-up has a nifty feature where you can tell the burglar you're watching them through speakers in the house.'

'Does it?'

Caz thinks of Marcy's abductor – or Marcy herself, she doesn't know which is worse – watching her moving around the house, using the bathroom. Her face reddens. In bed with Mark...

The shame. 'I'll switch off the system.'

'No, don't do that,' he says. 'It'll arouse suspicion. But always remember that you could be being watched.'

'And whoever it is will have seen me go to you again, then. There'll be even more trouble.'

'Let's hope they're not an early riser and don't go back over every recorded minute.'

'I've got everything crossed.'

'You said something about Marcy's dog. The fur in the box?'

'Whoever's got Marcy has also got Bridget.'

Caz shows him the sheep parts under the shrub, the DJ studio where she found Joe, and the blood on the unlocked back gate.

'What does he want?' she asks him. 'Why is he doing this to me?'

'From the cards, the first thing he wants is for you not to tell anyone.'

'I really need to tell the police, though.'

Peter holds up his hand. 'That may not be the wisest move right now. Listen. Going by the first card, he doesn't want to harm you. Quite the reverse. He seems to want you to have a good time.'

'If that's the case, it's not working.'

'What I'm trying to say is that he is not going to be a threat to you.'

'But Marcy! I've got to tell the police.'

Peter nods. 'You do. But we know what he's capable of, and the last person you want working on this is Dave Collins. You need someone with more discretion.' He frowns, thinking hard, then puts his hands together. 'My old DI and mentor is very senior in the Brighton force these days. I'll take all this to him and he can start a covert investigation from a higher level. It's what we – I mean they – do in cases like these. That way we can keep Marcy safe.'

Caz heaves a great sigh of relief and hugs him. 'Thank you, Peter. That's so kind of you.'

He squeezes her tight, then lets her go.

'Have you got any Ziploc bags for the evidence?' he says. 'I'll take it in.'

'I'll have a look.'

Together they head back to the house.

'So, we won't tell the police,' Peter says quite loudly when they are inside, nodding at the camera.

'No. We won't. We'll keep it quiet,' she says. 'I'll follow all instructions.'

She disappears into the utility room to look for plastic bags.

When she comes out, she is dismayed to see Mark coming into the kitchen, wearing nothing but his boxers. Peter is standing in front of the table, blocking his view of the jewellery box and its contents.

'What the hell is he doing here?' Mark says.

Is he *jealous*?

'Can we go outside?' Caz glances at the camera.

'What the fuck?' says Mark.

'Just do what she says,' Peter tells him. He has the natural authority of an ex-copper, and surprisingly, Mark responds to it.

They file down to the end of the garden.

'Well?' Mark says, his arms folded.

'We've evidence that those two young men Caz found were murdered by the same, very dangerous person,' Peter tells him. 'And there's a clear link to her.'

'Who the hell are you?' Mark says.

'He's Ezra's nephew, remember? You met him on Wednesday. He's police,' Caz says. Mark's hostility astounds her.

'I just want to warn you, so you can take care,' Peter says.

'What the *fuck*?' Mark says again.

'Keep your voice down, mate,' Peter tells him.

'We think the house is bugged,' Caz says.

'What?' Mark says. 'Jesus Christ. Does that mean I'm in danger now? That some murderer is going to track me down and slaughter me because I'm sleeping with her?'

Caz looks at him, her eyes wide. He's like a spoilt, whining child.

'Hold on,' he goes on, grabbing his beautiful curly hair. 'Did they see what we did last night?'

Peter holds out a hand. 'Calm down. This isn't doing anyone any good.'

Mark steps forward, pushes his face right in front of Caz's. 'You've put me in danger, you little idiot.' She can smell terror on his breath.

'You weren't taking no for an answer, I seem to remember,' she says, her voice trembling with anger and disappointment.

'Have you told the police?'

Before Caz can speak, Peter steps in. 'Of course.'

Mark backs away, holding up his hands. 'I want nothing to do with this,' he says. 'I don't want to be killed and I don't want the police getting involved in my life.'

'Why not?' Peter says.

'That is none of your business, mate. Just back off, right?' Mark looks like he is about to hit Peter, so Caz gets in between them.

'I think you'd better go,' she tells him.

Mark chokes out a hollow laugh. 'Don't worry, Caz. I'm out of here.'

He turns and hurries back into the house, leaving Caz and Peter looking after him open-mouthed.

'Wow,' Caz says.

'Sorry if I was out of order telling him that,' Peter says. 'I just thought...'

'No. You did the right thing. And I got a chance to see his true colours. Jesus.'

'A self-centred man.' He looks at her almost as if he is apologising for Mark's behaviour.

'Let's not talk about him any more.'

'I thought it best we keep the Marcy thing to ourselves for now. For the sake of discretion. We don't want to put her in any more danger.'

'Absolutely.' Caz holds out her hand and looks at her little finger. 'Poor Marcy. Would that have hurt?'

Peter sighs. 'The adrenaline shock would have numbed it when it happened, but yes, she's probably in pain now. Let's hope she can keep it clean.'

'We have to find this monster,' Caz says.

'We will.'

'I don't know what I'm going to do. Poor Marcy. Poor Bridget.'

Caz thought Marcy was behind her own disappearance. And she snooped in her private journals. Wished her the most awful things...

She is the worst person.

'You only have to wait until my old DI gets to the bottom of it. Just carry on as normal.' Peter puts his hands on her shoulders. 'Why don't you take Joe off for a nice long walk somewhere away from here. Stanmer Park, say? And I'll go round the house finding out where all the cameras are, so that you'll at least know if there's anywhere you can be unobserved.'

'Won't he be able to see you, though?' Caz asks.

'I'll switch off the system just for an hour or so. He'll think it's a power cut,' he says. 'Then I'll switch it back on and he'll not suspect a thing.'

Caz nods. She's not convinced, but if it means she can have a bit of time to herself to process, she'll go along with it. And Joe needs to go out. Stanmer is a perfect place to clear her head. She hands Peter the plastic bag. 'I'll find you the other card, too,' she says. 'The one with the heart on it.'

'Good plan.'

They hear Mark's footsteps thundering down the stairs, then the front door slams. A few moments later, his car starts up with its stupid, air-shattering roar.

They look at each other as the droning engine disappears, winding its way through the streets down to the Old Shoreham Road.

'That's him gone, then,' Caz says. And despite everything that has happened in the past twenty-four hours, her overriding feeling is one of relief.

'Just goes to show,' Peter says, 'money doesn't always make a man. Disappointing, isn't it?'

THIRTY

Caz crunches the van over the gravel entrance to the car park tucked away behind Stanmer church. On the drive up here, she tried to make sense of what has been happening. It's clear that everything this murdering, kidnapping monster has done is because of her.

Two overriding questions clang in her head: *Why?* and *Who?*

She is stumped on both. She has discounted Edwin because she really can't see him doing any of this. And it can't be Mark – can it? He was so horrified, so frightened and so, so disappointingly cowardly just now. She knows him too well – such fine acting is beyond him.

Could it be some random psychopath she has just stumbled across without realising it? But where? She's generally a boring little stay-at-home. She has no enemies, and apart from Mark, and creepy, weedy old Edwin, no one is particularly interested in her one way or the other. She's depressingly dull, really.

But it's got to be someone.

Is it Jon? But why? What's his connection to her? Why does she think she recognises him?

She wants to know what that hole he was digging is about. And she wants him to stop staring at her. But does any of that make him a murderer?

Again, she wonders what he did that got him put in prison.

Whoever it is, one scrap of comfort is that, as Peter said, they clearly don't want her to come to any harm. God knows, if they did, they've had every opportunity to do her in, with her out on the Downs most days alone but for a bunch of pampered hounds. Or here in Stanmer.

And it seems they have a set of keys to the house.

She switches off the van. She has to keep her head, for Marcy's sake.

And Bridget's.

She slides out of the van and lets Joe out of the passenger side. He looks awfully forlorn. She puts her arms around his neck. 'I wish you could speak, Joey,' she whispers into his fur.

At least whoever it was didn't hurt him. More proof that they mean her no harm. It would have been easier to take him than to lock him up.

Or to kill him.

She shivers. It doesn't bear thinking about.

She slings her dog walking bag over her shoulder and heads off, past the row of chocolate-box cottages of Stanmer village and up the hill into the wilder part of the park, where ash trees rise like reedy giants from beds of fern. The early leaves and branches dapple the morning light, filtering it across the muddy track, making Caz feel like she is walking through a stage set. She wishes she was. She wishes this were all some horrible fiction, rather than her own life.

She envies Joe his resilience. He has completely put behind him the trauma of being lured out of the house, Bridget's kidnap, then being locked up in the studio. While she strides hunched up, hands deep in pockets, nerves almost visible on her skin, he forges on, nose to ground, hoovering up the scent of mole, fox, badger.

She shuffles through last autumn's leaves. Without consciously thinking about it, she comes to a halt in the middle of a crossroads, where five paths branch out around her. Even though she could take any and not get lost, the decision is too much for her right now. She closes her eyes and breathes in the spicy, earthy leaf-mould air. Her shoulders relax and, in their release, make her aware of just how tightly she was clenching them.

'Everything will work out,' she tries telling herself. 'There will be a happy ending to this.'

But she knows it's too late. There is no happy ending for Ash or Harry. And Marcy will forever be scarred by whatever is happening to her. If she gets through it alive.

If she gets through it alive.

She opens her eyes. If there were any wind today, the mighty trees arching over her would pose a threat because of ash dieback – *God*, she thinks, *poor Ash*. It's ravaging these woods – any one of them could suddenly fall. But all is still and silent. She can almost hear the rustle of woodlice and beetles in the undergrowth. Almost but not quite.

Not quite.

There is no sound. But she feels something.

She looks round.

Where's Joe?

She calls him – 'Joey!' – the two-tone sounding of his name that usually brings him running straight towards her, eager for his treat.

But he doesn't come.

She ramps it up the whistle that means absolutely no nonsense.

Still no Joe.

No. Not again.

She carries on crying out, now running a hundred or so metres down each of the five paths, so that her calls can be heard in all directions.

'What do I do?' she finds herself saying out loud. 'What do I do now?'

She stands back in the middle of the crossroads and, holding her breath, strains to listen. Again she has the feeling of being watched, but she often does in forests and woods, all the beings that inhabit them.

But is there something else?

Then it's upon her. A crashing through the bracken and the undergrowth. Quickly she bends and picks up a sizeable branch. Holding it like a samurai with a sword, she wheels round until she pinpoints the direction of the sound.

As whatever it is approaches, she is ready.

Her hands tighten on the branch, her knuckles white. She is ready to swing it; she will not hesitate.

The ferns to her left part and she swings round...

And it's Joe.

He's panting, the tufts of white fur around his mouth red with blood.

She falls to her knees to inspect him. 'What's happened, Joey?'

He lets her look at his mouth. The blood is not his, and she doesn't know what to think about that. Every part of his being is straining away from her.

'What have you seen?'

He pulls away. Her heart is in her mouth as she follows him back down the track he appeared from.

And all she can think of is Mark, his face up against hers.

You've put me in danger, you little idiot.

Has she? Is that what she has done?

Or has Joe found Marcy?

She stops. She doesn't want this to happen again. Up ahead

of her, Joe too comes to a halt, turning back and looking at her, one of his front legs raised.

No. She has to face this. She reaches inside her bag for the pepper spray she always carries with her. It's the closest she has come to thinking about using it, but if her worst fears are confirmed and Joe has found Mark, then whoever killed him can't be far away, because it was only two hours ago that he roared off from Marcy's house.

But how did they know she was coming here? She thinks back to Peter suggesting it to her. Was he overheard? Or could it *be* Peter?

'Don't be ridiculous,' she says out loud to herself. Besides, even if he were a realistic contender, there would absolutely be no time for him to have found Mark, killed him and got his body up here.

The casual way she has just imagined Mark being killed shocks her. Has she become so inured to murder that she can picture it so easily?

As Joe leads her into a dense part of the undergrowth, where in the summer brambles and stinging nettles would make it impossible to pass, the green forest hum is pierced with a sudden horrible wailing.

He picks up pace and she follows him, leaping over fallen ash trees.

'No, no, no, no.' She repeats it like a spell as she runs.

Joe arrives at a thicket of prickly bush at the gnarled base of an oak tree set up against a broken barbed-wire fence. The plant is shuddering with movement, and behind it is the screamer.

It is not human, this sound.

It is not human!

Then she remembers Bridget.

Joe has dived behind the bush, and all she can see is his tail, wagging.

She joins him and carefully parts the branches, and there,

all caught up in thorns and barbed wire, is the source of the screaming.

It's not Mark.

It's not Bridget Jones.

She sees with relief that it is a terrified King Charles spaniel. He's cut and bleeding, but very much alive.

His screaming stops as Joe steps towards him and nudges him with his nose, gradually calming him enough so that Caz, with the aid of a fistful of treats, can disentangle him. He has a collar on that tells her his name is Buddy and gives his owner's phone number. She slips her spare lead on him – she always carries one after a lost lead disaster in a park in London forced her to use her bra to keep Joe safe on the road.

Buddy is beyond walking, so she sits with him as she calls the number on his tag and arranges to meet his highly distressed owner – who says she has been running around the park shouting herself hoarse for an hour – by her van in the car park.

Buddy is small, but by the time Caz carries him down to the van, her arms are aching. His owner, a well-heeled woman in a Barbour and Hunter wellies, is beyond grateful. She scoops him up, offers cash – which Caz declines – and takes a business card

'I was so scared,' she says. 'While I was searching, I bumped into a man in the field up there carrying a gun. Said he was looking for a stray mauling his sheep. Found one dead with its leg ripped off yesterday. Buddy couldn't do that, but I was terrified that if he saw him, he'd shoot him.'

Caz gasps.

'Horrible, isn't it?' the woman says.

She has no idea how actually horrible it is.

Gathering herself, Caz suggests she should take Buddy to the vet – one of his gashes might need stitches.

She watches the woman drive off in her big Lexus MPV,

then opens the van and Joe, truly the hero of this moment, hops in. She'll get him a lamb bone tomorrow.

Or perhaps beef.

If only the rest of what she is facing were as easily resolved as Buddy's predicament.

Chewing on a muesli bar she picked up at the little café in Stanmer Park after realising that she hadn't eaten since yesterday lunchtime, she turns into Marcy's driveway and almost runs over Clive and June, who appear to be talking to someone standing behind the magnolia tree. When they see the van, they jump out of the way and smile at her, laughing in a way that appears too forced, too jolly.

'Hello?' she says, climbing out.

'We've got a surprise for you!' Clive says.

'You do?' Caz lets Joe out of the back. She's really not in the mood.

'Surprise!'

A horribly familiar voice makes her belly lurch, and the muesli bar nearly makes a reappearance.

'What the hell are you doing here?' she says as she takes in the sight of Edwin standing there in head-to-toe shit-coloured corduroy, holding a bunch of service station carnations.

'Edwin's my old school mate,' Clive says. 'He told me all about you, and when you turned up at Colette's and said you were a teacher in London and that you'd come down here recently, I couldn't believe it. It's why I checked with you. I don't have a niece!'

'No shit,' Caz says.

'I came as soon as I could,' Edwin says. 'It's like fate, isn't it, Caz?' He smiles, showing a row of vile yellow tombstone teeth.

Caz cannot speak. She grabs Joe's collar and together they

run into Marcy's house, where she slams and bolts the front door and leans her back against it.

Her whole body shakes. She wonders if perhaps she is having some kind of fit.

'Peter?' she calls out, hoping he is still here checking out the security system. But there is no reply. She runs into the kitchen, where she finds a hand-drawn floor plan of the house showing the location of cameras and microphones. *You're safe in the bedroom and en suite you're using, and the one next to it*, he has written in a careful cursive script.

Someone bangs on the front door.

Peter has been in her bedroom after her night with Mark. She has little memory of what went on, only that it was quite active, and the place must be in a bit of a state. If she weren't already in a one hundred per cent fight-or-flight mode, she would combust with shame.

But Peter will forgive her, she is sure.

'Caz!' Edwin calls out. 'I know you're in there. Come out and say hello at least. I've come all this way to see you.'

She gets out her phone, ready to call Peter, to tell him about Edwin, to get him to tell him to go away.

Edwin bends to speak through the letter box. 'I forgive you for sending the police to talk to me. I understand how my previous behaviour might have given you cause for concern, but I've changed. I can prove it to you.'

She pulls up Peter's name on her phone, but stops herself pressing the button to make the call. She has leant on him too much. Looking out at the back garden, she sees he has cleared up the sheep, a job she was dreading.

Edwin hammers again. 'Caz!'

Even though it's not yet midday, she's suddenly so weary she can barely stand. She heads up to the bedroom with Joe at her heels, and is pleased to discover that when she shuts the door, Edwin's hammering is barely audible. He's persistent, she knows that, but he will give up eventually.

She turns to throw herself on the bed, expecting to see it all askew from the night before. But it is neatly made, with plumped-up cushions on the cover. The room is as tidy as a hotel bedroom after the chambermaid has been.

Did Mark do this?

She heads for the window to draw the curtains, to shut out the world. But when she looks out, she sees Jon in Colette's garden. She flattens herself against the wall so she can watch him unobserved. He's carrying what looks like a body wrapped in a duvet. She holds her breath, her mouth hanging open in shock, as he hoists the white bundle from over his shoulder and lets it tumble into the grave.

Because it is now, without any doubt, a grave.

She gets the camera ready on her phone, then jumps out in front of the window to film what she sees. This could be important evidence. Of what, she doesn't want to think – the death of Marcy? Or Mark? Her sudden movement, combined with Jon repositioning himself to pick up a spade standing in the earth at the side of the grave, means that she catches his eye.

Her insides turn to ice as he looks up at her, his mouth set in a grim line.

This time, he doesn't wave.

She pulls the curtain shut, dives under the duvet and sends the video to Peter, with a message:

What the hell is Jon doing?

Edwin continues to bang on the door.

'Please let it all stop,' she wails into her pillow.

THIRTY-ONE

Miraculously, Caz manages to sleep, albeit tangled in the usual nightmares. She is woken a couple of hours later by the buzz of a new message. It's Ruth, asking her to add almond milk to the shopping list and also to stop by at Piers's house on her way over this afternoon.

She had forgotten about her shopping promise. Such a mundane, everyday task doesn't feel like it belongs on the same planet as the rest of her life right now. However, the stopover at Piers's place on the way from Sainsbury's to Ruth's adds a touch of weird that at least brings it into the same orbit.

Piers is one of Ruth's exes. He lived with them for a couple of years while Caz was growing up, but he and Ruth decided that they were better off as friends than lovers. Caz likes him, but she has difficulty with how he makes his living, which is selling weed. Because of her neuropathic pain, Ruth has a specialist prescription from her doctor for a cannabis-based spray, but she says it doesn't work nearly as well as what Piers can get for her.

So Caz's weird and twisted world has now thrown up being her mother's drug courier.

Another message pings in. This one's from Peter.

Very interesting. Have passed it on to my old DI.

'Good,' she says. At last things are happening. She peels Joe
off from where he is lying on her chest, hauls herself out of bed,
strips off and has a shower, dresses in fresh clothes and heads
downstairs.

No more hammering from Edwin, but there is a snotty little
note pushed through the door saying how disappointed he is
in her.

Disappointed.

Disappoint was the word used on the most recent card. She
opens the photo she took of it and zooms in on the writing.
Because Edwin's note is not all upper case, it's hard to tell if it is
from the same hand, but it could be. It slants slightly backwards,
like in the cards.

She writes a message to Peter about Edwin turning up –
Could it be him? she asks – and puts it in a plastic bag with the
pathetic little note. More evidence to give to his old DI.

She opens the front door like a thief escaping. The driveway
is empty, so she scurries along the pavement, hugging the edges,
and pushes the plastic bag through Peter's letter box. She
doesn't want to disturb him again today, and she really has to go
and do her mum's shopping. As she slips back to Marcy's house,
her eye is caught by a movement at one of the upper windows in
the house at the end of the turning circle. An elderly, pale
figure, who, but for the dyed turquoise hair, could be a ghost, is
looking down at her. It must be Nicola, the agoraphobic neighbour who didn't come to Colette's dinner party. Nicola puts a
finger to her lips and shakes her head, then disappears behind
her net curtains.

What – if anything – does that mean?

Shuddering, Caz fetches Joe and heads off to the supermarket, glad to put a small stretch of distance between herself, Edwin and creepy Nicola.

With Ruth's modest weekly shop in the back of the van, she heads up to Moulescoomb, the sprawling estate on the wild north-eastern edge of the city. Piers's ex-council house is towards the top of the estate, and his garden backs onto an expanse of downland that rises like a green wave above his raised vegetable beds and ramshackle sheds.

Although she's not a fan of buying illegal drugs from him, she likes seeing Piers. He was fun to have around when he was with Ruth, and Caz had high hopes back then that he might become her permanent stepfather. Almost every weekend, they would go out to the countryside for walks and wild camping trips in his dilapidated old van.

That same van now stands in his driveway, propped up on some breeze blocks with its wheels off. Behind it there's a rusting Renault 4, which he has been doing up for eight or so years. 'That's for you, Caz,' he said when he bought it from the scrapper. 'A little beauty, lovely bones on her.'

'Hello, darling,' he says now, standing on his doorstep and enveloping her in his wiry brown arms. His unique smell diesel and weed and sweat – makes Caz feel like she has crept back into her childhood. She has a sudden, intense longing to be running around a field while Ruth and Piers sit by a campfire drinking tea and sharing a spliff. He beams at her, nodding in the way he has that makes her feel totally welcome and listened to. 'Long time no see. Your mum said to expect you. Want a cuppa?'

'Lovely.'

He bends to scratch Joe behind the ears, then leads them through into his functional bachelor kitchen and puts the old-fashioned whistling kettle on the gas hob. He grabs an old tartan blanket from a hook on the back door and throws it into a cosy corner on the floor for Joe to sit on.

He's using a stick, Caz notices, and as if reading her mind, he says, 'Another bloody flare. Got my right leg and my left hand. Total bastard.'

Piers has multiple sclerosis, which is the reason he first got into using cannabis. Like Ruth, he prefers the organic stuff to 'the poxy spray the doc gives you'. He swears he only sells it so he can subsidise his own needs. Even so, he rarely charges Ruth. They are still truly fond of each other, but his line is now that they split up because there was no future for 'us two crips' living together. Caz's theory is that, with the unknown quantity of his condition, he was scared of becoming a burden to Ruth.

'Can I help?' she asks him as he struggles to one-handedly sort the tea bags out.

'Nah, mate. You sit on that stool there.' He stops what he's doing and nods at her. 'You look proper knackered.'

'Too many earlies,' she says. She's certainly not going to trouble Piers with the true details of her situation, particularly because he is the world's worst gossip, which is not the most useful attribute for a drug dealer. But then there are many ways he doesn't fit the stereotype. He may drop his Ps and Qs when he remembers, but as his name suggests, he was born slightly upstream of middle class. Abuse suffered at a boys' boarding school meant that he dropped out of all that, rejecting his father's expectations of following him into finance, and instead started tinkering with engines.

'How's Ruthie?' he says, as he places a chipped mug of strong tea in front of her, with a plate of digestive biscuits between them to share. 'Nasty fall she had the other month.'

'It's set her back, but she's getting physio. And your wares help, as usual.'

Piers chuckles. 'I wish I could get down and see her, but I'm not going anywhere at the moment with this leg.'

'Hopefully it'll sort itself out.'

'Yep. No wheelchair yet.' Wincing, he sits opposite her, gets his Rizlas out and starts rolling a spliff. 'How's the rail holding up now?'

'Eh?'

'The one that gave way. I fixed it when she had the accident. Before this bastard flare.'

Caz nods. 'Seems to be doing the job, but of course like you she doesn't go out much at the moment because of the pain.'

'Poor Ruthie. Course, proper rawl plugs'll keep the thing secure now.'

'What?'

'Rawl plugs? You know, the things you put in the wall to keep a screw in place?'

Caz shrugs. DIY is not one of her skills.

'Whoever put that grab rail in didn't use any. Criminal.' Piers licks his papers and smooths down the joint.

'I think the council did it. Years ago'

'That's what Ruthie said. Surprised it held that long. She should sue.'

'I thought it was just bad luck.'

'Nah. This was negligence. Poor old girl, always getting done over by other people '

'I look after her.'

'I know you do, love.' He lights the spliff, inhales deeply, then lets a slow stream of smoke out of his nostrils. 'I'm still big fond of the old bird. How's her spirit these days?'

'You know... so-so.'

'Is she seeing anyone other than the physio?'

Caz smiles. 'Dating, you mean?'

'Nah.' Piers taps his temple. 'Head doc. I've told her so many times she needs more therapy. She's never got over the trauma of the attack, has she?'

'No.' Caz doesn't correct Piers for calling the car crash an attack. Due either to his condition or the steps he takes to self-medicate, he sometimes gets things muddled.

'Not surprising, though,' he goes on. 'It's hard enough the physical stuff she has to deal with, but the memory of the violence and what he did to her and poor old Dan, that's what she finds hardest, isn't it?

Caz frowns. She has no idea now what or who he is going on about.

'How anyone can do that to someone else, particularly someone they supposedly love, I have no idea... Another digestive?' As he offers her the plate of biscuits, he sees her confusion.

'Do what?' she says. 'Who are you talking about?'

He blinks. 'Fuck. You don't know, do you?'

'I don't know what?'

He gets up and leans on the sink, his back to her, smoking. 'She said she was going to tell you when you came back to help her after the thing with the grab rail. Said you were old enough to hear it. But she didn't, did she?'

Caz has a ringing sound in her ears, like she's just walked out of a too-loud gig. 'Tell me *what*, Piers?'

He takes a deep breath in and, steadying himself on the worktop, turns to face her. His gentle eyes are bloodshot, wide. 'I can't say anything else, love. I've done too much damage already.'

'I'm thirty. I'm old enough.'

'That's for Ruth to decide. She's the only one can tell you.'

'You mean there's something you've both been hiding from me?'

'Hiding you from, love.' A tear rolls down Piers's cheek.

Caz stands and heads towards him. He was never a big man, but now he seems wizened and tiny, like she could just blow at him and he'd fall over. She puts her face very close to his. 'You have to tell me.'

He slides along the counter, away from her, and grabs a large matchbox – the kind you would keep by the gas stove or fireplace – and holds it out like a shield between them. He gives her one of his sweet little nods. 'This is for your mum, Caz. I don't want no bullshit between her and me, so I'm not going to ask you to lie. Tell her I said what I said in all innocence, thinking she'd finally got round to telling you. Personally I think it's way past time she did. But I've always tried not to interfere in what she's got going on. She has her reasons for doing what she does, and I've always respected them. Always respected *her*. Top bird, your mum.'

He is nodding so much now that she fears his head might fall off. She takes the matchbox from him. 'How much does she owe you?'

'On the house, love. Always has been for our Ruthie. Always will be.'

THIRTY-TWO

'What haven't you told me?' Caz says as, Joe at her heels, she steams down Ruth's hallway towards the conservatory, where her mother is sitting half dozing in the afternoon sun, one hand resting on the Mother sculpture.

'What?' Blearily, Ruth sits up and smiles to welcome her daughter. 'Oh, hello, Joey.' He comes to her and puts his chin on her lap. The room smells stale, and Caz wonders whether Ruth is able to get in the bath any longer. Should she see about putting in a walk-in shower?

'What haven't you told me about how you got to be like this?' She gestures at Ruth's broken body, her missing fingers, her scarred face. 'It wasn't a car crash, was it?'

She almost throws the matchbox full of weed at her.

Ruth catches it and slumps back against her chair. 'Jesus Christ. Bloody Piers. He's been blabbing on, hasn't he? I'll bloody kill him.'

'It's not his fault. He let slip some things he thought I knew. When he realised that I was completely in the dark about what happened to you, that it was an attack rather than an accident, he didn't say anything else.'

'Well, that's something, I suppose.'

'I'm going to get the shopping in – your ice cream is nearly a milkshake. Give you time to gather yourself. And once I've put it all away, I want you to tell me everything.'

Ruth sticks out her bottom lip.

Caz has tried to be reasonable. But the anger that bubbled up in her as she drove over explodes in a vicious burst. 'What happened to "we've got no secrets, Caz"?' She cruelly mocks her mother's voice. '"We act as one"?'

Ruth lowers her brow, clasps the claws of her hands together. 'Hiding things seems to run in the family, doesn't it?'

Caz snorts. 'You stay there, Joey.' She turns on her heel to bring in the shopping.

'When I was pregnant with you,' Ruth says, exhaling smoke – she hasn't wasted any time opening Piers's matchbox and making use of the contents – 'I was attacked by my husband.'

Caz, who is sitting next to her mother in the other conservatory armchair, slaps her hand over her mouth. 'Dan?'

Ruth reaches out and puts a hand on her arm. 'No, love, not Dan. I've always told you the truth about him. He was the kindest, sweetest man. And he loved me. And because of that, he paid the highest price anyone could pay.'

'Tell it to me straight, Mum. I can't bear all this mystery. What happened? Who was your husband if it wasn't Dan?'

Ruth sighs. 'It was going to be Dan. That was the plan, after I got a divorce. My husband's name was Steve. Stephen John Nicholls. He was all right when we got together – a charmer, tall, good-looking, solvent. I was very young. Just twenty. Met him in a pub in Leeds, just round the corner from my art college. He was a proper grown-up, couple of years older than me, a computer programmer rather than a starving artist. Swept me away. Like they do. All dark brown eyes that sucked you in

like the sunshine, dazzling white-toothed smile. I was alone in
the world, with your grandma just died on me. Easy prey, see.
We married within six months. Then the moment he got me
home from the registry office – it was just me, him, and two of
his mates for witnesses – he changed. It was like I was his property. He beat me up if I looked at another bloke when he took
me out. Or if I got in later than I'd said I would.' She looks at
Caz and swallows. 'He raped me, too. But it was considered a
man's right then. The law didn't change until just before you
were born.'

'I didn't know that.'

'People forget. Not that it's all roses for women these days,
but even so.'

Ruth sips her tea, takes a toke. Caz is keen for her to get on
with what she has to say. She's had enough of rambling old
hippies for one day, and she is feeling impatient.

'I had quite a few years of that. Well, nearly a decade. From
the outside, it didn't look too bad. I was making work and selling
it, and that paid for a studio in a converted warehouse where at
least I could be myself for a few hours – so long as I got home in
time. Made her there.' She points to the Mother statue. 'When I
was pregnant with your brother.'

'I have a brother?' Caz says. She can't believe this.

Ruth shivers, and her eyes shine as she shakes her head. 'He
died. I got kicked in the stomach and he died.'

'By your husband?'

She nods.

'But didn't the hospital find out it was him? Didn't you tell
them?'

'I couldn't. I didn't dare. He told me to say I fell down the
stairs.'

'God... Jesus.'

'He'd cut me off from other people, so I didn't have many
friends. But having my studio in that warehouse meant I saw

the other artists working there and learned that life could be different. That's where I met Dan.'

The language Ruth is using, the order of events, make Caz feel like she is standing on quicksand. Everything she thought was fact is being shown to be very much the opposite. But what is worrying her the most is that in the past, Ruth always referred to Dan as 'your dad'. Now he is just Dan.

'I've not lied to you about Dan. He was such a lovely man, and we would have had a very different life, you and me, had Steve not...' Ruth puts her hands over her face. The familiar nubs of her missing fingers force Caz to remember Marcy's blue-nailed finger in the box she received just this morning.

Coincidence or link?

Coincidence or link?

Please let it be a coincidence.

'Had Steve not what?'

'I'd been seeing Dan for two years. First just as someone kind to talk to, but I very quickly fell in love with him, and we made plans to escape. We knew it wouldn't be easy, and that Steve would put up a fight, but it had to be done. Particularly when I found out I was pregnant with you.'

'Who's my father?' Caz says quickly.

Ruth sighs. Then she looks Caz straight in the eye. 'Honestly? I don't know. I look at you and see a beautiful, kind and wise girl, and I think it has to be Dan. But like I say, Steve insisted on having sex with me, right up to the end, and he didn't take no for an answer.'

'You never did a DNA test?'

She shakes her head. 'I want Dan to be your father, so that's how it is.'

Caz has no ground beneath her feet now, not even the shiftiest of sands.

'So tell me what happened,' she says, her voice barely able to escape her.

'I pretended to go to work, but then I snuck back to pack a suitcase of what I needed to survive – basic clothes, my passport and birth certificate, the money I'd made by selling my work in cash, which I'd squirrelled away into an escape fund. I'd handed in my notice on my studio, packed up my work and tools and put them in storage. The plan was that I'd go to Dan's place, then the next day he and I would move down south, to France perhaps. Get right away. But what I didn't know was that Steve was on to us. He kept closer tabs on me than I ever feared. He knew I didn't go to work that day. He knew about Dan. He knew where he lived.'

'How?'

Ruth shrugs. 'He was a total fantasist. Had a strange relationship with the truth and the real world. He loved all that private detective stuff, spy equipment, gadgets, disguises, guns.'

'Guns?'

'He never got his hands on one, thank God. Just a replica of the pistol Clint Eastwood used in the movies – a Colt, or something. It was all very glamorous to him. Pathetic boy stuff.

'He gave me a key ring, and what I didn't know was it had a tracker on it. Even back then, in the early nineties, you could get things like that if you knew where to look. And later, the police found a microphone in the lining of the handbag I carried everywhere. I didn't know! He followed me all over the place. Getting angrier and angrier.'

Caz is feeling a little faint now. This talk of stalking, of trackers, of being overheard and eavesdropped on all sounds far too familiar. She sits with it, though, letting it fester.

With shaking hands, Ruth stubs out her joint and picks up her cup of tea. 'This is so hard to talk to you about. I don't know if—'

'You have to go on.'

She drains her tea and folds her arms around herself. 'That night, I really thought I'd escaped. Dan and I had a beautiful evening. The car was all packed up ready and we were due to set off really early, at the crack of dawn. Everything at that moment seemed possible. He'd cooked a really nice curry, we drank a bottle of champagne.' She smiles at the memory. 'Curry and champagne! Though I only had half a glass because of you. Then we went early to bed.'

'OK.' Caz doesn't want more detail about that.

'It must have been about three in the morning. I woke up, and there was Steve, just standing there in the bedroom, looking at us.'

Caz shudders and thinks of Jon, watching her through the bedroom window at Marcy's.

'He had a jerry can at his feet and was pointing his stupid replica gun at us. I was so angry. I jumped out of bed and went for him. Dan woke up, and he didn't know the gun was a fake, so instinctively he launched himself at Steve. All this happened at once. Neither Dan nor I saw that Steve had a meat cleaver in his other hand. Later they found a receipt for it from a kitchen store.'

Ruth breathes in, then shakily lets the air out. 'He brought the cleaver down on Dan's neck, and there was blood everywhere. My hands were on Steve's chest, trying to push him away, and they were soaked with Dan's blood. Then Steve just lifted me up and slammed me against the wall, like I was a rag doll. I remember it so clearly, that bit – it all went in slow motion, like I was flying through blood and air and thinking only about keeping you safe, yet knowing that the impact was coming towards me. Which it did.' She slams her fingerless left hand into the palm of her right.

The sound makes Caz flinch.

'I'm sorry,' Ruth says. 'You see, this is why I haven't been able to tell you.'

'Go on,' Caz says.

'The next thing I knew was that everything was red and

smoke and stinking. The police said he'd put me and Dan on the bed and thrown petrol on us and set it alight. They found rope, too, which had been his original plan, but he had no use for that, because he thought he'd killed us both. But I was still alive. And when I woke up, I had nothing left but the urge to get out of there.'

Ruth's voice cracks. 'I left Dan in the flames. I had you, you see. I needed to save myself to save you. After losing your brother...'

Despite her anger at not being told, despite her horror at these revelations, Caz reaches out and takes her mother's hand. It is hot, clammy, like her own.

'The police said that Dan had been killed by the cleaver. But still, the guilt... Anyway, the postman saw the flames because they were leaping out of the open window. He'd called the fire brigade, so as I got out of the bedroom, I almost fell into a firefighter's arms. He said later that he'd barely recognised me as human, I was so badly burned.'

'Oh, Mum.' Everything has left Caz's body. All the anger, all the horror. The only thing she feels right now is enormous love and pride for this tiny, damaged woman, who, despite everything, has done so exceptionally well at being her mother.

The sun has dropped low in the sky and cooled the conservatory. Despite the warmth coming from Joe, who has curled up on her feet, Ruth is shivering.

'We need to get you inside,' Caz says. 'By the fire.'

'There you go, looking after me again.'

'And you didn't tell me this because you were looking after *me*, weren't you? Protecting me.'

Ruth looks at her with her fierce mother-eyes. 'Well, of course. You are the most important thing in my life.'

THIRTY-THREE

'So what happened to Steve?'

It feels so wrong giving a monster like that such an innocuous-sounding name. It would be even worse to use 'Dad', though.

They sit in front of the fire in the living room. Ruth is on the sofa, wrapped up in the big fake-fur throw they call 'the bear', and Joe is out in the kitchen, noisily eating a bowl of kibble from the big sack Caz left here when she moved into Marcy's, thinking she'd only be gone for a week.

Right now, all she wants to do is snuggle up next to her mum like she did when she was a child. Burrow into her side and feel once more the safety and security that she took for granted back then.

All she's got at the moment is the large glass of wine she is hugging to herself as they sit and watch the flames. Her foot, however, touches Ruth's leg: a sort of tentative grounding.

Ruth takes a drink from her own glass and sighs. 'They got him, of course. He didn't think I'd survive to name him, but it was pretty cut-and-dried. Apparently the hospital had noted their concerns when I went in with the "stupid, clumsy accidents" I kept having. There was no hesitation, no question that what I was saying wasn't true.'

'So he's in prison?'

She laughs, but with no joy. 'He got life. With a minimum of twenty-five years. Once he was inside, he was a model prisoner. Turned to Jesus.'

'Hell.'

'He quickly charmed this woman prison visitor into a relationship. Married her when he came out. Loaded, she was.'

Caz thinks of Jon again, and Colette, and like a game of Tetris, things start to fall into place.

'He got her looking for me, too. Being in with the nick, she managed to find out where I was living. She took pictures of me with you when we were in the park. She told him about you, and he was sure you were his.'

'Ugh.'

Ruth grabs her arm. 'Listen: you're not. You can't be. You look like Dan, not him.'

'Go on.'

'He sent you presents, through some charity. I'd had enough. I changed our names to Dan's surname – it felt right – and we moved down here. As near to France as possible. I didn't have the confidence to go to another country, with how I looked, and without Dan, who was the one who'd spoken good French.'

She stops and looks at her hands.

'You were so badly injured,' Caz says. 'And grieving for Dad – I mean Dan. And you had me to look after. How did you do it?' She has never really thought about this before, from Ruth's point of view.

'I just did. You just do.' Ruth sighs. 'One of the conditions of his licence when he got out was that he wasn't allowed to contact us. I thought we were safe down here, with the different name, but he was clearly on to us. He could hack computers, remember. And once he set his mind to something... Anyway, his new wife was braver than me. He'd started on his old abusive tricks with her, and although she had originally agreed with him about his right to see you, she found out what he was up to and realised that we were in danger. She tipped off the police and they picked him up at London Bridge station waiting for the Brighton train. He got banged up for another five years.'

'What happened to her?' Caz says, thinking of Colette.

'I found out through her Facebook that she died soon after he was sent back inside. From liver disease. He'd probably been slipping something in her tea.'

'You don't mean...?'

'He inherited all her money, I should imagine, being married to her. I wouldn't put anything past that man.' Ruth grabs Caz's hands again. 'I was so angry he'd found out we were in Brighton. All your life I tried to keep you safe from him. That's why I've always been so careful with you, never allowed the school to post pictures of you, never let you have social media accounts.'

'That's why?' Caz always thought it was something to do with Ruth's own issues around her facial disfigurement.

'And I'm so glad you don't.'

She takes a deep breath. 'I do, though.'

Ruth looks at her, open-mouthed. 'You do?'

'Everyone does, Mum,' Caz says, feeling like a teenager.

Ruth picks up her phone and shoves it into Caz's hand. 'Show me.'

Caz winces. 'No.'

'Show. Me.' Ruth fixes her with her stare, and Caz has no option but to obey. She calls up her genuine Facebook account, which is mostly about dog-walking, and hands the phone back to her mother.

'Fuck,' Ruth says, looking at the page.

'What?' Caz's inner fourteen-year-old bristles.

'You say you're from Brighton.'

'Yes.'

'And you have this as your profile picture.' Ruth stabs at the phone and pinches the photo until it zooms in on what Caz is standing next to.

'What?' Caz says.

'Mother.'

'It's a beautiful sculpture.'

'That lived in the hallway in Leeds when I was married to Steve. I put it there to silently punish him for what he did to your brother. He went past it every day on his way out to work.'

'So...?'

'Do you know how easy it would be for him to find you by searching "Caroline, Brighton", and then looking through the profile pictures until he sees my sculpture?'

Caz puts her hands over her face.

'How long has this been up?' Ruth says, pointing at the picture.

'Couple of years.' Caz had Mother in her flat in London, and she came with her when she moved back down.

'Couple of years?' Ruth looks at her, eyes wide.

'Could he be out now?' Caz asks, her throat so dry she has to take another slug of wine.

'I don't know. They don't tell me. I look at the papers on the internet, but nothing's come up. Or I haven't seen anything.'

'Are you sure?'

Ruth holds up her hands. 'OK. I've been an ostrich about it. I didn't want to know anything about him, or even hear his name again. I told the Probation Service not to tell me. I thought you were safe in London. I thought that was it.'

Caz has taken her phone back and is googling fiercely. 'Here,' she says, holding up a small article in the *Evening Standard* from eighteen months ago.

Police are looking for ex-offender Stephen Nicholls, who
failed to attend a meeting with his probation officer earlier
this week. He is described as 62 years old, 6ft tall, white,
with greying hair and a full beard. He is potentially dangerous, so if you see him, please don't approach him, but call
Crimestoppers on 911.

'Jesus,' Ruth says. Her face appears to close in on itself.

The article is accompanied by a grainy photograph of an old
man with long grey hair, his face mostly hidden by a beard. It
reminds Caz of the breastfeeding man on the nauseating card
that came with Marcy's finger. But there's also something
familiar about the angry dark eyes that she can't put her finger
on. She turns her phone camera to selfie mode and looks at her
own eyes.

'You don't look a bit like him,' Ruth says, because she knows
what Caz is thinking before she says a word. 'You're not his.'
She levers herself round so she is facing her. 'But he thinks you
are. So he's out. I think he could be behind your dead boys. It
could be him, you know, getting at me through you.'

'But I've been getting love letters from whoever killed Ash
and Harry.' Caz knows it's about her, not Ruth.

'What?'

'And there's more I need to tell you.' It's full disclosure time.

Ruth's face grows darker as Caz tells her about the cards.
About Marcy and Bridget going missing. The finger. About how
she now has proof that it's all the same person. About Jon and
the grave.

'You haven't told me any of this,' Ruth says.

'You're not exactly in a position to complain about that,
Mum, are you?'

Ruth harrumphs. 'What do the police say?'

'It's complicated.' Caz tells her about the bugs, about Peter,
about how calling the police would endanger Marcy. 'So he's

gone to a colleague high up in the Brighton police to start a covert investigation.'

'And you trust this Peter?'

'With my life,' Caz says.

'Well then, I need to see him. We need to tell him about Nicholls.'

'We do.'

'And I need to see this Jon. See if he's Steve.'

'And if he is, what's in that grave?'

Ruth shudders. 'I don't want to even think about it. All I know is he's dangerous, and if it's him, we need to get this colleague of your Peter doing whatever they can to save poor little Marcy.'

Caz nods. *Poor little Marcy.* It's not what Ruth called her when she stole Mark.

'And you're staying here,' Ruth says. 'There's no way you're going back to Marcy's place.'

'I have to. I've been told I have to stay there and stay quiet. If I don't, I don't know what will happen.'

'Then I'm coming with you.'

'What?' Caz is thinking about the cameras, the microphones, the very few safe spots according to Peter's map.

Ruth stands, swaying, with her glass of wine. She is really quite drunk, or stoned, or probably both. But her intention and determination are entirely sober. 'If it's me he wants, then I'm going to give him me.'

THIRTY-FOUR

It's gone nine by the time they get to Marcy's with a suitcase full of Ruth's meds and some basic clothes to keep her going for a few days. They Uber there because Caz has had too much wine to drive. It's a pain because she'll have to get a cab back over tomorrow morning before she picks up the dogs, but she has rules. Besides, she's not putting herself or her mother in any more jeopardy than is strictly necessary. As well as being two sheets to the wind, Ruth is really too worn out to do anything useful tonight, so Caz shows her to the bedroom next to hers. According to Peter's map, it too has no bugs in it.

'Nice gaff,' Ruth says as Caz hands her a nightcap of chamomile tea and sits beside her on the bed.

'I don't think Marcy is happy here,' Caz says.

Ruth nods and looks around. 'Yeah. There's sadness in the walls.'

'We have to get her back. And Bridget.'

'If this Jon *is* Steve, and if that's a grave in the garden, then...' Ruth looks like her whole body is itching.

'Don't, Mum.'

'I can't let it lie.' Ruth throws back the bedcovers and swings her feet round onto the rug. 'Help me up,' she says.

'You've done too much today.'

She picks up her little butterfly bag, threads it over her shoulder. 'I want you to show me. You saw it through your bedroom window, yes?'

'But it's dark.'

'There's a big moon. The sky's clear.'

Caz is astonished at how alert Ruth is. She follows her through into her own room, and they stand in the dark, peering at Colette's garden.

'That's it there.' Caz points to the mound of freshly dug earth. 'We can't see anything else in this dark, though. Let's leave it till tomorrow.'

'We could just sit here and wait for a bit.'

'If you want.'

Caz fetches a couple of chairs and they sit by the window. Ruth leans against a chest of drawers to her right and in doing so knocks over a framed picture sitting on top.

'Oops.' She reaches to pick it up, but instead of setting it back in place, she holds it in front of her, angling it so it catches the moonlight.

'Ugh. *Roman Charity*. Why's Marcy got this in her spare bedroom?'

Caz frowns. She's not noticed a picture on the drawers before. 'Let me see.' She takes it from Ruth. When she sees what it is, she instantly throws it onto the floor.

'What's the matter?'

'That's the picture on the card that came with Marcy's finger.' Fighting back nausea, she reaches down and picks it up so that she can shine her phone torch on it. 'It wasn't here before tonight, I swear. I'd have noticed.'

Ruth looks at her, her mouth set in a straight line. 'It's from Steve.'

'How do you know?'

'It's pretty obvious if you know the story.'

Caz tuts, annoyed at her mother's obtuseness. 'I don't know the story, though, do I?'

'It's a horrible image for us today,' Ruth says. 'But when Rubens painted it in 1612, it signified piety and great sacrifice.'

'What is it?' Caz says.

'See how the old man is breastfeeding from the young woman?'

'I know. Gross.' Caz bends to look at the painting. 'I'd not realised how old he was.'

'No? He's bald and grey with a grey beard!'

'Damian's bald. His beard's got grey in it, too. And he's only thirty.'

'Well, that's Damian for you.' Ruth rolls her eyes and smiles. She has always liked Damian. 'So this old man with his hands shackled behind his back is Cimon, who was imprisoned for stealing bread. His sentence was that he was to be starved to death.'

'Harsh.'

'They give murderers less these days,' Ruth says with a bitter laugh. 'So, anyway, he didn't die, and this is the reason why.' She stabs the picture with a finger. 'One of his visitors gave him a special, secret gift each time she came to see him.'

'Ugh.'

'But that's not the worst part,' Ruth says.

'How can it get worse?'

'God, you're dense, aren't you?'

'That's no way to talk to your brilliant daughter.'

'That's exactly it. This lovely young woman in billowing red satin, her tits out for old Cimon, is Pero, his daughter.'

'Ugh.' Caz actually feels quite sick.

'This confirms it,' Ruth says. 'It's Nicholls sending you a message about how you keep him going.'

'Really?' Caz says. 'It seems a bit far-fetched.'

'It's *exactly* what he would do. Exactly! And it's by Rubens. He knows I was a big fan. Wrote my dissertation at art school on him.'

There is an explosion of light outside the house. 'What the hell?' Caz presses her face against the window.

'Whoa,' Ruth says. Colette's back garden lights – festoons, plant uplighters, spotlights on seating areas – have all popped on. It looks like the setting for a play. And on walks one of the actors. It's Colette, in a long, flowing kaftan, a scarf covering her hair.

'She looks like some sort of cult priestess,' Caz says, her mind going off in all kinds of directions about what could be going on next door.

'Or a woman of a certain age in her off-duty gear,' Ruth whispers back. 'We don't all wear Nike in our downtime.'

'I wear Nike all my time, down and up.'

Ruth laughs softly. It's amazing how, even in this perilous situation, she and Caz can bat around like this. Of course, what Caz didn't know before today is that her mother has always lived with threat hanging over her. Indeed, her whole existence has been underpinned by a trauma unimaginably and horrifically worse even than the fictional car crash she used as her cover story.

'She's heading for the grave,' Caz says. 'What's that in her hands?'

'Lilies,' Ruth says. 'Jesus.' She reaches into her little butterfly bag and pulls out a ready-rolled spliff.

'I don't think Marcy would like you smoking in the bedrooms, Mum.'

Ruth presses her lips together. 'I don't think Marcy is in a position to complain right now.'

'Don't.'

She puts a comforting hand on Caz's arm. 'We'll air the rooms before she gets back.'

'Which she will.'

'She will.'

They return to watching Colette.

'She's crying,' Ruth says. 'Look at her shoulders.'

Colette stumbles across the uneven ground at the bottom of her garden and kneels at the grave. She takes the lilies and places them at what must be the head end of the mound of earth. Then she pulls a candle from the pocket of her kaftan, drives it into the earth and lights it with a box of matches from the other pocket. She puts one hand on the soil and the other on her heart and appears to recite a prayer, or some sort of poem. Then she looks anxiously up at her house, stands, and hurries back inside.

'What the hell was that about?' Ruth says.

'She's heartbroken about something,' Caz says. 'Which makes me think that whoever is in the ground, it can't be Marcy.'

The doorbell rings, and Caz and Ruth jump as if an electric current has zapped through them. Joe, who has been dozing peacefully on the floor by the bed, leaps up and runs for the stairs, barking.

They look at each other. 'It's gone ten,' Caz says. 'Everyone's usually tucked up fast asleep in their beds round here by this time.'

'We have to get it,' Ruth says.

'You stay here.'

'No way.'

Together, and because of Ruth, slowly, they make their way down the stairs. The shape outside the glass front door is male, but the shadow cast by the magnolia makes it difficult to see any more detail.

It's only when she's at the door that Caz remembers she

could have checked the app to see who it was. Being with Ruth has sent her back to analogue door-answering. She'll be only using the landline next.

'Hello?' she says.

There is no reply.

She hooks on the security chain and gingerly opens the door. There, outside, still clutching his stupid bunch of carnations, which are looking very much the worse for wear for sitting a whole day in their cellophane wrapper, is Edwin. His face is grey, his breath stronger than ever.

Emboldened by her mother's presence, Caz unhooks the chain and throws open the door.

'What do you want, Edwin?'

'I... I... I didn't know if you were back. Your van's not here...'

'And?'

'I've got to go home tomorrow first thing.'

'Good.'

He stands there with the flowers, as if she should somehow feel guilty for making him feel so downtrodden. She can't bear it. Something fires in her. The tension and stress of the past days explodes all niceties away.

'Get out of my life, Edwin,' she says. 'You're a pathetic old man and I never, ever want anything to do with you. I wouldn't date you if my life depended on it.'

'No need to be so nasty,' he says, curling his lip.

She steps out onto the doorstep, so that he has to move backwards. 'No need? There's every need. You arrogant little prick, thinking you can just track me down and I'll be all "oh, hello, Edwin, come in and be my boyfwend".'

She pushes him, hard, against his shoulder, then she grabs the carnations from his startled hand and whacks him round the head.

'Get out of my garden,' she says.

'It's not your garden,' he says, holding his hands up to defend himself.

This really sets her off. She grips the crappy bouquet and swipes it at him again and again, beating him back towards the road. He squeaks and squeals like a frightened girl. Her fist may well have come into contact with his skull a couple of times.

A hand lands on her shoulder. It's Ruth.

'Chill, Caz,' she says. 'He's not worth it.'

At the sight of Ruth, Edwin shrieks, and this reaction makes Caz batter him more, until the carnations are in red tatters around her feet.

'Stop it, stop it,' Ruth says, grabbing at her arms.

Eventually, Caz gathers herself, and Edwin backs out of Marcy's gates.

'Go back to London,' she says. 'And if I ever see you again, you'd better bloody watch out.'

'I'm going to call the police,' he says.

'Yeah, good luck with that, stalker,' she says.

He turns and runs into the darkness.

Ruth turns to Caz, her mouth open.

'What's happened to you?' she says. 'It was like you were possessed.'

Caz puts her hands on her knees and bends over, trying to catch her breath. She doesn't know what's happened to her. She doesn't know who she is any more.

'And who the hell was that?' Ruth says, once Caz has recovered.

Caz sighs. 'Long story. But not Steve Nicholls.'

Ruth laughs, for the first time today without bitterness or irony. 'He's certainly not Steve Nicholls!'

Caz catches her mother's laugh and, cracking up, they hug, the two of them against the world, like it always has been.

But then she sees Jon, who is coming up the driveway towards them.

She pushes her mother behind her and, her anger and fear peaking again, says, 'What do you want?'

He holds up his hands. 'Whoa, whoa. Nicola just called Colette. She heard a lot of shouting and asked me to come round to see if you're OK.'

'We're OK, thanks,' Caz says, her voice a strangle.

'You don't look OK.'

Ruth struggles out from Caz's protection, and as she does, she gasps.

She recognises Jon.

'Jonny Cursed,' she says, pointing at him.

'What?' Caz looks at Ruth, who is smiling.

'Fuck me,' Jon says. 'It's not often someone calls me that these days.'

'I was a big fan,' Ruth says. 'Saw you at the Fenton a dozen times when I was an art student.'

'What?' Caz says again, pointedly. 'But this is Jon. Colette's boyfriend from next door.'

Ruth steps forward and takes him in. 'He was also lead singer in the Cursed, the best punk band to come out of Leeds, and that's saying something.'

Jon is blushing with pleasure. 'Yeah. That's me. More folky these days. Singer-songwriter, though I've changed the stage name to Jonny Blessed, because I reckon I really am. Colette doesn't like me to spread it about. Doesn't want everyone thinking she's some kind of groupie.'

'So he's not...?' Caz says.

Ruth shakes her head. 'Certainly not,' she says, still beaming like a star-struck teenager.

'And this is the marvellous artist mama,' Jon says, squeezing Ruth's good hand.

Caz's shoulders drop. The immediate threat has passed. But it's time for explanations, not for Ruth to amble down memory lane. She squares up to Jon. 'What's been going on in Colette's garden?'

'Eh?'

'I heard her crying the other day. And that hole you've been digging...'

'Oh God, yeah. That's poor Roget. He carked it. Just keeled over. He was seventeen, mind. Good age for a dog that size. Colette's in bits.'

'Oh!' Caz says. For a second, the rush of relief takes her breath away.

'So are you OK?' he says. 'The shouting?'

'Oh yeah. My daughter's dealt with that problem,' Ruth says, a hint of pride in her voice. 'He won't be coming back.'

'Well, better get back to my grieving lady,' he says.

'Bye.' Ruth waves as he walks away, a definite strut in his step.

'So he's not Nicholls, then,' Caz says.

'That's a relief.'

'But don't get carried away. He's not a nice person.'

'He's great!'

'He went to prison for doing terrible things.'

'We've all done a bit of naughty in our time.'

'No, I mean *awful* things.'

Ruth waves her hand. She clearly doesn't believe Caz, or she thinks she's being a typical millennial puritan. 'Well, whatever he's done, he's served his time. Who would've thought it. Jonny Cursed.'

Caz shivers. 'We need to tell Peter about Nicholls. Right now, so he can let his colleague know.'

Ruth closes her eyes. 'I am so whacked, Caz. Today has been too much. I don't think I can tell that awful story again tonight.'

Fatigue works in a strange way on Ruth. Her pain threshold lowers, and her body gradually seizes up until she literally can't move. Caz can see it happening now, so she helps her gently back up the stairs and puts her to bed.

Back in her own room, she messages all her clients for the next three days to tell them she has tested positive so won't be able to work. That's a weight off her mind. She has no idea what to do next, though. Sleep is gnawing at her edges, but she has a growing sense of urgency, like something will happen if she just sits still.

Her phone rings. It's Peter.

'Is everything OK? I heard noises.'

'Can you come round?' she says.

'Give me ten.'

THIRTY-FIVE

She waits by the front door, Joe at her side, until Peter appears in the gateway.

'Hi,' she says, hurrying to join him before he is in range of the house cameras.

'What is it?' he says. 'Are you OK?'

Caz nods. 'I just had a visit from Edwin, the creep who sent me that little note.'

'Oh God.'

'He won't be coming back. I made sure of that.'

'Good,' Peter says. 'I was putting the rubbish out and I thought I heard Jon's voice, though?'

Caz smiles. 'We can rule him out. He's just some old punk star.'

'Eh?'

'I need to update you on something,' she says. 'Do you want to come round the back, and I'll make coffee for us both.'

Peter looks around, then nods.

'Where's your van?'

'At Mum's.'

He raises his eyebrows, as if waiting for an explanation.

'Wait there. I'll let you in round the side.'

'Mum told me something last night that changes everything.' Caz puts a tray with coffee, whisky and chocolate down on a table by the pool. The night is quite warm, and she would have chosen to talk to Peter out here even if there weren't any cameras.

'What?'

'We think the person who has Marcy, the person who killed Harry and Ash, is Stephen Nicholls, who was imprisoned thirty years ago for murder and attempted murder.'

'What?'

'My mother's ex. He attacked her and my father.'

'Your father?'

Caz nods. 'He killed him.'

'How awful.' Peter winces. He gets out his phone and starts taking notes. 'Stephen Nicholl, yes?'

'Nicholls. He's out now. Has been for nearly two years. And there's so much evidence pointing to him.'

'But why?'

'He wants to get to my mum through me? Or Mum says it could be that he thinks he's my father.'

'Sounds a bit desperate.'

'So we need to act quickly.'

'I'll pass this on to my colleague. Set up a meeting at the station first thing tomorrow. And do you want me to pick up your van for you? I could run and get it now if you give me the key and the address.'

'Ah, thank you, but you wouldn't be insured. In any case, I've taken a couple of days off, because of everything. I brought Mum back with me last night.'

Peter looks alarmed. 'You what?'

'She's staying with me. Safety in numbers.'

He shakes his head. 'That's the worst possible thing, Caz. He wants you here on your own, not speaking to anyone about what's going on. What do you think he's going to do if he knows your mum's here?'

'We're being really careful,' Caz says. 'And anyway, it's Mum he really wants, I'm sure of it. And we're acting so quickly that your colleague will be on to him in no time.'

Peter holds her by the shoulders. 'Take care, Caz. You are playing with fire here.'

'Believe me, I know that.'

He drains his coffee and stands. 'I'll set up the meeting at the station first thing. I'll let you know when I have a time.'

Caz stands on tiptoes and kisses him on the cheek. 'Thank you so much. I don't know what I'd do without you.'

He touches his cheek and blushes like a schoolboy.

She lets him out of the back gate, then returns to the seat by the pool and, turning over what has happened today, eats the chocolate with a capful of the whisky.

When she's finished, she goes inside and locks and bolts the house completely. No one can get in, not even if they have a key.

With Joe at her heels – he's not letting her out of his sight at the moment, nor would she want him to – she trudges up the stairs, exhausted. The rush of the day, the revelation she's had to contend with and the relentless worry about everyone's safety are beginning to overwhelm her. She needs to sleep, so that she can better face the challenges of tomorrow.

Somehow, she does.

She wakes early and makes her way through Ruth's bedroom. The bed is empty, the covers thrown back. Joe is not around either. Panic gripping her chest, Caz runs downstairs calling out for both of them. She skids to a stop in the living room: the bifold doors to the back garden are wide open.

'Mum!' she calls out. There is no response. Sunlight streams through the open window, warming the room and ushering in the scent of the wisteria hanging from the pergola on the terrace, which has just come into full bloom. It feels like the first day of summer, and for a brief second, she remembers the joy she used to feel at that realisation that winter was over at last.

Joy would be good in any form right now.

'Mum! Joe!'

Barefoot, she runs out across the terrace and down the steps towards the lower part of the garden. To her great relief, Joe hares around the hedge that encloses the pool and almost knocks her over, so pleased is he to see her.

She drops to a squat and wraps her arms around him, like a mother greeting a son returning from war. 'Have you seen Mum? Is she out here?'

He appears to want her to follow him, so she stands and lets him take the lead. When she rounds the hedge screening the pool, she cries out.

Ruth is floating naked, face-down, in the water, her pale, scarred body hovering like a ghost, her arms stretched out, her beautiful grey hair suspended in fronds around her.

Caz doesn't even stop to think. With a massive splash, she's in the pool in an instant, in her night attire of yesterday's T-shirt and knickers. She surfaces to set out towards her mother... but then Ruth is in front of her, bobbing in the water, her hair slicked back from her face, smiling at her.

Joe, who has been barking furiously at the edge of the pool, jumps in and joins them, circling them, splashing with his paws, trying to herd them towards the edge.

'Pool party!' Ruth says, treading water. 'It's so warm.'

'Don't do that, Mum! I thought you were...'

'I was just enjoying the float. Zero gravity. What a joy! I

don't usually get the chance. People stare too much at the public pool.'

'I thought you were drowning.'

'I'm sorry.'

'No, no. It's me.'

'Float on your back. The sky is so blue this morning.'

'I can't, Mum. We've got too much to do.'

'It's all right, Caz. It's coming to an end. We've nearly got the bastard.'

'Shh,' Caz mouths. 'Microphones.' She knows from Peter's map that the area round the pool is fine, but Ruth is not being careful with her voice. 'I spoke to Peter last night and he's setting up a meeting at the station this morning. We're so close, so we have to be super-careful. Stay out here and I'll get you a cup of tea, then you have to get dressed so we can be ready to go down there as soon as we get the word.'

Ruth nods.

Caz swims to the edge of the pool, which pleases Joe greatly, and hauls herself out of the water. She splashes towards the pool house and grabs one of the clean towels from where they are stacked in a wooden stand. Rubbing herself dry, she turns and sees a towelling robe hanging on the hook on the back of the door. She takes off her wet things and slips it on.

She heads to the kitchen, leaving a towel on a sunbed for Ruth, who is now lying in the water on her back, everything exposed to the sky. It's been a few years since Caz has seen her mother fully naked, and the extent of her scarring takes her breath away. Her body is covered in a web of white ridges, uneven pigmentation, and textured patches where she needed skin grafts. Despite this – or more likely because of it – she was always very free with nudity around Caz, never trying to hide what had happened to her. When Caz, aged fourteen and fed up with her mother wandering from the bathroom to her bedroom without even a towel wrapped around her, asked her why she insisted on parading herself around like that, Ruth said that if she didn't, Caz would only wonder what was going on under her clothes. She wanted to show her daughter that no one should be ashamed of their body, whatever it looked like. She did buy herself a dressing gown after that, but Caz has to admit that the lesson worked, and unlike almost every one of her female friends, she has rarely had any body image issues – beyond the annoyance of Marcy's clothes being so much smaller than her own.

She has a flash of Marcy, perfectly groomed in her beautiful outfits. But what sort of state is she in right now? Is she in pain? Caz's guts knot. She crosses her fingers for her.

When Caz returns with the tea, Ruth is out of the pool and, with her nightdress held across her front to preserve her modesty, stands talking through the fence to Colette.

'Sorry to hear about Roget,' Caz says.

'They take a piece of your heart, don't they?' Ruth says.

'They do.' Colette noisily blows her nose. 'He was so big; I didn't know what to do with him. I don't really like cremation – my family were pretty orthodox, and although I'm non-practising, certain cultural things stick, you know? Anyway. Still no Marcy?' she asks.

'No,' Caz says.

'Parents still in trouble, then?'

'Yup.'

'I hope she's not putting you out too much, leaving you stuck here,' Colette says.

'It's no trouble,' Caz says.

'She likes it so much she's moved me in,' Ruth adds.

They all laugh.

· · ·

Ten minutes later, Caz is pulling on her bra when she is interrupted by a text from Peter.

> *Sorry, Caz. Ex-colleague out on an emergency call. Suggests 2 p.m. I'll pick you up. Sit tight. X*

Caz hits her forehead with her hand. She doesn't know how she can bear this.

Her phone buzzes again. Hoping it's Peter with a better plan, she picks it up.

It's not him, though.

This text is from Mark.

> *I'm sorry, sorry, sorry, Caz. I am such an idiot, a stupid moron. I should never have gone off like that. It just freaked me out so much, those poor guys, and I didn't even give a moment's thought to how you must be feeling. Poor you. I'm a pathetic coward. Please, can we just meet up? I need to see you. I want to make it up to you. And I've got some important information about Marcy. Somewhere neutral so you don't feel under any pressure. Cafe Coho Ship Street? Ten today?*

Caz looks at the message. He's got some cheek. But she needs to find out what he's got to say about Marcy. She texts him back.

> *Can't you tell me what it is now?*

He gets back immediately.

> *It's a thing. I need to show you in person.*

She sighs. If she makes Ruth bolt herself into the house with Joe until their meeting at two, she might just be able to manage it. This new information on Marcy might be important. Damn Mark and his bloody mystery. And his cowardice. He's probably too frightened to come here.

She gives Ruth instructions, then, checking behind her before she pedals off to make sure she isn't being followed, she heads off on a City Hire bike to meet Mark.

THIRTY-SIX

Bang on ten, Caz orders a flat white and a healthy breakfast flapjack and positions herself at the rear of the coffee shop, her back to the wall so that she will know if she's being watched. Every older man is a suspect now. Has she just been sleep-walking through her life for the past couple of years, not noticing that same face in the background of photographs, standing behind her in a queue, following her as she walked the dogs?

She sips her coffee but can't face the flapjack. Her stomach is churning. A man in his mid sixties walks in and joins the line. He's tall, bearded, long-haired, wearing Ray-Bans and a face mask. Her hand shakes as she puts her cup back on its saucer. The man looks around. His gaze behind his shades appears to linger on her. She lifts a menu to conceal her face in a way that automatically draws the attention of a small child in a stroller a couple of tables away, who points at her and asks why that lady is hiding. The child's mother throws a dirty look at Caz, and she couldn't feel more exposed if she were sitting there fully naked.

The man continues his survey of the café, until he is looking towards the door, where another older man, bald with an elaborate moustache, enters. He waves at the first man and squeezes past the tables towards him. When they greet, they kiss each other on the lips, and the first man puts his arm around the second man's waist as he shows him the cakes on display.

Not Nicholls, then.

For a second, Caz relaxes, but then she remembers that she can't let her guard down.

Ten minutes later, there is still no Mark. He was always one for punctuality. In the past, when she turned up more than five minutes late to meet him, he would say, only half jokingly, that she was betraying him.

She waits another ten minutes. And another.

Still no Mark.

She texts him. No reply.

The café is now full, and her cup is empty. A couple about her own age – they can barely keep their hands off each other – have just arrived and are scanning the room for a free table. She screws her face up and hates them for their uncomplicated, loved-up existence.

Where the hell is Mark?

She pretends to drink from her empty cup, to be absorbed in her phone, when all the while her nerves feel as if they are sticking out of the surfaces of her.

An hour passes. Still no Mark, still no reply to the ten messages she has now sent him. If he appears now, she thinks she will punch him and storm out. How dare he stand her up. How dare he.

His last bridge, burned.

Unless. Unless...

When he walked out on Saturday, he was angry because he said she had put him in danger.

He was right.

She remembers how scared she was up at Stanmer that Joe

was going to turn up their third body, and that it was going to be Mark.

She moves her empty cup around between her hands, gazing at the dregs of milk and coffee inside it. The café is still busy. The hip young woman behind the counter keeps shooting looks her way that are partly sympathetic because she has obviously been stood up. But she's also clearly wondering if she is going to give up and vacate her table.

Caz leaves a pound coin on the table and walks out, avoiding the eyes of the customers and staff, all of whom she is certain are looking at poor, stood-up her.

They don't know the half of it.

Out on the street, blinking in the bright sunlight, she realises that she is just round the corner from Fox & Hunter, and Damian. Suddenly, she needs him, his familiarity, his strong sense of what is wrong and what is right. The needle of her own moral compass is spinning so fast it is in danger of flying off.

She scurries along the street, glancing right and left to look out for older men, then slips inside the shop.

It's late Monday morning – not a busy time for an upscale menswear shop, Caz should imagine. Indeed, Damian is on his own, sitting at a laptop behind the counter. The sun streams through the big plate-glass display window behind her, and he clearly can't see her, because when he looks up on hearing the tinkle of the bell above the door, he smiles at her like a stranger.

'Good morning!' he sings. He looks like a different person wearing this impersonal yet welcoming shopkeeper mask. 'Can I help you, or are we just browsing?'

'It's me, Dame.' Caz steps forward.

He stands and slips out from behind his counter. 'Caz? Are you OK? You look awful.'

'I don't know where Mark is.'

'You and me both. I need him to sign off some orders, with

Marcy off on her flit, wherever she is. I've been trying to get in touch with him since Saturday.'

'Oh, Damian.' Caz falls into his arms.

'What is it, babe?'

She looks at him and feels like she is going to break into a thousand pieces. Damian nods. He steps behind her and bolts the shop door, flipping the closed sign over. 'I'll put the kettle on, and you can tell me all about it,' he says.

He thinks he is going to hear a story about how awful Mark has been to her, but instead he gets the full double barrel of everything. About Marcy's finger, about Steve Nicholls, about Mark not turning up, about the link to Ash and Harry. As she speaks, his mouth drops, he puts his hand on his cheek, his chest, and finally on her knee.

'Why haven't you told me any of this?' he says.

'He told me not to tell anyone. And you were mad at me. And I was ashamed about *not* telling you. And you're always so busy here.'

'Apart from the fact that she must be scared to death, Marcy has had part of her finger amputated without any medical care whatsoever. What about infections? Has it been stitched? Has he even given her an Elastoplast?'

The thought of Marcy's kidnapper putting a plaster on the stump of her finger almost makes Caz break down into hysterical laughter, but one look at Damian's horrified face stops her from even smiling. 'I'm sorry, Damian. I've had a failure of imagination, haven't I? I've been so deeply buried in the tunnel of this all that I've forgotten how it actually is from the outside.'

'You have to go to the police,' he says. 'I can't believe you haven't.'

'We've got this meeting at two this afternoon. It's all being done secretly because Marcy's house is bugged.'

'I don't understand.'

'Collins is not to be trusted.'

'Who the hell is Collins?'

'The officer in charge of the Harry case. You know how that sergeant treated you after St James's Street?'

Damian's eyes darken. 'Like I was a pervert and a criminal.'

'This guy Collins, he's like that. One of the bad ones.'

'How do you know?'

'Peter told me.'

'Peter?'

Caz explains who Peter is and how he is helping her. 'The meeting today, that's all his doing. And we've got so much now that we're going to find Marcy for sure. It needs to be hidden from Collins.'

'Huh.' Damian doesn't sound convinced, and his doubt has added another prickle to Caz's discomfort.

'And now I'm worried about Mark. He said he had something to show me about Marcy, but he didn't turn up. So where is he? What if he was right and I've put him in danger, and now Nicholls has got him, too? What if he's going to end up like Harry and Ash?'

'I'm more worried about Ruth,' Damian says.

'What do you mean?'

'If this Nicholls guy is on the loose and he's using you to get at Ruth, and if the house is bugged, then he'll know she's there.'

'We tried to keep away from the cameras.'

Damian looks unconvinced.

'I need to go back, don't I?' she says. 'Check up on her.'

'And then you need to go directly to the police. Demand to see someone other than this Collins if you must, but you need to let them know as soon as possible.'

'Yes.'

'Do you want me to come with you?'

Caz shakes her head.

'You stay here. But can you keep your phone on and nearby? Just in case I need you?'

'Of course. Now go.'

It's midday when Caz lets herself back into Marcy's house. Joe bounds up to her, even more pleased to see her than usual. His enthusiastic welcome almost manages to lift her spirits. She needs to go and see Peter, tell him about Mark, tell him it's urgent that they speak to his colleague, get him to take them immediately to the station.

But first she needs to find her mother. With Joe running ahead of her, she hurries out to the pool. One of Marcy's fashion magazines, crinkled with pool water, lies on top of a sunlounger, and a towel has been flung damply across the flagstones.

But there is no sign of Ruth.

Joe runs around the pool, his nose tight to the ground. Caz goes inside and calls out for her. She checks the downstairs cloakroom, then runs up to look in all the bedrooms. Back downstairs, she makes an increasingly frantic circuit of the living spaces.

No Ruth.

She tries phoning her, but hears the phone she is calling ringing. She follows the tone and finds it upstairs in the room Ruth slept in. To add to the stress of the moment, Joe is barking like a wolf out in the back garden.

'Joe, *quiet!*' she shouts out of the bedroom window. He's over by the gate into the twitten. She runs downstairs and out of the bifold doors to haul him inside by the collar. The last thing she can deal with right now is Colette complaining.

She grabs her phone and starts to call Peter, but is distracted by an envelope on the kitchen worktop. She knows exactly who it's from. She picks it up and rips it open.

It's another card, another printout of a painting of a young woman breastfeeding an old man. It may be because she knows the story behind it, but this picture seems to show the age differences far more clearly. It's also painted in a starker way. She can see the woman's nipple in the man's mouth. He has his head through the gaps in his prison bars; she is wearing red satin, painted so that it looks a little like meat. It's horrible, horrible. But what's inside the card is even worse.

HE WAS WRONG FOR YOU. I WILL NOT SHARE YOU
ANY LONGER, NOT WITH HIM, NOT WITH HER.
I WANT YOU TO MYSELF.

Shuddering, Caz finds a Ziploc bag to put the card in, then, holding it at arm's length like she might one of the many dog poos she has to bag up in a normal working day, she runs round to Peter's house and leans on the doorbell.

There is no response.

'Come on, Peter. Come on,' she says.

She tries again, and still no one comes.

Has Nicholls taken Peter, too, perhaps thinking that they are having an affair? Does every man she likes have to pay?

She walks along the front of Ezra's house, tapping on the windows, but the curtains are all drawn. The back garden is behind a locked gate with razor wire on the top – presumably something to do with Ezra's prepping arrangements, to stop zombies or something after the end of the world.

Zombies would be so simple right now. A clear and identifiable threat, instead of all this shifting of horror, where everyone she knows has gone missing.

Been taken.

By a shadow man.

She runs back to Marcy's house, grabs her phone from the kitchen counter and calls Damian.

While she waits for him to pick up, Joe bellyaches behind

her, scratching and whining at the back door, trying to get out to the back garden.

Shutting him in the living room, she runs out to the front garden, out of earshot of the cameras and microphones.

Finally Damian answers. 'Caz?' he says, concern in his voice.

It all comes out in a rush. 'Mum's gone, and I think Peter has, too. I've had this horrible new card from Nicholls. I'm so frightened.'

'You have to call the police, Caz.'

'I'm scared he's going to hear me do it. Can you do it for me?'

'Who do I call?'

She screws up her face. Her only contact is Collins. Indeed, he is her only option right now. But she can't bring him to the house. It's too much of a risk.

'I'll send you a photo of his card. Tell him to meet me at the fingerprint maze in Hove Park in half an hour.'

'Sure. You sure you're OK?'

Caz nods. 'I feel sick.'

'I'll come to you as soon as I can after the shop closes. I'm on my own here today. Kind of feel I owe it to Marcy to keep it going.'

'You mustn't come here. I don't want to lose you, too.' Her voice breaks. First Marcy and Bridget. Now Ruth, Mark and probably Peter. All lost. What if he's actually going to do the same to them as he did to Ash and Harry?

'It's going to be fine, Caz. You just have to stay strong.'

'I'll send you that card.'

'Stay in touch.'

As soon as she has messaged Collins's business card to Damian, she goes back indoors and grabs the most recent *Roman Charity* card and the picture from upstairs. Collins needs to see them.

She puts Joe on his lead and grabs her dog-walking bag. There's no way she wants to let him out of her sight.

And anyway, if Nicholls is watching, it just looks like she is taking him on an innocent walk.

Acting normal.

THIRTY-SEVEN

Caz sits on a park bench just a short distance from the maze and worries about her choice of rendezvous. It's a labyrinth of limestone paths laid out in the whorls and curves of a fingerprint. But unless you're familiar with the area, you might not know where it is, because when you're close to it, it just looks like a load of random curving lines.

A bit like her current situation, really. There has always been a pattern, but only now has she begun to see it.

Joe is being a proper pain, pulling at the lead. He appears to want to get back to the house.

Her phone dings with a message from Damian.

Collins on his way. Bit cross. Very concerned.

She has just begun to wonder what *bit cross* might mean when Collins himself texts.

Be with you in fifteen minutes. Be vigilant.

Be vigilant!

Despite everything, Collins still has the capacity to irritate – no, infuriate her.

She unclips Joe from his lead, pulls his ball from her dog-walking bag, and throws it. His instinct kicks in and he runs to fetch it, but she can see his heart isn't in it.

'You must have been with Mum when she was taken. If only you could tell me what happened,' she says when he returns with the ball in his mouth. Something in the way he looks at her tells her that he wants to let her know, too. He turns in the direction of the house, growling.

'We'll go back in a bit, boy, but we've got to speak to DS Collins first. He's going to sort us out.'

She hopes she's right on that point.

He was good about her not mentioning Ash, concerned for her safety. How will he be now he's found out that she hasn't told him about Marcy, Ruth, Bridget, Peter and Mark going missing?

Yes, he's going to be furious, but she hopes he will be on her side, and understand why she hasn't felt able to speak.

And here he is, striding across the park, grubby raincoat flapping in the breeze, a seagull dive-bombing him as he stuffs what looks like the last portion of a sausage roll into his mouth.

Caz suddenly feels very small and very stupid, like she is the class troublemaker about to meet the headmaster.

She clips on Joe's lead and puts her foot on the end of it, telling him to settle. Her wave brings Collins steaming over in her direction. She stands to greet him.

He comes very close to her, looks over his shoulder, then leans right into her space. 'Why the hell didn't you tell me about Marcy Jones going missing?' His breath smells of pork, and as he speaks, he showers greasy pastry crumbs onto her hoodie.

Joe barks and snarls and tries to jump up at him.

'Down, Joey!' Caz brushes the crumbs away. 'He said if I did, no one would be safe. And it was being looked after. We were talking to Peter's old DI, who's very senior in the Brighton police...'

'Peter?'

'A friend. An ex-policeman.'

'Give me strength. Why didn't you just come to me, Caz? Why didn't you report all this to the policeman on the team officially investigating the murders of the men whose bodies you found?'

Caz looks shamefaced. She can't tell Collins what Peter said about him. Not right now. Not when she desperately needs him to be on her side.

'Stop it, Joey!' she says. He is chewing now, trying to get through his lead.

'Sit down,' Collins tells her in a way that gives her no choice but to obey. He sits next to her, angled so that she feels like he is bearing down on her. 'Now tell me everything.'

She starts at the beginning, unloads the whole lot. He listens, head lowered, occasionally prompting her for a detail. When she tells him about Marcy's finger, he frowns and asks her to say it again, like he can't quite take it in first time round.

When she's finished, when she's told him about how she fears Peter and Mark have now been taken, too, he puts his hands together and looks at her.

She is amazed what a relief it is to finally say it all out loud to someone who can directly help her.

'Look, Caz, I don't know who this Peter is, but I don't understand why you trust him more than you trust me.'

'He's a friend. I'm so worried about him.'

'But why go behind my back? And who is this "old DI" he's got working secretly against me?'

'Not against you, but putting all the pieces together.'

'If he's in the same force as me, and he's secretly working on my cases, then he is working against me.'

'I'm sorry.'

'Did you actually ever think this through, Caz?'

'I—'

'And I've looked this Steve Nicholls up – your friend Damian gave me the name. He's a dangerous bastard and he's been out now for two years. Why the hell didn't you tell me about him?"

'I didn't know! My mum always said she got her injuries in a car crash.'

He shoots her a brief look of such withering contempt that she feels like she just wants to run away and hide. But she has to go through with this. She has to keep him on her side.

'Do you think your Peter could be Nicholls?' he asks.

Caz shakes her head. 'He's got to be at least twenty years too young.' She pulls the card and picture out of her dog-walking bag and shows him the images of the young woman breastfeeding the old man.

He runs his fingers over the Ziploc bag. 'You bagged this up like evidence, but you didn't show it to me?' he asks as he extracts the cards, carefully handling them by the edges. 'What is this? Amateur detective hour?'

'And there was this, too. Peter has the originals.' She hands him her phone showing the photos of the last heart-shaped card and the one that came with the finger.

As he reads the cards through, his tight jaw softens, and instead of continuing to bitch at her, he looks at her with pity.

She's not sure which she prefers.

'Look, Caz.' He puts a greasy hand on her knee. She looks down and sees dirty, bitten nails and red-raw knuckles. 'You've been through a lot, I know. And it can be confusing and frightening. But you have to let me know, and truthfully this time: have you told me everything?'

'There's the neighbours,' Caz says. She tells him about Jon and Colette, Nicola, June and Clive, and how Edwin appeared from nowhere.

'Jesus,' Collins says, as he notes down the names. 'We're going to do the intel on this lot then, too.'

'I didn't think it was relevant,' Caz says. 'I mean, there are creeps everywhere, aren't there?'

He shakes his head in disbelief.

'So what am I going to do now?' she says.

'You're going to lock yourself in the house, act as if nothing's happened.'

'Because of the bugs?'

'Bugs?'

'In Marcy's house. Nicholls is spying on me. He must be, because he knows who I'm talking to. That's why we're here, rather than in the house.'

Collins looks as if his patience is wearing very thin indeed. 'You've been living like this for ten days and this is the first you tell me? Unbelievable.'

'Please don't go on at me.'

He holds up his hands. 'OK. So you go back, bolt yourself in, act normal, because of the bugs, and I'm putting an unmarked car outside. I'm also doing the background on all your neighbours.'

'But it can't be them, can it? Mum said Jon wasn't Nicholls, and although he's the right age, Clive looks all wrong.'

'Nevertheless, it's all we've got to go on right now. And I'm going to check out your Peter guy, too. Do you know which force he was with?'

Caz shakes her head and starts to say something, but Joe, who has continued to whine and pull during all of this, tugs his lead out from under her foot and is off, running across the maze.

She calls out to him, and he doesn't respond. Doesn't even look back. And then he's out of sight, disappeared behind a clump of rhododendrons. Caz tries to go after him, but Collins holds her back. 'You'll never catch up with him,' he says. 'And you've got to look after yourself right now.'

'But Joe's a part of me!' she says. Apart from Damian, he's potentially all she's got left.

'He'll turn up. I'll put a call out. Dogs do this all the time, and nine times out of ten they're back home within twenty-four hours. This is an emergency, Caz. You have to do as I say. Go back to the house. Act calmly, as if everything is normal. Lock and bolt all the doors and windows. I will contact you as soon as I have any information. I'm pretty certain Nicholls will come to you soon. And when he does, we'll be ready for him.'

'And Joe?'

He tuts. 'He's just a dog, Caz. He'll be fine.'

THIRTY-EIGHT

Of course, Collins's assurances don't work. On her way back, Caz runs through the park shouting for Joe. She looks behind bushes, stops strangers and asks if they have seen him.

A boy steps out from a gaggle of rucksack-toting kids just let out of school. 'I saw him,' he says. The way he eyes Caz makes her wonder just how mad and dishevelled she must look right now, how desperate.

'Which way did he go?'

The boy points straight up in the air, and his crew collapse into cruel giggles.

'That's not funny,' she shouts, which only doubles their laughter.

She runs on, calling Joe's name.

'A Border collie–type dog?' a woman with a pushchair says.

Panting, Caz stops and nods. The woman looks like her life is so perfect, in her snappy Boden outfit, pushing her baby in one of those battleship-type buggies, dangling her beautifully behaved pug on a velvet lead. Caz wants to rip her apart, climb inside her skin and enjoy her marvellous, wonderful, uncomplicated life.

'He went that way.' The woman smiles and points in the direction of Marcy's house. 'I hope you find him. He looked like a lovely boy.'

'Thanks,' Caz says, flushing with shame at what she let run through her mind. 'He is. The loveliest.' A sob catching on her breath, she sprints off to escape the perfect woman and follow Joe.

A frantic running wraith, she rounds the corner to the close and suddenly remembers Collins's instruction to act normally. Everything looks so peaceful here, the big houses sitting behind their privets and subtropical plants, their monkey puzzle trees. You would have no idea if you were walking down the street what was going on behind these lovely detached facades.

'Joey!' she calls out softly.

Nicola's net curtain twitches and her ghost face peers out. Caz fires her a stern look.

It's coming up for quarter to two, just before the meeting Peter arranged with his colleague. As she nears his house, she decides to try one more time to see if he's in, see if he's OK, see if she can find out who this colleague is so she can tell Collins. She rings on his doorbell as if it were the most normal thing in the world and waits, hopping from foot to foot, looking around for Joe.

Still no Peter.

Still no Joe.

Her heart somewhere around her navel, she trudges back to Marcy's. Clive steps out of his driveway and stands in her path. She flinches as if he has just drawn a gun on her.

'Whoa!' he says, holding up his hands like she's a bolting horse.

'What?' she says, panting and sobbing and fighting for breath.

'I need a word with you, missy.'

'*What?*' she says. No one has ever, in her entire life, called her missy.

'My friend Edwin was most disappointed in you yesterday. You really upset him. It doesn't cost anything to be polite, does it? I know you young women. You just breeze through life thinking the sun shines out of your arses. But let me tell you, it doesn't.'

'What the hell are you talking about?' she says.

'I beg your pardon?'

Her terror tips over into rage. She can't even pretend to be polite. She puts both hands on his chest and shoves him. 'Oh, just piss off.'

'June! June!' Clive calls out as he staggers into a thorny pyracantha.

Caz tears into Marcy's driveway.

Despite trying to visualise Joe waiting at the door on her way here, he's nowhere to be seen.

That's the end, then.

He's gone, too.

Her hands trembling, she unlocks the front door and bolts it behind her, then, tripping over the post lying on the mat, runs to the kitchen, where she sticks her head under the tap to try to wash away some of the stress.

It doesn't work. Standing dripping and swaying, her eyes half closed, she remembers that it is now the afternoon. Post arrives in the morning. Shaking her head in disbelief that she is going to have to face another unexpected horror, she goes back to the front door and eyes the manilla envelope on the mat.

Leaning away from it, she picks it up by the corner. She carries it to the kitchen and thinks about calling Collins, but her curiosity gets the better of her and she opens it, then gingerly slips her hand inside, pulling out the contents and laying them on the table.

It's a British Airways wallet and a card with another

horrible image of a young woman breastfeeding an elderly man. This one looks ancient, far simpler, worn at the edges. Just how she feels right now.

Fury roiling inside her, she opens the card. This one is in straightforward handwriting. No more hiding behind capitals.

You know who I am and what I am to you.
During all those years that were stolen from me, you have given me succour.

She makes a vomiting gesture.

I understand you've had the art history lesson. Your mother always knew a lot about paintings, didn't she? She was a clever lady who just didn't know how to love properly.

The use of the past tense to describe Ruth shoots ice through Caz's veins.

This one is from Pompeii. It's a story old as time.
You're alone now. And we have a lot of catching-up to do. So this is the plan. Take this plane tomorrow to Guarulhos International Airport in São Paulo, Brazil, and go to the hotel I have picked out for us – it's a fifteen-minute drive. I'll see you there once I've tidied things up here.
This is the next chapter, our new life together. What I am owed. If you do this, everyone here will be safe. If you don't, if you put one step out of line, Caz... Well, I don't need to spell it out, do I? You've seen what I do.

She flings the card down and rifles through the wallet. Inside is a one-way plane ticket leaving Gatwick tomorrow. A hire car reservation, details of a hotel booking.

She shudders so hard the world goes wavy.

Nicholls is convinced he is her father. She holds her hand out in front of her and examines the bitten nails, the rounded fingertips at the end of fingers she has always thought of as fairly spidery. Has this body of hers been built with the genes of this madman? This violent, vindictive psychopath?

She thinks back to when she attacked Edwin. She could have ripped his head off, she was so furious.

If only her mother had done a DNA test.

She wipes her arms down as if she is trying to rid herself of something horrible clinging to them.

She has no idea what to do.

She needs to tell Collins.

Her phone rings. It's Damian. Behind him, the cool beats of the shop soundtrack don't even touch the edge of her nerves.

'Hello, darling. How are things?' he says. 'I'm knocking off in ten minutes. No one in, might as well. Do you want me to come round?'

Caz shakes her head.

'Caz?'

'No. I've got to act normal,' she whispers. 'Not make him suspicious.'

A hellish thump from the living room makes her shriek and nearly drop the phone.

'What is it?' he says. 'Caz?'

'Stay on the line, Dame,' she says. 'Just in case.'

'Speak to me! What's going on?'

But she's got the phone by her side and his words are only a faint buzz. With her other hand, she grabs a kitchen knife, and holding it above her head, ready to strike, she slides along the wall and into the living room.

Another thump makes her yelp.

'Caz? Caz? Are you all right?' Damian shouts from the phone.

And then, the tightly curled knot of her heart opens like a

sunflower. The thumps are coming from Joe. The ultra sound insulation of Marcy's window has hidden his barks from her, but the clever boy has worked out that throwing himself against the glass of the bifold doors will make a noise she can hear.

She runs to the doors and, after a short fumble with the locks, flings them open and falls to her knees to welcome him. Damian yells her name from her phone as she buries her face in Joe's familiar earth-scented fur.

'It's OK,' she tells him. 'It's Joe. He's come back!'

'Had he gone, then?'

Joe pulls himself away from her and runs out into the garden, coming to a stop in the middle of the lawn, facing her like he does when he wants her to throw a ball.

'Gotta go,' Caz says, leaning against the door. 'Joe's got something to show me outside.'

'Leave me on,' Damian says. 'Just in case.'

A text comes through on her phone. It's from Collins.

Unmarked car positioned outside. Text if you need me.

Does that mean it's Collins himself out there, not another officer? Isn't that above and beyond the call of duty? Is he going to enjoy spying on her?

She is just about to reply when a screech of over-loud feedback coming from within the house makes her drop the phone and put her hands over her ears. She wheels round, and as she does so, a booming voice sounds from the walls.

'YOU'VE GONE TO THE BASTARD PIGS!' The voice is crackled, distorted, but definitely male. And it's an accent that Ruth recognises well – like her mother's when she's tired. It's pure Leeds.

'What?' Shaking, terrified, Caz runs indoors, towards the point where she knows the nearest hidden camera lurks. This must be the two-way sound feature Peter told her about, the facility to speak through the security cameras in the house. 'Where are you?'

'You've messed everything up,' the voice says. It's coming from speakers all around the house, so it echoes madly, like there are ten men talking. Does she recognise that voice through the distortion?

'Everyone's got to pay now,' he goes on.

'Please don't.' She drops to her knees. 'We can still go away. I'll pack a bag and leave, and I'll be your daughter for ever more, just please let everyone go. I'll do anything you ask.'

Another swoop of feedback and the crackling and distortion suddenly stops, leaving a silence that rings in her ears.

'What do I do now?' she says. 'What do I do?'

Joe runs into the living room, grabs her sleeve and tugs at her. It's like he wants to play, but his intention is deadly serious, so serious she can see it at once. He wants her to come, to follow him.

She does, running across the terrace and down to the very bottom of the garden, where she finds the gate to the twitten standing wide open.

Back in the living room, her phone lies on the floor, Damian shouting for her through it.

Unheeded.

THIRTY-NINE

Caz follows Joe through the gate. He turns left, runs on, stopping to wait for her about forty paces ahead. As soon as she catches up with him, he's off again. It reminds her of when he found Harry, which compared to now seems like the days of innocence.

Again she catches up with him, but this time he stays where he is, scratching at the ivy-covered fence in front of him and looking up at her.

'This is Peter's place, Joey. Is this where you want me to go?'

Again that look, as if he is expecting her to throw a ball. Then he is gone, shimmying under the fence through a dip, which from the smell of it has been used by foxes.

'Joey!' Caz hisses. 'Come back!'

He growls softly from the other side. He wants her to join him.

This is indeed Peter's place. But Peter has disappeared, presumably taken by Nicholls. Unless he's had an accident or something and is lying hurt in his garden.

Her first ever imagined better-case scenario.

It seems unlikely.

She reaches into her pocket for her phone to call Collins and tell him about the voice through the speakers, but then she remembers that it's back in the house. She should really go and get it, but she doesn't want to lose Joe again.

Dog or people? Which does she choose?

What if Peter *is* the other side of the fence and desperately in need of medical attention? She could just go in and see, then dash back and get her phone.

She tries the gate, but it's locked. It has been used recently, though, because the ivy growing over it is bent backwards and snapped. But that's no use to her now. She grabs onto the remaining ivy and uses it to scrabble up to the top, where rolls of rusty old razor wire block her way, like at the front of the house. Hanging onto the ivy, she tugs off her hoodie and lays it over the metal. It's not perfect, but she manages to get over with only a few scratches. She drops to the ground and is joined by Joe, who has been waiting for her.

The garden is as she remembers it, overgrown with weeds and bushes and ratty fruit trees, the rusty old crane with its giant hook dangling above a block of stone. Ezra's workshop is shut up now, its door locked, well-used mallets lined up against it.

She can't see Peter collapsed on the ground, so that's something.

As she's pulling her hoodie on again, Joe starts tugging at her, dragging her towards a clump of bamboo. 'What is it, Joey?' she says, but she's stopped short by the slam of a door up at the house. Instinctively she slides behind the bamboo and crouches down.

It's Peter, healthy and well, backing away from the building, dragging a wheelbarrow. With some effort, he manages to circle it round so that he is facing forward.

Relieved that he's still there and looking OK, Caz nearly jumps up to greet him, but Joe puts a paw on her arm and growls. And anyway, this doesn't look like the Peter she has come to know and like. This man has an altogether different aspect. His mouth is set in a grim line. His hair is askew, his eyebrows lowered. His trademark gentleness appears to have melted away. His wheelbarrow bears a shape wrapped in tarpaulin. A shape the size of Colette's dog. A shape the size of a human.

Holding her breath, Caz watches as Peter wheels his cargo towards a clearing in the tangle of trees and bushes on the other side of Ezra's back garden. Muttering to himself, he tips the barrow up and the contents thump out with a sound that, because of the weight and heft it implies, hits Caz in the bottom of her stomach. She doesn't want to even begin to bring together the lines of conclusion forming in her head.

It's probably just a roll of old carpet, a couple of bags of soil.

But why wrap them up? Neatness, perhaps. Peter always struck her as a tidy man.

She realises that she is thinking about him in the past tense. The Peter she thought she knew is receding, and she doesn't like the thoughts building inside her head. She should get back to Marcy's and call Collins and tell him about the plane tickets, the voice over the speakers in the house.

But she is rooted to her spot.

Dusting off his hands, Peter returns to the house.

Once he is inside, Caz creeps out from behind the bamboo towards whatever he tipped from his barrow. But then the door opens again, and he is back. Seeing what he is carrying, she springs back under cover.

Slung over his shoulder is a rifle. It looks more like a museum piece than a working gun – it was probably Uncle Ezra's. In one hand he is carrying a Nutribullet jar with its lid screwed on, full of what looks like bright green smoothie. In the other, he holds what appears to be the knife part of a bayonet. Caz glances down at Joe, who is crouching low, like he could attack at any moment. She puts her hand on the scruff of his neck to stop him should he decide to do so.

Instead of heading towards the tarp bundle, Peter veers to the other side of the garden, to a gravel area beyond the prepper store shed, about ten metres away from where Caz and Joe are hiding. Placing the knife and gun on the ground, he kneels, scoops away a few handfuls of gravel, and digs around until he hooks his fingers around something. Then he lifts.

It's a hidden manhole cover.

Is he going into the sewers?

He stands at the edge of the hole.

'It's time,' he says, angling his head so that his words disappear into the ground. His soft Bristol burr has gone, and it's the same Leeds accent that came over the speakers in Marcy's house.

Under the manhole, a dog starts barking, and someone shouts at Peter, using all the swear words under the sun.

Every single hair on Caz's body spikes.

She knows that voice and the bark.

It's Marcy and Bridget.

'It's not going to be the happy ending I wanted,' Peter says, not sounding like anything she has ever heard from him before.

'Just get the fuck away from me!' Marcy screams at him.

'All this swearing,' he says. 'I won't miss that.' He kneels and drops the Nutribullet jar into the hole. 'Your last supper. Tinned spinach, tinned carrot and powdered egg smoothie. Too bad you're not going to reap the full healthy benefits, but it's out of my hands. I'll leave you to eat it while I deal with my other problems up here.' He reaches into his pocket, pulls out a sachet of dog food and throws it so that it joins the smoothie. 'And I didn't forget Bridget's last meal. I'm not a monster.'

Marcy swears some more.

Caz creeps a little nearer.

'Yes, but if things don't turn out how you want them,' Peter is saying, 'you have to change your plan. Make things happen. You'll know this as a businesswoman. I'll be back soon, Marcy. A little firing squad, I think. Nothing personal, but I need to make room for my daughter.'

Even though she has already caught up with the realisation that Peter is Nicholls, hearing this confirmation spoken out loud makes Caz gasp.

He's too young, surely?

He backs away, picks up the knife and heads over to Uncle Ezra's studio. Caz shrinks back into the greenery.

Taking a large ring of many keys from his pocket, he opens the lock, leaving the keys dangling from the door as it swings open. A whimpering noise comes from inside. Whoever is making it has a gag on.

'Our daughter has ruined everything,' Nicholls says. 'She brought you into the house, and now she's gone to the police. I don't want to do this, Ruthie, but what choice do I have? She's put my back against the wall.'

The sound of a struggle – metal things falling from table-tops, something tearing – comes from inside, then there's a slap and a scream.

FORTY

It's too much for Caz, but Joe is up first.

'Joe!' she calls, but he's off, snarling, snapping, towards the studio.

Caz follows as fast as she can.

As she nears the door, she grabs one of Uncle Ezra's stone-carving mallets from where it stands propped up against the studio wall.

However quickly she has processed Peter being revealed as Steve Nicholls, she is not prepared for what she witnesses inside.

Bound up with gaffer tape like a battered and bloody chrysalis, Ruth is being manhandled to her feet by an angry, frustrated Nicholls.

'What the...' he says as Joe launches himself at his legs. From the scream Nicholls lets out, Joe has got his teeth into more than just a mouthful of trouser.

He wheels round and sees her.

'Caz, oh, my Caz. What have you done?'

Careful to take the side of him furthest from Ruth, she

swings the mallet towards his head, where it connects with his temple with a mighty thwack.

He tumbles to the floor, catching his head on the corner of a solid wooden workbench, dropping the bayonet as he falls. When he's down, he is still. Stone-cold unconscious.

'Oh, Mum,' Caz says as she carefully peels the tape from the papery skin around Ruth's mouth. 'We'll get you out of here.'

'Marcy...' Ruth says. 'Must save...'

'Once I see to you.'

She works to free her mother, using Nicholls's knife to slice through the tape binding her arms and legs.

'I don't understand,' she says, nodding her head towards him. 'He's too young.'

'He's had a bloody facelift and hair implants,' Ruth says, gasping. 'The bastard left me looking like this, then used his dead wife's money to "claim back the years prison stole from me". And those blue eyes are just contacts. And he changed his accent. He's so bloody pleased with himself about how you didn't suspect a thing.'

'He was right, though. Come on.'

Caz rips the last piece of tape from Ruth's legs and they hobble towards the manhole.

There's a ladder inside. Caz throws herself down the rungs.

'Stay away from me!' Marcy cries from inside. Bridget barks and barks, but Joe, who is standing next to Ruth at the top, replies, and this reassures her.

It takes a moment for Caz's eyes to adjust to the gloom inside what she now realises is Ezra's hidden Armageddon bunker. Her nostrils pick up the heady stink of human and dog waste mingled with something sweet and rotten. On the far side of the chamber – which is about the size of a single garage – is a filthy bed, and on it, manacled to the headboard, sweating and shivering, is Marcy. Within her reach is a padlocked dog crate, in which Bridget cowers and whimpers.

'Get the keys from the studio door,' Caz shouts up to Ruth. 'Take Joey with you, and the knife, just in case.'

She turns to Marcy. Her skin is grey, her eyes bloodshot. She is drenched in sweat.

'Where is he?' Marcy says, her voice an urgent, hoarse croak.

'Unconscious up there. We have to move quickly.'

'My hand...' she says through cracked lips.

The stump where Marcy's finger was amputated is wrapped in a dirty Elastoplast, but her hand is swollen, and towards the base of the finger, the flesh is yellow and green. A thick, angry red line tracks all the way up her arm.

'We'll get you to a hospital as soon as we can,' Caz says.

'He used garden secateurs,' Marcy says. She narrows her eyes. 'He knows you went to the police. That dog collar he gave you. It's bugged. He thought he was so fucking clever.'

'What was he going to do?'

'Kill me and Bridget. After he got rid of your mum. Make way for you.'

'He told you that?'

'He's kept me up to date with all his plans. He's been following you since he got out of the nick. Didn't you notice?'

Caz shakes her head. 'I don't see what's going on under my nose, remember?'

Marcy looks at her and nods. It is a sort of apology. 'He cracked into Mark's shitty app and followed you out on dates.'

'Of course! He was a computer programmer when he met Mum.'

'You were with some bloke called Ash? He sat behind you in a bar, where you told him all about how I stole Mark from you. Batman and Robin. On a first date, Cazzer. TMI.'

'And then he killed him.'

'Because he wasn't good enough for you. Because he was married.'

'Yeah, I found out.'

'But what you said about me gave him ideas. He looked me and Mark up and worked out how he was going to put the world back to rights for you. Starting with some grab rail thing to make Ruth fall over.'

'He did that?'

'So you would come back. You're welcome to Mark, by the way.'

Caz wishes Ruth would hurry up with those keys.

'He's furious that you disobeyed his instructions. He doesn't want to take you to Brazil now. Says you don't deserve it.' Despite the situation, despite the state she's in, Marcy laughs. Because it really is laughable.

Caz can't quite believe all this. 'He's mad, isn't he?'

'Off his fucking rocker.' Marcy laughs again, but it dissolves into a painful hacking cough.

The keys clatter to the ground in the bunker. Ruth peers down through the manhole. 'Be quick,' she croaks.

Caz fumbles with the keys – there are so many of them – but eventually she gets Marcy's handcuffs undone and releases Bridget from the cage.

Marcy can barely stand, she's so weak. Bridget isn't too good either. Caz carries the dog to the manhole first and lifts her up for Ruth to take. 'We'd better get a move on,' she says to Marcy as she supports her towards the ladder. 'I don't know how long Peter's going to be out.'

'Peter?'

'I mean Nicholls.'

'Whatever his name is, I never want to see the bastard again.'

She stands behind Marcy and more or less pushes her up

the ladder, then hurries to join her. But before she reaches the edge of the hole, Bridget and Joe start barking and snarling.

'Careful, Caz!' Ruth calls out.

'What is it?' Caz rushes to clamber out, scrambling over Marcy, who has more or less collapsed onto the ground.

Then she looks up and gasps.

Staggering, with blood running into his eyes from a gash on his head, Nicholls holds Ruth, her back against him, his arm clamped around her neck. He's pressing the bayonet against her throat and has the rifle over his shoulder again.

Joe and Bridget try to get hold of his leg, but he kicks out at them.

'Keep the fucking dogs off me, or I'll kill her.'

'Joe. Come here,' Caz says. Joe steps obediently towards her, his tail between his legs. Bridget follows.

'Don't worry about me,' Ruth says. 'Just save yourselves.'

'She's not going to do that, are you, Caz?' Nicholls says.

Caz shakes her head.

'No, she's a good girl, our daughter. Follow me.' Keeping hold of Ruth, he backs towards the bundle he emptied from the wheelbarrow. 'All of you.'

Caz helps Marcy up, and together they follow him, with the dogs taking up the rear.

'Stop there,' he tells them. 'By the crane.'

They do as he says. Nicholls keeps going, Ruth against him, until he reaches the tarpaulin. Then he lets go of her, takes the gun from his shoulder and points it at her. 'Undo my parcel.'

Clearly in a lot of pain, Ruth kneels and slowly pulls off the tape holding the tarpaulin in place. She turns back the cover and Caz and Marcy gasp. It's Mark. He is deadly still and pale, his eyes slightly open, rolled back into his head so just the whites are visible.

'No!' Caz says.

'He's not dead. Yet,' Nicholls says. 'Just nicely roofed.'

'Why have you got Mark?' Marcy says.

'It was the genius part of the plan,' Nicholls says. 'I set Mark and Caz up to get back together. I knew it would happen, given the right conditions, so I established those conditions. He looked like the perfect mate after those losers I had to get rid of. You and I, Marcy, we know how useful it is to be married to someone with loads of dough, don't we? She'd have been set up for life. It was going so well.'

He pushes Mark with his foot.

'But you turned out to be a fucking disappointment, didn't you, Mark? Like those other wasters, Ash and Harry.' He puts on an effeminate voice as he says the names. 'So something has to be done, doesn't it?'

He turns to face the three women.

'Eh, girls?'

He grabs Ruth, pushes her away from him and cocks the gun, pointing the barrel at Mark's head.

FORTY-ONE

It all happens so quickly Caz is barely aware of her role in it.

She steps away from Marcy, who stumbles and falls, then grabs the big hook dangling from the stone-lifting crane and in the same movement pulls it back as far as she can to give it a serious amount of backswing. Then she lets go. The hook flies through the air with a metallic shriek, flaking rust down onto the overgrown garden beneath it.

The sound and movement distract Nicholls, and as he looks up, the hook slams straight into his face. The gun goes off, he is sent flying, and Caz finds herself standing over him holding another, bigger mallet.

She has no idea where she found it. But it is there, ready in her hands.

Nicholls is flat on his back, his arms out at either side of his body, his nose smashed like a bloody piece of meat in the middle of his face. Amazingly, he is still conscious. Unable to move – perhaps his neck has been damaged – but he can speak.

'My baby,' he says through a mouthful of blood and loose teeth. 'We could have had a lovely life together, my little girl. I was making things better for you.'

'You're not serious?'

'We got on so well, didn't we?'

'That wasn't you.'

'I would have gradually shown myself to you. You would have loved me so much.'

'You murdered two people! Kidnapped Marcy!'

'I would have got rid of her, too, and you'd have understood. You could have had the life you deserve. You said you deserve it. Mark, the house. You do!'

'You're mad.'

'I just want what's best for you. I love you so much.'

Caz has had enough of this man. She raises the mallet.

But just as she is about to bring it down on his despicable head, something stops her, and she is stuck with her arms up in the air, gripping the handle.

'What the...?'

Trapped and struggling, she glances to one side and sees her mother, who is lying on the ground where Nicholls threw her.

Ruth is staring at her in horror, her mouth open, her eyes wide. She looks as if her worst fears about her daughter have been confirmed. 'You would have done it,' she says. 'Wouldn't you?'

Caz would have done it. She would have brought the mallet down on his head again and again, until it was nothing but a bloody pulp. She still burns with the desire to obliterate him, but now the mallet is being prised from her fingers and strong hands are pulling her away from him.

'He's no threat to you any more,' the man holding her says. She turns and sees Jon. 'I was in the garden. I heard,' he says. 'I ran round here and smashed my way in.'

A shout makes everyone look towards the house.

'Stop! Police!'

It's Collins. With two uniformed police shooters at his side, he rushes through the back door out into the garden. He is clearly not expecting the scene that greets him, but he's a professional and reads it entirely correctly, and within what seems like minutes, the guns are stood down and the garden is filled with paramedics and more police officers. Nicholls is taken away in an ambulance with a police escort. Mark too is stretchered away – thanks to Caz's swing of the crane, Nicholls's gunshot missed him entirely. Ruth and Marcy are wheeled to yet another ambulance.

'I want to go with you,' Caz says to Ruth, grasping her hand. She doesn't want to let her out of her sight ever again.

'I'll be fine,' Ruth says. 'You see to those dogs.'

'And I need you here to tell me exactly what's been going on,' Collins says.

Dazed, Caz sits on the ground, stroking the sleeping Joe and Bridget as she waits for Collins to interview her. He's busy right now coordinating a team who are cordoning off areas of the garden to get forensic evidence. She doesn't mind waiting. In fact, she can't really move right now.

Jon comes out of the house with two cups of tea.

He sits next to her and takes out his cigarettes. 'Do you mind?' he asks.

'Be my guest.' Passive smoking is the least of her concerns right now. 'In fact...' She holds out her hand.

He gives her a cigarette, takes one for himself, then lights them both.

'You OK?'

Caz exhales and nods.

But she's not. She is dizzy with how blind she was to what was actually going on right under her nose, how she was so completely taken in by 'Peter'. But worse than that, sitting in her head like the most extreme sort of vertigo, is the fact of what she would have done to Nicholls.

'Thank you for stopping me,' she says.

She looks again at her hands. Her nearly killer's hands.

'That Collins bloke told me all about it. Bloody hell, Caz. He fooled us all, didn't he? I thought he was a harmless arty type. Woke, even!'

Caz frowns. 'Can I ask you something?'

'Sure.' Jon sips his tea.

'How did you and Colette meet?'

'Why do you want to know?'

'Peter... I mean Nicholls told me something about you.'

'What?'

'That you were in prison. That you'd done something unspeakable. And she was a prison visitor.'

'Colette? A do-gooder?' Jon laughs so much he splutters tea all over his trousers.

'So it's not true?' she says.

He gathers himself together. 'Colette came up to me after a gig. She'd been a big fan. Proper little punkette back in the day. We'd even had a fling, apparently, one night after we played the Marquee in Soho, though to my shame, what happened in those years is a bit of a mystery, Colette included.'

He nudges Caz's shoulder. 'Full disclosure, though: I did spend a year or so inside, when I was younger. Where I got my kitchen experience. Never again, mind.'

'But it wasn't for something unspeakable?'

He laughs. 'Nah. Bad-rock-'n'-roll-boy drug things. Or rather, forgetting I had something naughty on me when we tried going on tour to France and getting hauled over by customs. Haven't touched the stuff since.'

'So yet another lie by Nicholls?'

'Yet another lie by Nicholls.'

Collins hurries down the garden towards them. Perhaps it's because she's not seeing him through Nicholls's eyes, but it seems to Caz that his whole persona has changed. He looks like he is alight from inside. Even though he has been working non-stop, he seems cleaner, younger, more alive.

That's what having such a neat solution to a series of horrible crimes must do to a policeman.

He could even be quite attractive, but she doesn't allow that thought to spend a second in her head.

'Can you spare me an hour or so?' he asks her. 'We want to gather evidence and I need your statement, but I promise you, we'll throw away the key this time.'

Caz nods.

She hopes so.

She really hopes so.

FORTY-TWO

'It's all go down the turning circle today, girls!'

Damian, who is sitting in the passenger seat of Marcy's Mini, is not wrong. Caz manoeuvres past the private ambulance parked outside Ezra's house and swerves round the car of the guy who is putting the For Sale sign up outside Marcy's place. A small crowd of gawpers and photographers have gathered around the ambulance.

'They're taking him away, then,' Marcy says from the back seat, where she is huddled wrapped in blankets, clutching her bag of hospital discharge meds. She had sepsis, but after just two weeks is recovered enough to come home. There was talk about having to amputate her arm, but luckily the intravenous antibiotics they gave her in the ambulance on the way to hospital saved it.

'They had to dig up the whole back garden to find him,' Caz says as she pulls into Marcy's drive. 'Poor Ezra.'

'Nicholls definitely killed him, then?' Damian says.

'He didn't bury himself.' Caz parks the car right by her van.

'Duh,' Damian tuts. 'What I mean is, it wasn't natural causes.'

'Stabbed,' she says, jumping out of the Mini. 'And they found poor Roop beside him.'

'Eurgh,' Marcy says.

'Bastard,' Damian says.

'I know.' Caz lifts her seat so she can help Marcy out. 'Let's hope that's the end of the horrors.'

Caz and Damian support Marcy as she returns to a hero's welcome from Bridget, who is so excited she wets the hall floor. Joe is more sanguine. It's like he knows his time in this house is coming to an end.

They set her up on the sofa with a cup of tea and a plateful of fancy macarons. Damian nips back out to the car to get her suitcase. After everything that happened, he took over the house-sitting from Caz and will be staying until Marcy is strong enough to look after herself.

As he comes back in, Marcy's phone dings.

'Ooh. An offer already,' she says. 'Thirty grand over asking.'

'That'll please his nibs,' Damian says as he puts the case down.

'It'll help with the Swiss clinic bills,' Caz says.

'Poor Mark,' Marcy says.

They all look at each other, and even though it feels cruel, they laugh.

Because really, compared to what Marcy has gone through, Mark has had a walk in the park. However, although he hid it well, he had been close to another burnout when he was seeing Caz. An Apple OS update had opened up a security gap in SeeMe, and his company were firefighting that when Nicholls hacked into it. His kidnap ordeal was the final straw.

'No, really. Poor Mark,' Caz says. He's not a robust person, she realises now. She also realises he is the worst possible news for her. Never again.

'Are you sure you won't stay?' Marcy holds out her good hand.

Caz shakes her head. She doesn't want to spend one more night in this house. And despite everything, she's not keen on becoming any closer to Marcy. She can't talk about the journals, of course, but the knowledge of what Marcy put in them has tainted their friendship – even the part before she went off with Mark.

The clincher was when she found out that Marcy hadn't actually reached out to her when she moved back to Brighton. The message suggesting they meet had of course come from Nicholls, as part of his madman masterplan to get Caz back into Marcy's life. He'd hoped, correctly, that since he had asked Caz to reply to Marcy via the unsuspecting Damian, the two women would be too English to bring up who had initiated contact.

Anyway, she can't stay. She needs to get back to Ruth.

She has made a decision and she needs to tell her what it is.

On her way out, she sees that Jon has joined the gathering outside Ezra's house. Unlike the others, he has the air of someone paying their respects. He spots her reversing out of Marcy's drive and strolls over. She winds down her van window.

'You off then?' he says.

She nods.

'Don't blame you. Send my regards to your mum.'

'Will do.'

They shake hands through the window, and he starts to head back to his post outside Ezra's house. But she calls him back.

'There's one thing I wanted to ask you,' she says. She has wanted to confront him about this since their moment in Ezra's garden, when she felt a real closeness to him. She hates the idea that he might just be another cheating creep.

'Fire away.'

'What were you doing looking into my bedroom window?'

'What?'

'I saw you do it a couple of times. It made me really uncomfortable.'

'Oh! Oh God,' he says. He looks horrified. 'Did you think...? Oh no.'

'What *were* you doing, then?'

'I'm so sorry. I was sky-watching. It was a stretch of lovely clear nights when you were staying, and Venus and Mars were beautifully visible just above Marcy's house. If I'd known you thought that... Oh God.'

She looks at him. He appears genuinely mortified. But is he? Really?

She doesn't know if she believes him.

It's going to be a long time before she can fully trust anyone again.

'Guess who's here,' Ruth calls out as Caz and Joe battle past the big old boots and leather jacket thrown on the floor. Caz doesn't need to be told. The gear and the diesel-weed-sweat smell tell her immediately that Piers is in the house.

She goes through to the conservatory and there they are, sitting in the armchairs, holding hands as if all the intervening years hadn't happened and they had started to grow old together.

They both turn to her and smile, Ruth exhaling from the joint she is, of course, sharing with Piers. She's come out of her ordeal pretty much unscathed. For her, she says, it was just a minor blip compared to what she went through thirty years ago. And she's beyond glad that Nicholls can't touch Caz any more.

But there's still one way left that he could affect Caz's life. It has been the burning issue in both their minds since Ruth told her about him.

'Well?' Ruth says.

Caz knows instantly what her mother is referring to.

She smiles at her. 'I've decided not to.'

Ruth smiles and heaves a great sigh of relief.

'Good girl,' Piers says.

'I don't care about DNA,' Caz says. 'Dan was my dad, even though I never met him.'

'Yes.' Ruth nods at Piers, and he levers himself up with his stick, reaches a shoebox out from behind Mother and hands it to her.

'This is my Dan box,' Ruth says. 'Piers has been minding it for me for years. It's photos of him, a couple of his paintings rolled up, a few other bits. Things I haven't been able to look at until now, because it seemed so cruel that he wasn't with us. It's for you.'

She hands over the box. Caz lifts the lid on the treasures. On the top is a photo of Dan that she has never seen before. He is handsome, wild, his eyes full of love.

'I took that,' Ruth says. 'The day before...'

Caz holds the photo up beside her face.

'He looks just like you, girl,' Piers says.

Ruth takes her hand. 'Yes, love. You've got his eyes. You've got Dan's lovely, kind eyes.'

Joe leans against Caz's leg and looks up at her. Every part of his dog body and soul is saying, 'Yes!'

A LETTER FROM JULIA

Dear Reader,

I want to say a huge thank you for choosing to read *The Perfect Date*. If you enjoyed it and want to keep up to date with all my latest releases, just sign up at the following link. Your email address will never be shared, and you can unsubscribe at any time.

www.bookouture.com/julia-crouch

One of the reasons I became a crime writer is that I suffer from a dark and vivid imagination. This means that I always picture the worst possible thing that could happen in any given situation. Useful for a crime writer; not so great, for example, for staying in a remote house alone at night, or for solo expeditions to the countryside.

However, two years ago, we got a dog, and now I am out early every morning, all over the hills, woodlands and deserted beaches around Brighton where we live. I also go out after dark around the city streets for that 'one last walk' and its attendant functions.

The combination of necessity and a hound at my side – albeit a soppy, fluffy, bewitchingly cute dog whose default response to strangers is to roll on her back for a tummy rub – means that I no longer fear what might find me.

However, what I might find – that's another story. Dogs run

around in the undergrowth, their noses drawing them to all the dark and terrible things. In the case of my dog, Uncle, the worst has been a long-dead fox. She found him under a low branch, and before I could stop her, she had rolled on him, anointing herself with his pungent scent. It was a fun car ride home, I can tell you.

Before I go any further, I have to explain: yes, Uncle is a girl. This is what happens when you ask your kids to name your dog.

Even when those kids are in their late twenties...

But that canine impulse to explore can unearth other, more disturbing discoveries. Google *dog-walker finds body* and you'll see what I mean. Dog-walkers are out early and late, with a nose on legs, in out-of-the-way places. Is it any wonder that we often beat the police in their searches?

I hope the fox is the worst of Uncle's finds. I would never, ever want to be in Caz's walking boots.

It may sound like a stretch, but in some respects, dating through an app is like dog-walking. You are out there in the wild, not knowing what you are going to discover. Will it be a beautiful vista scented with wild roses? Or have you found a stinking dead fox?

While I have been out of the dating game for a very, *very* long time, my friends tell me stories that make my eyes pop. I'm not going to repeat them here because I'm saving them for the future.

I hope you enjoyed Caz's journey, and I'd love to know what your theories were about the mysteries she encounters. I've really enjoyed connecting with readers through my other books – *Cuckoo, Every Vow You Break, Tarnished, The Long Fall, Her Husband's Lover, The New Mother* and *The Daughters* – so please, if you have any comments or questions, do get in touch on my Facebook page, through Twitter, Instagram or my website.

Finally, I hope you loved *The Perfect Date*. If you did, I would be very grateful if you could write a review. I'd love to hear what you think, and it makes such a difference in helping new readers discover one of my books for the first time.

Thanks,

Julia Crouch

www.juliacrouch.co.uk

 facebook.com/JuliaCrouchAuthor
twitter.com/thatjuliacrouch
instagram.com/juliageek

ACKNOWLEDGEMENTS

First, I want to thank Uncle, Minnie, Little My, Soot, Tessa and Blanche, who taught me all I know about dogs and dog-walking; the dog-walkers of Queens Park, Brighton, and their pets, who have filled in the gaps; and All Paws Dog Walking on YouTube, whose great videos about her daily life made thoroughly enjoyable research material (https://www.youtube.com/@allpawsoutdoors/videos).

Then I want to thank my dear friends Hannah, Sue, Emma, Liz, Sam, Graham, Stephen and Hayley for all the meaty chats and stuff about writing and life and art. And Colin Scott, of course.

Thanks also to all at Curtis Brown, especially my agent, Cathryn Summerhayes, Jess Molloy, Annabel White and Anna Weguelin. And to my brilliant, brilliant editor, Ruth Tross, who has turned the sometimes lonely work of novel-writing into a massively fruitful partnership. I'm also massively grateful to Jane Selley, who has done great work on the copyedit, erasing typos and sorting out tortured sentences, and Maddie Newquist, who as proof-reader has mopped up any remaining errors. Anything that remains is my own damn fault.

Thanks also to my many creative writing students – at UEA, the National Centre for Writing, Faber Academy and the Professional Writing Academy, as well as my private mentees – who teach me at least as much as I teach them.

Massive gratitude to the publicity team at Bookouture – Kim, Noelle, Jess and Sarah – and all the other people at Bookouture who make being an author with them such a dream. And I particularly want to thank Jo Thomson for the striking cover design. From the moment I saw it I loved it, and had no comments whatsoever – a complete first.

Thank you to my father-in-law, Colin Crouch, who supported the writing of this novel with a roaring fire, a quiet study and delicious little lunches.

Finally, love and thanks to my mum, Jane, and my kids and their partners – Nel and Rob, Owen and Eva, and Joey – for making life such fun. And last but absolutely the reverse of least, my husband, Tim Crouch, for his unerring belief in me, his support and his willingness to be one of my first readers, even after eight novels' worth of me acting weird while he sits with the manuscript.

Printed in Great Britain
by Amazon